D0052117

THE HOB'S BARGAIN

PATRICIA BRIGGS

ACE BOOKS, NEW YORK

THE HOB'S BARGAIN

An Ace Book / published by arrangement with
the author

PRINTING HISTORY
Ace edition / March 2001

All rights reserved.
Copyright © 2001 by Patricia Briggs
Cover art by Duane O. Myers

This book, or parts thereof, may not be reproduced in
any form without permission.
For information address: The Berkley Publishing Group,
a division of Penguin Putnam Inc.,
375 Hudson Street, New York, New York 10014.

The Penguin Putnam Inc. World Wide Web site address is
http://www.penguinputnam.com

Check out the ACE Science Fiction & Fantasy newsletter
and much more on the Internet at Club PPI!

ISBN: 0-441-00813-5

ACE®
Ace Books are published by The Berkley Publishing Group,
a division of Penguin Putnam Inc.,
375 Hudson Street, New York, New York 10014.
ACE and the "A" design
are trademarks belonging to Penguin Putnam Inc.

PRINTED IN THE UNITED STATES OF AMERICA

10 9 8 7 6 5 4 3 2

To Michael,
Dreamkeeper and Songsmith, with all my love.

SPRING
Rᴇʙɪʀᴛʜ

ONE

Changes are frightening, I thought, even when they're changes for the better. From the doorway of my cottage I looked across the yard and garden to the barn where my husband was harnessing our chestnut workhorse. *My* husband. *Our* workhorse. I tasted the thought in my mind and smiled. Frightening, yes, but exciting and wonderful, too.

The barn wasn't far from the house, but the distance was great enough that I couldn't see the lacings on the harness or the faint, pale lines near my husband's eyes where the sun didn't reach his skin when he smiled. But I could see the horse cock an ear back, listening to Daryn's soft, slow voice. I could see the wheat-gold of Daryn's hair, newly cut in honor of our wedding.

We'd been married all of a night, and though we'd been betrothed this past harvest, I still couldn't quite believe it. I'd never expected to wed at all. The morning was still chilly this early in spring. I drew my shawl more tightly around my shoulders, hugging the warmth closer.

Daryn tied the traces to the croup strap high on the horse's rump so they wouldn't drag the ground all the way to the high field where he'd meet his brother and my father to continue the plowing they'd already begun. The muscles of his back flexed under the wool shirt he wore as he pulled himself to the chestnut's back in one smooth motion.

"Daryn . . . ," I called tentatively.

He saw me in the doorway and grinned. I smiled back with relief. When he'd left the house, I'd been busy cleaning up after breakfast, pretending I fixed morning meals every day when it had always been my mother's task. Near to thirty years old, and I still couldn't make toasted bread without scorching it.

Cleaning had given me a reason for my red cheeks other than the embarrassment that had first caught my tongue when I awoke in bed with him this morning and worsened dismally with the advent of the blackened bread. I'd expected him to be grumpy, as my father always was. I should have known him better than that: Daryn didn't hold grudges.

He spun the horse on its haunches, a trick he'd taught it during the last year's long winter months while I'd watched from my parents' house. If I half-closed my eyes, I could almost see a warrior on his mount preparing for battle rather than a landsman off to work. With a snort, the horse galloped to the small porch where I stood, his heavy feet thundering on the ground like the great horses from Gram's tales of ancient heroes.

Daryn was handsome enough to be a hero, perhaps some lost prince or noble. A clever twinkle seldom left his eye, and good humor colored most of his expressions—attributes all proper heroes should have. The muscles he'd earned tilling the fields were no less impressive than those of a soldier, and probably better than any prince would earn seated upon a throne.

Truth was, he was prettier than I, and the better part

of a decade younger. His age had worried me when Father brought him home last fall. I should have remembered how shrewd my father was. Only an idiot could have found fault with Daryn, and I hope I've never been that—or at least not very often.

"Aren, my lass?" Daryn asked after a moment. I realized he'd stopped in front of me some time ago, and I'd been staring at him without speaking.

I started to say something light and funny, something to let him know it was shyness, not moodiness, that I felt, but the words stopped in my throat. A familiar chill settled into my stomach. *Not now*, I thought desperately. I reached out to his normalcy and warmth, gripping the cloth of his pant leg, and hoped for the feeling to pass. When I closed my eyes against dizziness, I saw . . .

. . . *a winter lily, scarlet flower drooping and edged with brown, bobbing as something dripped on it.*

As an explanation of the dread feeling that choked me, it was a complete failure. Most of my visions were like that. Later, after whatever event the *sight* had warned of took place, I could nod my head to myself and say, "Oh, *that's* what it meant." Not very useful.

If I had to be stricken with magic, I would rather have had something like Gram's talent for healing, or my brother's knack for finding things—especially because the consequences of having magic were so deadly. My brother had died for his when I was thirteen.

He'd been in town with Father, trading fresh milk for leather to mend a harness, when Lord Moresh's bloodmage saw him and spoke my brother's death sentence. Quilliar had been fifteen, and he'd had a day to choose whether he would apprentice to the bloodmage or refuse and be put to death.

If he'd chosen to become a bloodmage, he'd have learned to kill and torture for power. After a while he'd have begun to go insane, as all the mages did in the end—

some immediately, some after years of a gradual decline into madness.

He'd picked death, but not one delivered by the blood-mage. The bloodmages would have used his death, his dead body, to power their magics. So my brother walked into the middle of a snowstorm and found a place where his body would be safely hidden for three days: enough time to ensure the bloodmage had no power from him.

I couldn't tell Daryn I had the *sight*, though I'd had all winter to do it. Caution learned so harshly would not drop from me after a few months of exchanged confidences and growing love. After a night of being man and wife, I would have trusted him with my life, but I couldn't risk losing the growing softness in his eyes when he looked at me.

Looking into his eyes, I couldn't tell him what I'd *seen*.

"Aren?" he asked, concerned. "Is something wrong?"

"No. No, just be careful." I released his leg and stepped back. I hugged myself as if it would help keep my mouth from telling him everything. I wrestled with my conscience, finally deciding that if whatever happened was catastrophic, I would tell him about the *sight*—punishment for being too selfish to tell him now.

He grinned at me, not seeing the seriousness of my warning. "I'll keep my feet out from under the plow-shares and be back at dusk after a dangerous day of plowing fields with your father and Caulem."

The warmth in his eyes kept his speech from being patronizing. He took my words as an expression of concern, perhaps the implied apology for my moodiness this morning that I'd meant to give him when I'd called him over.

Well, my foreseeing was not exact, predicting small harms as well as great. Perhaps someone would twist an ankle today or cut themselves on a sharp rock. Maybe it would rain. I hoped it would rain.

I set the worry to the back of my mind and kissed him when he leaned down. "See that you do," I said.

When I patted his cheek with a motherly hand, he grinned suddenly. He gave me a warm look and turned his head to bite my forefinger gently. I ducked a bit, not wanting him to see the heat in my eyes. He wrapped his hand around a strand of my hair and tugged me close again. This time his kiss left me too breathless to talk, sending the dark warning from my heart as if it had never been.

The horse shifted, pulling us apart.

"Don't fret so much, Aren," he said, and his voice soothed me as it did any of the other beasts he used it on. "You and I'll do very well."

He kissed me again and set the gelding up the path to the field before I recovered enough to speak. He knew I watched him, because he pulled the big horse into a controlled rear just before he rode out of sight. The harness was more hindrance than help in riding, but Daryn sat the horse easily. He blew me a kiss, then horse and rider plunged forward and were lost in the trees.

I shut the door of the cottage and looked about. Daryn had built the little house himself, and each joint of wood and brush of whitewash showed the care he'd taken. There was a loft for our bed, and the kitchen was set in its own nook. I'd helped to sand the wooden floor (along with everyone else in both our families), and I'd woven the small green rug that covered the trapdoor of the cellar which would keep our food cool during the summer. There wasn't much furniture. Daryn promised that when next winter came, he'd build more. Possessively, I ran my hand over the wooden back of my grandmother's loveseat.

Everyone in the village knew there was a strain of magic running in my father's family. That hadn't stopped my sister's wedding. There weren't so many folk around that a taint to the blood kept people from forming alliances, not when it was properly buried a generation or so back. My brother's death brought shame to the forefront; there were no families who would have me after that.

If anyone had found out I was mageborn, they'd have killed me. By the One God's sacred commands, mages are an evil to be eliminated, and since Lord Moresh's great-grandfather's conversion, everyone in Fallbrook followed the teachings of the One God. Death to mages was more popular than some of the other edicts.

I still had nightmares about the old woman who was pressed to death by her family when I was five or six. They'd used a barn door and piled it with stones until she was crushed beneath the weight. I wasn't there when it happened, but the stones still stood. When I passed them, I always tried not to see the remains of the barn door underneath the heaped mound of rock.

Like my brother, I'd still prefer such a death over what a mage would do to me—which was just as well, for I wouldn't be given the choice of apprenticeship. All bloodmages were men.

I stayed away from town when Lord Moresh and his bloodmage were in residence. Fortunately, Fallbrook was neither his only nor his most important holding, so he was seldom here. This year there'd been a war someplace and he hadn't come at all.

I'd expected Quilliar's death to leave me an old maid no matter how hard I tried to appear mundane, but fourteen years had been enough time for memories to fade. My father needed someone to take over the land he held. My sister Ani's husband, Poul, had as much land as he could work. So Father traveled north to Beresford, which was even smaller than our own Fallbrook, and found Daryn and his younger brother Caulem, tenth and eleventh sons of a farmer with only a small plot to divide among his children. So Caulem and Daryn came to my father's house last fall to help with the harvest.

Neither old memories, the pall of the *sight*, nor the equally dismal embarrassment of burning the toast this morning could rob me of my happiness for very long. The past was gone: Quilliar's death was unchangeable. When I went to the fields at midday with food for the men, I'd warn my father to be careful. Though Ma tried to pretend I didn't have the *sight*, Father would give proper weight to it. Tomorrow I would do better with the toast.

I looked around the cottage for something to do until lunchtime, but there really wasn't anything. We hadn't been living there long enough to get much dirty. My earlier fit of cleaning had taken care of our few morning dishes.

I pulled out the quilt I was making for my sister's baby. After years of barrenness, Ani was preparing for the birth of her first child in late summer. As fast as I sewed, I might get it done by the child's twelfth year. Even so, the rhythm of sewing was familiar and relaxing.

At midday I folded the blanket and set it aside with a smile and a pat. I was not the best seamstress, but this blanket was going very well. Ma said it was the simplest pattern she knew, and even I couldn't ruin it. Stretching the stiffness of a morning's stitchery out of my shoulders, I started for the cellar to prepare a meal.

I slid the rug aside with my shoe and tugged the trapdoor open. A haunch of salt pork awaited me on one of the shelves. Sliced onto some of Ma's bread, it would make a good meal.

I'd already taken a step down the ladder when I heard a commotion outside.

Hooves thundered, and a male voice shouted something I couldn't quite make out. Horses at this time of year were bad news. Good news could wait until planting was over. I started toward the door.

"Check the barn," rumbled someone. I didn't know his

voice, and his accent was odd. "See if they have any horses."

I'd just been ready to call out a welcome, but that stopped me. *Bandits*, I thought. We hadn't had robbers for a long time. Even though the King's Highway passed through Fallbrook, we were isolated on the outskirts of civilization.

The sound of boots on the porch shook me from the stillness of shock. I pulled the rug across the outside of the trapdoor and held it in place with one hand as I climbed down the ladder. I let the door close almost completely before releasing the rug and pulling my fingers out. I hoped it would conceal the door from a cursory search; it had no lock or bar to keep anyone out.

I heard a crash that might have been the cottage door opening. Daisy, our milk cow, lowed in alarm from the barn. I hunched in the corner of the small cellar behind a barrel of flour. Boots thudded dully on the floor above me. I couldn't tell how many people there were, but certainly more than one.

I remembered the big butcher's knife sitting beside the ham, and I scurried out of my hiding place to get it. I wished Quilliar had shown me how to fight with a knife when I'd asked him, but he'd been growing increasingly conscious of the differences between boys and girls. He told me to ask Father, knowing it would be useless.

Wood splintered above me, and I ducked, certain they'd smashed through the floor—it sounded like someone had thrown our bed from the loft. The floorboards were new and tight. I couldn't see through them to assess the damage the thieves were doing, but they couldn't see me either.

I heard them laughing, and I scuttled back behind the barrel. I hoped they wouldn't think it odd there was no meat in the house, or they might start looking for it. Maybe they wouldn't notice the hollow sound of their boots on the floor.

Who'd have thought the *sight* had tried to warn *me* of danger? It never had before. I hunched down against the earth floor, and something more than cold began to seep in my bones.

Magic. I knew what it had to be, thought I'd never felt it before. The ground began to glow dimly, sullen red with small bits of gold here and there. As I watched, the bits of gold began to grow bigger and the red duller.

I worried for a moment that the raiders would see it, or that they'd caused it somehow, but the force of the emanation soon drove all thoughts of raiders from my head.

My body vibrated from contact with the earth. Power wrenched through me, making it hard to breathe. Did the bloodmages feel this way as they stood over their victims? By all rights I should have been terrified, but the sweet taste of magic prevented fear from touching me.

Red was woven over the gold in layers like a giant woven cloth, holding the gold back.

I stared at it, and suddenly knew what it was I saw.

Magic hadn't always been wrestled from pain and death. Once, so long ago the memory of it had disappeared except for Gram's tales told in secret on dark winter nights, one mageborn child to another, magic had been a joyous thing summoned from the earth. But jealous bloodmages had bound it until no one could use the wildling's power.

Beneath the red blanket, gold magic called to me, singing tenderly in my soul. Something snapped, and one thread of red came unbound. Then another.

Layer by layer the bands of red were being torn away, and the power of it lifted me off the ground. I hovered a fingerspan off the earth as one by one the angry red cords gave way. When the crimson ties broke, I could feel the corrupted touch of bloodmagic pull in places I'd never felt before—like a hair caught deep in my throat. It didn't hurt, but I could feel it all the same. The blood

cords pulled me by their ties to the land of my birth, until
I *saw* . . .

*. . . a tower, dark with the force of the mage within.
He called the magic tied to the land. I felt the strength
of him like the heat of the smithy forge. Madness lurked
in the heart of his call, adding its strength to his purpose.*

Then the vision was gone. With it went the last of the
binding spells of the bloodmages. I felt them go—as any
mageborn native to this land would have. For a moment
the floor glowed brilliantly gold, then the light traveled
up the walls as if driven by demons, fading, leaving me
sitting, exalted, on the ground, alone in the dark cellar.

My eyes told me the magic was gone, but where I
touched the ground, my body still tingled with its sweet
warmth. I felt clean, though I'd never known I was dirty.
I put my fingers against the dirt of the cellar floor and
knew the bloodmage's hold on the magic of the land was
gone.

A loud shout drew my attention to the raiders above
me: I'd forgotten about them. Without the protection of
the magic, fear returned apace. For a moment, I thought
they'd seen the light as well, and waited for them to
storm the cellar to investigate.

My heart pounded, my breath came in quick pants, but
they were only fighting over some piece of loot. Gram's
silver mirror, probably.

Let them fight about it. Let them just go. The longer
they were here, the better the chance they would find me.
They'd been here for a long time now: they should be
getting nervous. The men might be coming down from
the field.

*An immense pot in the cellar fell to the floor with a
crash. The sound quieted the men who stood above.*

*"There's something below us—look for a door outside.
These kinds of places usually have a cellar. There could
be valuables in it."*

I jumped to my feet and ran to the far side of the cellar.

It was dark, but the dirt floor was clear of things that could catch my feet. There was a violent boom from above. They'd knocked over the big shelves near the fireplace.

Without actually seeing it fall, I caught the big soap-making cauldron as it slipped from the peg Daryn had worried was too small for it. I'd have to remember to tell him he had been right. Men liked that—at least Ma said they did. The weight of the cauldron made me stagger, and the handle flipped down and bruised my thumb where it rested over the edge of the pot—but I managed to hold it and my knife without making any noise.

I set the cauldron carefully on the ground. As long as nothing else fell, I was safer now. The shelves had fallen across the trapdoor. There was nothing the raiders could do to the house that we couldn't repair. Nothing they could take we couldn't live without.

I could safely marvel at my vision of the pot falling. I'd never had one so clear, never had one I could use to prevent a disaster. It must be because of the unbinding.

I would tell Daryn about the *sight* tonight, I decided. Not to punish myself, but because I could tell him how it had saved me. If magic was unbound again, maybe I could use my bit of magic to help us, help the village—as Gram had done. I was still smiling when yet another vision took me.

Daryn held the horses in place while Father helped Daryn's younger brother, Caulem, attach the harness to the plow Lord Moresh had given the village two years ago. Father was patient, letting Caulem fumble with the unfamiliar double harness. Beresford had only the older style, single-horse plows.

Something caught Daryn's attention, and he held his hand to shade his eyes as he stared into the rising sun. His body tightened to alertness, and he said something urgently to my father.

Father dropped the leather strap into the dirt and stepped forward to Daryn's side.

After no more than a look, Father grabbed Caulem's shoulders and shouted something at him, throwing the boy onto the horse that hadn't yet been hitched to the plow. He shoved the reins into the boy's hands. Caulem shouted something back, protest written in the stiffness of his jaw. Father took his hat and slapped the horse, sending it running down the path to my parents' house.

The track was wide and the horse knew every rock and rut, sprinting full-out for home. The bandit waiting in the tree at the edge of the field had a finger missing from one hand, but it didn't affect the flight of the arrow that took Caulem in the throat.

The man leaped from the tree and tried to catch the horse, but it had been thoroughly spooked by the run and the scent of blood. It was a working horse, strong enough to pull the raider dangling by its reins as if he weighed no more than a twist of straw. The man held on until he lost his footing and the horse's iron-shod hoof caught him in the leg, throwing him to the ground.

Unhindered, the animal raced on. The message that the bandits had come covered its back in a red blanket of Caulem's blood.

The vision shifted abruptly.

My father was facedown in the dirt, an ax buried in his back. Daryn stood over him, work-hardened muscles lending strength to the blows he dealt with Caulem's walking staff. The men he fought appeared only as vague blurs and flashes of weaponry. Blood ran down Daryn's face and neck until it disappeared in a larger stain of red spreading from his shoulder.

The staff he held broke, and he threw it aside, taking a step forward to protect my father. Metal gleamed, and a sword sliced into his neck.

A winter lily grew out of the unbroken ground, brown-

*ing with the weight of time. A drop of Daryn's blood fell
on the faded, scarlet petals.*

The vision left me, and I sat where I was, stiff with
shock. It was too late for me to do anything. From the
position of the sun in my vision, I knew Daryn had died
before I'd hidden in the cellar, running from his killers.
The shock held me for a moment before the warm rush
of rage followed it.

My hand tightened on the butcher's knife, and I ran
for the ladder. I climbed up three rungs and pressed my
back against the trapdoor, but it wouldn't move. I stepped
up another rung and straightened my knees, forcing my
shoulder against the door and pushing, but the shelving
atop it was too heavy for me to move. I hammered it
with my fists, screaming with fury at the barrier that prevented me from attacking the raiders.

At last, knuckles bloody, I stumbled off the ladder and
sat on the ground—numb in body and soul. The raiders
were gone. If they'd been in the house, they'd have heard
me and opened the door.

I dropped the knife in the dirt and stood up again. A
rough table against the wall contained a few tools in need
of sharpening. One of them was a saw.

I fumbled in the darkness. My hands didn't feel quite
right after hitting the door. I found the saw and set to
cutting my way out. It took a long time to cut the cross
braces of the door with the dull blade angled over my
head. Once the braces were gone, I pulled the door into
sections that fell from the opening and dropped below
me.

With the door out of the way, I slid through the shelves
and climbed out into daylight. Bits of broken crockery
were everywhere, intermixed with chunks of wood and
scraps of torn cloth from Ani's quilt.

In the barn a few chickens, still spooked by the noise
of the raiders, scattered away from me. Daisy the cow
lay dead in the straw. They'd hacked off one hind quarter

and taken it with them, leaving the rest to rot. I looked away from the cloudy film that covered her warm, brown eyes.

Louralou, our riding pony, was gone from her stall, along with every bit of leather harness in the tack room. The piglet was gone as well. They'd left the sacks of grain.

Out of habit, I took out a fair measure of corn and scattered it for the chickens. There was a saddle blanket lying in the walkway where someone had thrown it. I stared at it for a moment.

I ought to cover their faces, I thought. *The crows will come.* The thought of Daryn's eyes eaten by the birds made me violently ill, and I vomited in the straw.

I rinsed my mouth in the bucket hanging in Louralou's stall, then picked up the blanket. I beat it clean against one of the stall walls, and set off to cover my husband's face.

The wind was warm, carrying with it the sweet perfume of spring flowers. Only the torn-up soil of the trail showed that this afternoon was different from any other.

I knew I wasn't thinking clearly. I should have been worried about meeting the raiders again. But it was a distant thought, and I ignored it.

Even so, when I heard men's voices and the creak of a wagon, I stopped, then found a hiding place deep under the bows of an old spruce tree, ignoring the sharp prickles of the needles through my woolen gown. For a moment, I had a strange feeling there were two of me: one here and now, kneeling in my favorite dress, and the other . . .

. . . wearing a stained tunic and a pair of men's trousers with a crossbow clutched tightly in my hand.

I wiped at my eyes with the rough saddle blanket and bit my lip until the pain drove the vision away.

As the sound of the wagon's squeaking drew closer, I recognized Talon the smith's smooth tenor as he shouted something over the rattle of the wagon. It was the villagers, then.

I eased out of the shelter of the spruce. It was much easier to go out than it had been to go in against the growth of needles. Dirt from the cellar stained my gown along with flour from the crock that usually sat on the shelves by the fireplace; the hem was covered with cow's blood. Pieces of spruce hung from my hair, brushing against my cheek.

When they came over the hill, I knew they'd been to the field before me. Knew it because the wagon was carrying something covered by a blanket.

I stopped where I was, unwilling to go any closer. Albrin, who lived closest to my parents, was there on his favorite mare. The wagon was his, drawn by his oxen. Next to him rode Kith, his son, who'd served under Lord Moresh as one of his personal guards until he lost his left arm. Kith had been my brother's best friend.

Three of the four other men also lived nearby; only Talon actually lived in the village. He must have been at Albrin's shoeing horses. Except for Kith, who still had his sword from his time of service, they were armed with scythes and long knives. There was a broken staff on top of the blanket that covered the contents of the wagon.

They slowed when they saw me. I couldn't tell what they thought because my gaze kept slipping past their faces and settling on the covered load in the wagon. My throat was dry and rasped uncomfortably as I spoke.

"They've gone on. The raiders."

"Lass," said Talon, though he was no older than I was. "Aren." The sorrow on his broad face made him look like the hound that lived on Albrin's front porch. "Your father. . . ."

I glanced at the wagon, noticed something dark dripping from the back of it, and hastily looked back at Talon.

"Dead," I said. "From the prints outside my home, one

of them is riding my husband's gelding. His shoes are new," I said.

I didn't remember looking at the ground when I walked out of the house. But I remembered the prints. Quilliar and Kith had taught me to track when we were children. I glanced at Kith, but, as usual since his return last fall, it was impossible to tell what he was thinking.

Talon looked a little disturbed at my change of subject. He spoke slowly. "Caulem must have been coming for help, but they'd posted someone on the main trail to your da's. His horse ran into Albrin's yard covered from ribs to croup in blood. Kith rang the alarm bell and we all headed out. We left some men at your ma's, and the rest of us followed the horse's trail."

I licked my lips nervously, wishing my thoughts weren't so clear. Father had just bought that horse from Albrin, but the track it had followed should have taken it past my parents' house before it ran to Albrin's yard. My parents had an alarm bell in the yard, too. Ma should have been out ringing the bell before the horse made it as far as Albrin's—if she'd been alive to ring it.

The raiders hadn't taken grain sacks from the barn because they already had enough grain, stolen from my parents.

"Ma?" I said softly, as if my quietness would change the answer I knew they would give me.

Talon looked around for help, but no one else took up the story. "They started at Widow Mavrenen's," he said as softly as I had, the way he spoke to fidgeting young horses. "Killed her and that old dog of hers. Took everything that wasn't nailed down. They hit your folks' place next. Mistress Ani was there and your ma. We figure they must have put up quite a fight from the looks of things."

He swallowed and looked uncomfortable. "Poul, he was with us, too. We left him and his da there to take care of things, but we were afraid, from the direction the raiders were taking, that they might decide to hit you up here before they left off."

I nodded dully. Ma, Ani, and her unborn child were dead, too.

"There's no one farther out than us," I said, telling them nothing they didn't already know. My voice was slurring, but I didn't care enough to correct it. "The old place up on the hill has been vacant since old man Lovik died of lung fever last winter. They didn't take much more from our place—just the pony, really. And Gram's silver mirror." I hadn't looked for it, but it must be gone, too.

"How is it that you escaped?" asked Kith suspiciously.

His harsh tones pulled my attention to him. I'd grown up with Kith, fished with him when we were children, danced—and flirted—with him before he'd been called to war. When he'd come back to us, he'd come back with a loss that was more than his arm. . . .

"Time for you to go home, can't fight with one arm. Too bad, really, you'd become quite a soldier . . . "

I swallowed, forcing Lord Moresh's voice away, knowing that they were all watching me. I'd never had visions like this before, as if all I had to do was think of something and the *sight* grabbed it for me.

"It was stupid," I said, finally. I knew another time I'd have been angry and hurt at his suspicion. "I was starting down the stairs to the cellar to get some salt pork for . . . for Daryn's lunch when I heard them outside. So I hid down in the cellar with a rug over the trapdoor. I waited until it was quiet before I came out."

I walked past them then, to the wagon. I think Albrin asked me something, but I couldn't focus on it. I lifted up the quilt—it wasn't one of Ma's, she never used flowers in her patterns.

I stared at the bodies lying in the wagon. Death had marked them so they didn't look like the people I had loved. Someone had closed their eyes, but I tucked the horse blanket over Daryn's head anyway, climbing on the wheel to get close enough to do it. Then I covered them back over with the flowered quilt.

"I think I have some information that the village elders need to hear," I said, stepping down from the wagon.

"About the raiders?" asked Kith. "From what you said, you didn't even see them."

"Mmm?" I looked up at him. If I'd told Daryn about my vision, he might still be alive. I'd promised to tell him about my *sight* if something bad happened. An atonement I couldn't make now except by proxy, with the village elders standing in Daryn's stead.

I even had a good reason to do it, to take my punishment. Magic was loose in the mountains again. I could feel the pulse of it under my feet. I didn't know exactly how it happened, or why. But Gram's stories had always ended. . . .

The old woman smiled at the children who were bundled in quilts on either side of her.

"But someday," she said, "someday, the magic will return. And with it will come the white beast, the sprites, and the giants. The gremlins, the trolls, and all that is fey."

"But Gram," piped the boy, "won't they be angry?"

If Quilliar had been right, Fallbrook needed to be warned.

I spoke quickly, hoping no one had noticed my lapse. "The quickest way to the village is back to our—to my home and down by way of the path next to Soul's Creek to the river."

"What do you want to talk to the elders about?" pursued Kith doggedly.

"I have the *sight*," I said.

There, it was said, never to be taken back. I could not have more effectively set myself apart from the villagers if I had slit my own throat. I couldn't bring myself to care. I would tell the elders, and pay the price they demanded.

The numbness that had protected me since I climbed out of the cellar was fading, being replaced by pain so great it made me want to scream. No one left of my family. No warm husband to huddle beside when I awoke to a crisp, spring morning—never again.

I had done my screaming in the cellar. I turned back down the trail toward—well, it didn't seem like home anymore. It had been that for—I glanced unobtrusively at the sun—only a little more than a day. The numbness settled back down again, like a soft quilt protecting me from the cold.

"What did she say?" asked one of the men I didn't know very well. I thought his name was Ruprick.

"She's in shock," said Albrin shortly. "She doesn't know what she's saying."

Kith's yellow gelding passed me and moved to block my path. Kith sheathed his sword and held out his hand. There was nothing in his face, but when I took his hand, he swung me up behind him, much as he had done in those long-ago days when I'd been his best friend's little pest of a sister.

His horse, Torch, danced a little, throwing me forward and giving me an excuse to press my forehead against Kith's back. If I cried, I could trust him not to tell. Though he'd become wary, behaving as if we all were strangers to him, he wasn't a stranger to me. I knew he could be counted on to keep secrets.

The group was slowed by the oxen, and Kith ventured ahead now and then, sometimes leaving the trail entirely. I could tell he was looking for signs of the raiders, though their trail had turned west just past the croft, away from the village. I hadn't seen any sign of them after that. Since Kith remained silent, I assumed he hadn't either.

Even insulated by my sorrow, I could sense the wild magic that had been gathering since I'd first felt it. The power caused me to sweat as if this were high summer rather than spring. The air was growing heavy with it. I felt as if I were breathing underwater—but no one else seemed to be affected by it. The animals knew, though. Even the imperturbable oxen started to act restless. The horses danced and skittered like untried two-year-olds.

Torch stopped abruptly, bracing himself. His hips dropped underneath me as he clamped his tail tightly against his legs. The oxen bawled and stopped as well, dropping to the ground despite the discomfort of the yoke.

"Raiders?" asked Albrin.

"I don't know, sir," replied Kith. "I wouldn't think they'd bother old Torch, not after the campaigns he's—"

The earth bucked and heaved beneath us. Kith's gelding let out soft little murmurs of distress, his dun coat darkened with the sweat of fear. After a moment the animal's noises were hidden by the roar of the earth's anger. The sound was indescribable. An immense tree dropped not an arm's length from us, but I didn't hear anything when it hit because of the earth's incredible roar.

The shaking slowed. The magic that had consumed me eased, and I could breathe again. A rumble drew my attention to the southern peaks of the mountains surrounding our valley. Silvertooth Mountain slid downward, almost gently. The noise of it was quieter than the earthquake, distant—until it fell across the pass with a thunderous crash, blocking the King's Highway. The earth shook again.

The second time wasn't as bad, but it seemed to go on longer. Albrin's horse had been dumped on her side as the earth buckled beneath her, but during the lesser shaking the mare regained her feet. When the second quake stopped, I could feel only the barest hint of magic.

Except for Hob's Mountain, Silvertooth had been the

tallest peak surrounding the valley. Now it looked as if someone had kicked it into Old Fortress, which was itself leaning aside. As we watched, dust rose from the fall, gradually obscuring the new landmark from view.

"This is a day of ill omens," said Talon soberly, his hands steadier than his voice as he reassured the oxen.

I couldn't see Kith's face, but Albrin looked as if he'd just seen the end of the world. The oxen heaved themselves to their feet. The resultant jostling of the wagon knocked the blanket aside, and I stared into Caulem's dead eyes. My world had ended before the earthquake.

The smith spoke softly to the oxen, and they threw their weight behind their harnesses. The wagon passed us, and Torch sidestepped closer. Kith leaned over, the reins in his teeth, and pulled the blanket back into place.

We followed the trail by Soul's Creek until after it forded the creek and turned to parallel the river. For the first few minutes of travel, the view of the river was blocked by thickets of willow. When the willow thinned out, it wasn't the animals that called a halt this time.

"By the gods," whispered Albrin hoarsely, forgetting we had been worshiping the One God for the last few generations.

Where the river had formerly run, there was nothing but the deep channel it had cut. Soul's Creek emptied into the rocky riverbed, and flowed where it would. Fish flapped weakly in the muddy river bottom, their gills fluttering uselessly in the open air.

"It will come back," I said involuntarily. For a moment the *sight* was more real than the shifting horse underneath me. "By tomorrow night it will flow with mud, and next week the water will rush freely."

Albrin gave me an odd look with a hint of coldness in his eyes. "What do you know of this, Aren?"

I gripped the back of Kith's shirt tightly and shook my head. "I need to talk to the elders," I whispered. "Can we hurry?"

• • •

BEFORE WE REACHED THE NARROW BRIDGE OVER
Canyon Creek, the sky had darkened ominously. Great
clouds traveled south to north, though the more usual
direction was west to east. A fine powder drifted down
like dry snowflakes.

"Ash," I said.

"From a fire?" asked Albrin, who'd been riding nearby
since we'd seen the empty riverbed.

"No," I answered, shivering a little. "Bodies."

After that Albrin dropped away from us. The space
between Kith and me and the rest of the group became
noticeable. I understood how they felt; if I could have
gotten away from me, I would have, too.

THE WOMEN AND CHILDREN OF THE VILLAGE WERE
standing in clusters along the edge of the river when we
came into Fallbrook—as they might well have been. But
the river had been gone for a while by then, so they were
ready to be distracted by the contents of the wagon.

Albrin told them about the raiders, and sympathetic
murmurs seemed to surround me. Someone tugged me
off the horse, but I clung to Kith's stirrup tenaciously.

"The elders," I said.

Albrin, who'd just dismounted, nodded, and said
grimly. "Go with them. It will be a while before we can
call them together. Planting must go on."

So I allowed myself to be hustle-bustled into the warm
inner sanctuary of the inn's kitchen by Melly, the innkeeper's wife. Everyone called her that, though the innkeeper had little to do with the inn. He spent his days
tending his turnips, carrots, and aristocratic pigs whose
pedigrees were longer than Lord Moresh's.

The inn had three sleeping rooms for infrequent travelers and several dining and drinking rooms that were in
use much more often. Food and drink were paid for
mostly by barter, though Lord Moresh and his armsmen

paid in hard currency. My father said Melly made little more than she spent, but it kept her happy.

Melly lived up to her legendary charity by settling me in front of a vast bowl of her husband's turnips.

"Here, child, keep busy with these if you like—or leave them. But your gram always said busy hands are life's great healers." Then she shooed everyone else out of the room, closing the door behind her as she left.

I took out the first turnip and concentrated on skinning the whole thing without breaking the peel. Apples were easy, but turnips required real skill. Melly's knife was sharp, and it slid easily over the turnips. It required all of my attention and no thought, so it worked very well to take my mind off of what had happened—and what I feared was going to happen.

TWO

It was evening before the elders met. Earthquakes, raiders, ill omens notwithstanding, this was planting season, and a farmer worked in the fields from daybreak to twilight.

They planted the lord's fields first; then the villagers could attend to their own lands. This high in the mountains the seasons were too short for dawdling. The elders divided the land, which was held in common by the village, among families for farming. After the lord's tithe, the harvest of each field belonged to the man who farmed it.

The land rights passed from father to son. If a man had no sons, he adopted, or passed them to his daughter's husband. Father's land would go back to the village. The elders might wait a season for me to remarry, but the village could not afford to let cropland lie needlessly fallow. Next spring the elders would give it to a new holder or split it among those who held land already. With the lord's tithe on the harvest and half the land fallow each year to keep it healthy, the village was sometimes hard put to feed itself through the long winter months. There was no emergency so great it could call the men from the planting.

My knife slipped, and the turnip skin, which was half-peeled, broke in two. I sucked on my right thumb where I'd nicked it as I examined the turnip to make sure I hadn't bled on it. My knuckles ached where I'd beaten them against the trapdoor, and my left thumb was bruised from the cauldron handle. My right thumb had been un-injured until I'd assaulted it with the knife.

I went on with my thoughts, distracting myself from what happened this morning even if it meant thinking about what I had to do tonight.

The elders could have met, despite planting. There were a number of elders who weren't farmers. Albrin bred and trained horses and dogs. Cantier, the oldest, still went out with the young men to fish, though his wife often nagged at him to retire. I didn't know how old he really was, but his eldest son was older than my father. Tolleck, the new village priest, was an elder by virtue of the office—though he helped in the fields, too, some-times. Merewich, the headman who presided over all of them, had been a shepherd until his joints became too twisted for the work.

For some things they would have been enough, but Albrin must have decided the earthquake, the disappear-ance of the river, and the blocked pass to Auberg, the village's major market, would require the whole council.

Sitting in the kitchen, I wondered what I would say to them. What if the magic I'd felt had only been the gath-ering earthquake? As time passed, the experience I'd had in the cellar became more and more dreamlike. But there were the visions. Visions such as I had never had before, coming one on top of the other.

My knife shook until I had to stop cutting for fear of doing more damage to my already abused thumb. I swallowed hard and sought the numbness that had protected me so far—but it was dissolving like morning mist.

Whether I addressed the council or not, I had already condemned myself as a mage. Kith wouldn't say anything, but there had been other people who heard my confession. The only way any good would come of my death would be if I could convince them of what I knew to be true.

Magic flowed though these mountains now as it had long ago. The wildlings who had lived when magic was bound were long gone. But I knew in my bones that Fallbrook's valley wasn't safe anymore. Not that it mattered to Daryn or my parents. Not that it mattered to me much, either—but I had a penance to make.

Melly bustled in and took the knife from me. "Sorry, my dear, but it's dark now and the council will be convening."

"I don't hear anyone," I said.

It was true. There should have been the sounds of heavy tables scraping across the inn's public room, where councils were held. The inn walls weren't so thick as to hide voices, and the inn sounded empty.

Melly stepped behind me, took my hair out of its braids, and began to brush it. "They've decided to hold the council out in the inn yard. You were out there when it happened, so I suppose you know old Silvertooth is blocking the highway to Auberg. The farmers are all going to be here to see what the council suggests about marketing the excess crops, and the fishermen will be there, too. Several of the village houses fell when the earthquake hit, and any number more will need work. Thank the One God the inn survived with little damage— though I'll have to have the innkeeper look at the window in the back bedroom. Add the raiders, and everyone in the village will be in attendance. The public room isn't large enough to house half of them."

She rounded the front of me, took a wet cloth from a

bowl, and scrubbed my face. "There, now. You still look like a woman who's lost her family, but now no one will be staring at you to see if they can see tear tracks. No one's business how you mourn, but your own."

I looked at Melly, but I *saw* Albrin's man talking to a group of villagers.

Unnatural, the way she stood there, talking to us as if her menfolk weren't stretched out in the wagon beside us.

"Aren?" Melly said.

I nodded my head, focusing on her face, which was closer to my own than I remembered it being.

"Stand up, now."

I did. She walked around me, hands on hips.

"We'll leave the dress as it is," she decided with a nod. "No harm reminding them what you've been through. The hair made you look wild, but with it braided again and tidy, you look about fifteen."

I felt a hundred and fifteen. She patted my shoulder lightly, and led me to the door.

"Best if you go out on your own," she said. "So they know it's your own idea."

Melly was right, the inn yard was crowded. My desire to address this mob was less than nothing. If Kith hadn't appeared just then to take my elbow, I think I would have walked right back to the safety of the kitchen.

The crowd parted to let us through, more frightened by Kith than moved by courtesy. With his cold eyes and hard face, he seemed more a dangerous stranger than a boy born and bred in Fallbrook. Well enough. I was frightened, too—though not of Kith.

The elders were still shuffling back and forth around the table when Kith set me on the far end of the bench; I would be heard first. The man who'd been sitting there scooted farther down without objection. Not even the woman who lost her place at the other end of the bench complained.

Kith stood to my left, resting one foot on the end of the bench. He folded his right arm across his chest, gripped his opposite shoulder, and closed his eyes. I wished I was calm enough to do that.

When I glanced at the elders' bench, I saw that Koret watched me thoughtfully. He was a big man with a bushy beard that I could remember being black as tar, though it was mostly iron gray now. Rumor had it that he had been a pirate until he was captured and enslaved by one of the southern kings. He escaped and turned up in Fallbrook, looking for work. He married the daughter of the man who hired him, becoming a farmer: a part of the community. He was a soft-spoken man with a gentle manner. The only sign of his past was the scars that encircled his wrists. Scars that might have come from slave manacles. Or not.

When the elders had sorted themselves out, and the people who could not fit on the bench had been lined up in some sort of order, Merewich took the acorn that lay in the center of the table and therefore spoke first.

"I sent Talon to see what damage the earthquake did to the houses. Talon, how did you find the village?"

"Good, sir," answered the smith from somewhere behind me. "Only a few of the houses in town took very much damage, and most of those were larger, two-story buildings. The worst I saw will take only a few days' work to mend."

"Good," said Merewich. "I trust the people in the outlying areas know to come to me with the damage they took. After the planting, I'll organize work crews to repair the worst of it."

He set the acorn down and Koret took it up. "Most of us saw the mountain fall. I trust that someone has ridden out to see if the King's Highway, by some miracle, is still clear?"

"I did," answered Wandel Silver-Tongue, stepping out of the crowd. He ran his harp-calloused fingers over his face tiredly. "As soon as it fell. You'd have to see it to believe it. Not even one of the king's sorcerers will have an easy time clearing it."

"Anyone know if Wedding Pass is clear?" asked Koret after Wandel sat down.

There was a silence, then Albrin, at the far end of the table, stood. "I'll check in the morning. If not, there is a secondary pass over The Groom. Even if the highway is clear through Wedding Pass, though, there is nothing to the north except Beresford. The King's Highway ends there, and the only way from Beresford to Auberg is through here. Wedding Pass isn't going to help us get goods to market. With Silvertooth blocking the road, Auberg is a twelve-day journey over the next best path. I know of a few trails that are quicker, but they're nothing you want to take a wagon over."

He sat down, and Koret set the acorn back on the table as the elders exchanged grim looks. Twelve days rather than two was fearfully long, especially with raiders in the valley. I didn't doubt that everyone in the village knew about the raiders by now.

I stood up, waiting to be recognized. Cantier took up the acorn and nodded at me sourly. "Might as well hear all the bad news at once. Tell us what you can about the brigands, Aren."

I bowed my head and took a deep breath. I'd had all the time I needed to think while I worked in Melly's kitchen.

"Today my parents, my sister, her unborn child, and my husband were killed." It sounded stark, and my throat froze with the truth that I spoke. I had to swallow hard to continue. "Without them I have no close blood relatives still living."

I had to stop. If I cried now, it would ruin my credibility because they'd attribute anything I said to grief or hysteria. Several of the elders relaxed, probably thinking I was going to petition for help. Unlike falling mountains, helping their own was well within their experience.

"My grandmother, Father's mother, died last spring. She spent her life working as a healer, doing it better than most." I looked at them. "I know you've heard stories about her—that she relied on more than her knowledge of herbs and splints to heal you. It was true. My grandmother was as fey as my brother—who died rather than become what the lord's bloodmage had decreed."

Albrin blanched, and several other elders stiffened to alert—this was not usual talk for so public a place. Koret rubbed his beard thoughtfully, and old Merewich just nodded. It was hard to shock Merewich.

"So am I," I said starkly.

Before I could say more, Cantier set the acorn back on the table with a snap. Koret, foreign-raised, snatched it up before the fisherman had quite let go.

"I expect you did not ask to meet with us here to be burned at the stake or pressed. Go on, child."

Tension and terror had held me for so long that I had gotten used to it. Licking dry lips, I said, "Gram said many of us no longer remember much about how and why this land was settled, and no one wants to know anything about magic."

Casually, Kith stretched; when he settled, his shoulder rested against mine. I concentrated on that touch and Koret's impassive face, ignoring the reactions of anyone else.

"Long and long ago, a king inherited a land full of too many people. To the west were the lands of the Black Duke; to the south was the sea; to the north was bitter cold; and to the east were wild lands. In the wild lands lived the magic creatures: trolls, goblins, dragons, and ghouls—things not conducive to human habitation. Wildlings." I relaxed a little as I settled into the familiar cadence of Gram's story.

"So this king called upon his mages, and they set spells upon the magic of the last of the wild lands. Here. The king's mages bound the magic of this land as well as they could, and after them successive generations of wizards tied the threads of magic so tightly that, at last, there were no more wild lands in the world at all, no more wildlings—for they cannot live without magic. This binding allowed human mages no access to the magic either, but they had another way of gaining power."

"Bloodmagic," said Koret needlessly.

I nodded. "Those of us who choose not to use that path have little power. And what they—*we*—have, we hide. Bloodmages are rightly feared—" I looked up, and as I spoke the next words, I met the eyes of each elder in turn—"and any mage can decide to take that path. You have no guarantees that I won't: none other than my word."

I paused, staring at Kith's boot. "Gram's talent was healing, but mine is the *sight*. This morning I could tell something bad was going to happen—but I thought it would be something . . . well, something like a storm or a twisted ankle. So I didn't say anything to Daryn when he left for the fields."

I paused, then said rawly, "He is now dead because of it. I won't make that mistake again.

"While I hid from the raiders, I *saw*"—I added emphasis so that no one there could have any doubt how I got my information—"the raiders kill Daryn, my father, and Caulem. Then I *saw* something else. A bloodmage tore the bindings of the land away, and one of the aftereffects of his spell was the earthquake that toppled Silvertooth."

I expected to feel relief once I'd told them my story—or, if not relief, then fear of my impending death. But I didn't feel anything.

Cantier held out his hand and, after an assessing look, Koret dropped the acorn into his hand.

"Can you prove you are what you say you are, girl?"

I looked at him stupidly for a moment—why would

anyone claim to be a seer if they weren't? When it was apparent that he was serious, I shrugged. "The *sight* comes when it wills. What do you want me to *look* for?"

He frowned, looking grumpier than usual. Finally he pulled up his sleeve, displaying a jagged scar. "How did I come by this?"

I stared at the scar for a bit, then closed my eyes and pictured it in my mind, but nothing came. At last I looked up, opened my mouth, and—visions came, if not precisely the ones I had sought.

Lord Moresh argued with another nobleman. There was no sound, but the smell of blood and death was overwhelming. Moresh gestured toward something lying beyond sight. The other man nodded and turned away as an arrow slid into Moresh's eye.

Glimpses of battlefields full of men one moment and ashes the next. Faces of people flashed by so fast that I could only know that they were strangers to me.

Sound came at last: screams and prayers of the dying. . . .

My face hurt suddenly, and I saw Kith, his upright hand a few inches from my face. But the screams in my head continued unabated. I pushed my face close to his and said, "The wildlings will return."

"Is she all right?" asked Cantier, kneeling on my other side and taking my shoulders in his hands. I realized I was sitting on the ground.

Kith raised his eyebrows and said, "How the . . ." He drew in a breath. "I don't know. I just don't know."

A man in strange livery pulled his gold-embroidered, purple cloak around himself, striking a heroic pose as he stood before his men. Something . . . something happened between one moment and the next. Where he had been was a skeleton in his uniform, standing in front of a skeleton army. Nothing moved but the purple cloak flapping gently in the wind. Then the skull of a horse, bitted and bridled, slid off the narrow bones that held it in place.

It dangled momentarily, held up by the reins. But the finger bones that held the reins fell apart. They all came apart then, the whole lot of them, one after the other. An army of bones in uniforms lying on a field of yellow flowers; bones that shifted to ashes and blew away in the spring wind.

I CLOSED MY EYES AGAINST THE ANGRY VOICES, ONE shouting over the top of another so none was heard. At last Koret's bellow rang over the rest, shouting them down until they were silent.

"Killing the mageborn is barbaric," said Tolleck the priest in his smooth baritone. "The One God does not demand it—he condemns the bloodmages and those who call upon their power from death. But a man . . . or woman cannot help how they were born. To condemn them for it is wrong."

"Brother Gifford did not agree with you," called someone from the crowd. "He had more experience as a priest than you."

"Brother Gifford is not here now," thundered Tolleck in a voice I'd never heard from him. It almost made me look, but I was afraid I'd *see* something else. There was power in his voice, and it subdued the crowd.

Calm and forceful, the priest continued. "It is not for you to condemn someone who has committed no crime."

I *saw* the priest's face, proving that I didn't need open eyes to see. The thought of living with these constant visions for any length of time made me wish Tolleck would be quiet and let them hang me.

"Drink this, Pest," said Kith, putting a glass against my chattering teeth.

I swallowed, tasting apples and poppy juice.

"She needs rest. My home's just around the corner, and that lot won't bother me." It was Cantier's voice, rough and unmistakable.

* * *

I WOKE UP ABRUPTLY, STARTLED BY THE STRANGE SUR-
roundings—though when I gave myself a moment to really look around, I realized I was lying on a makeshift
pallet in the main room of Cantier's house, which
smelled faintly of fish. It was dark but for the banked
embers in the fireplace. From the loft overhead came the
soft sounds of sleeping bodies. I wondered how he'd
talked his wife into allowing me here.

By the darkness and by the silence of the streets, it
was sometime past midnight. I was still wearing my
dress, but it took me a moment to find my boots. As
quietly as I could, I let myself out the door and into the
street.

THE HOME I SOUGHT WAS MY PARENTS' HOUSE RATHER
than my own. I needed to cling to something familiar,
somewhere safe. The house was dark and empty when I
got there. I had nothing to light my way into the interior,
so I fumbled my way into the main room.

Ma's bride chest was highlighted in the faint wisp of
moonlight leaking through the broken oilskin of the main
window. Someone had taken an axe to it, leaving its contents scattered on the floor. I wondered if it was the same
man who destroyed the furniture in my home, or if the
raiders specialized in hacking helpless furniture to bits.

There was blood on the floor, and I lost the humor I'd
been trying to summon. I turned away. A blanket lay in
a rumpled heap in the corner of the room. I snatched it
up and wrapped myself in it, though I didn't believe anything could make me warm again. I sat in the corner
where the blanket had been and stared into the night.

I STAYED AT THE HOUSE UNTIL LATE MORNING, GATH-
ering what I could use from the things the raiders had
left. There wasn't much. The house had been stripped of
food, weapons, and anything anyone could use to pack
things in: sacks, baggage, backpacks, even bedsheets. I

don't know how the blanket I'd used came to be overlooked.

I found an assortment of Caulem's clothing. Father's clothes were gone. I folded my brother-by-marriage's shirts and pants carefully and left them beside the remains of his cot. Perhaps his parents would want them.

My hands stopped as I folded the last pair of pants. I was tall for a woman, though skinny. Caulem had been a growing boy, almost as tall as he would have been as a man, but thinner. Caulem's pants would fit me.

I stood and stripped my clothing as quickly as I could, exchanging it for boy's trousers and a loose-fitting shirt. I had to tighten the drawstrings around my ankles and waist, and fold back the sleeves. The shirt, which had come to Caulem's hips, hit me just above the knee. I belted it to keep it out of my way. His boots were too big, but mine would work.

The boy's clothes made me different from the silly woman who believed in happy-forever endings. The woman who'd killed her husband because she'd tried too hard to be like everyone else.

It occurred to me that I was more than a little crazy. If the priest could have seen me running to my cottage and slipping through the shelves into the cellar, he might not have been so quick to defend me.

Over several days, the dark enclosure of the cellar became my shelter against the world. I left the main floor as it was, covered with the scattered remnants of my life. Like some half-mad animal I cowered in the dark of the earth, leaving its embrace only at night.

I couldn't run from the visions, for they came to me no matter how hard I tried to hold them away. They came with sound more often than not, and sometimes smells as well. I watched as the villagers buried my family in the plot behind my father's house and scattered fragrant petals on the disturbed ground over their graves. All from the closed darkness of the cellar.

I knew what the world outside my cellar was doing, whether I wanted to or not.

LIKE ME, THE VILLAGE BURIED ITSELF AWAY FROM THE truth of its isolation. The planting season was so much work, they were soon lulled into complacency. The raiders were quiet. The houses that could be repaired, were, and new houses were started to replace the one or two dwellings that were beyond fixing. There were a few more earth tremors, but they were weak and easily ignored.

Perhaps, opined the townswomen as they washed their clothes at midweek, the bandits had left altogether. Perhaps they'd wandered on to Beresford and kept going. Didn't Albrin's man, Lomas, report that Wedding Pass was clear, though he hadn't followed it all the way through to Beresford? Wasn't it sad about Hobard's daughter, Aren? Doubtless she was just maddened by the grief of losing so much so quickly, but what a thing to claim! She was lucky that the old priest had died; he would have had her burned for that—and some of the women whispered that the new man was too soft.

No one came from Beresford—but then the Beresforders, like the Fallbrook farmers, were in the middle of spring planting, and they were even farther north and higher in the mountains than we were. Except for Wandel Silver-Tongue, we seldom had anyone come through in the spring, even with the road to Auberg open. Melly usually left only the tavern open until after planting, for Wandel stayed in the manor house when he came. Lord Moresh was particularly fond of him and allowed Wandel free access to his library.

Six days after Silvertooth fell, Wandel had an argument with the steward (and didn't everyone at some time or another, for a more disagreeable man I've never known) and rode out for Wedding Pass.

He sang as he rode, mostly about nasty things that

happen to stewards who have no understanding of music and harpers. He used both hands on his harp. His white mare followed the cobbles of the King's Highway. As they neared The Bride and Groom, Wandel put his harp away.

The steep sides of The Bride rose to his left, casting her shadow over the road, and The Groom rose almost a third again as tall, though not half as steep, on the minstrel's right.

Up on the side of The Groom, the scar of the original road wound steeply to Beresford. The King's Highway was much more gradual because the king's bloodmages could clear through the thick thorn bushes that grew between the mountains as ax and scythe never could. I'd heard the farmers swear the stuff could grow a finger-span in a day and take root where only moss would thrive; but even after centuries, not a single sprig pushed up between the stones of the King's Highway.

Wandel looked at the path lying before him and began humming a soft tune. It was one of his favorite songs, having to do with a man whose house lay in the path of the road. He'd been so stubborn and tricky the mages had finally gone around his house. To this day, Wandel swore, there was a valley where the road traced a neat half-circle around a bare spot of ground where a hut might once have stood.

Goes to show you, the harper liked to point out, that a person could be more stubborn than the worst curse of nature.

Wandel was on the last small incline when he stopped the mare. He slipped off his horse and walked to the side of the road. One of the paving stones was kicked out of place, leaving a deep hole and several loosened stones around where it had been.

"Lass," he said to his mare, "in all my years of riding the Highway, I've never seen a cobble out of place before."

He remounted slowly, and watched the ground as he traveled; but there was nothing more amiss with the road. Not even when it disappeared under the still waters of a lake that occupied the valley where Beresford had been.

"Another rockfall," he said softly to himself or the mare. "Half the mountains in this region are cliff-sided, with boulders falling every spring. I thought Silvertooth might not have been the only one to fall. At any rate, something dammed the river and flooded the valley, which is why the water level in the river has fallen so drastically."

The lake in the valley was deep—only the drooping tops of trees broke the surface where Beresford should have been. The water was mucky with rotting vegetation and worse.

Tight-mouthed, Wandel turned his mare and rode back the way he'd come. By the time he rode into the yard of the inn, he was dusty and looked tired. The innkeeper's boy gave the harper a curious look as he took the Lass, but was too well trained to ask the questions on the tip of his tongue.

There was no one in the public room when Wandel entered. He set his harp and his travel bag down in an inconspicuous corner and ventured into the kitchen, where Melly was cleaning some pots.

"Mistress Melly?"

She turned and wiped her wet hands on her apron as she hurried forward. "Why, Master Wandel, I thought you'd be in Beresford by now."

"So I would," he said without his customary good humor, "if there were a Beresford to be at. Lord Moresh's steward and I had a falling out. Would you be so kind as to give me a room in your inn?"

"Of course, of course, but it'll take me an hour to air it out. What do you mean about Beresford?"

"The whole valley's flooded, mistress."

Her face whitened, but she nodded and led him out to the main room, by tucking her arm under his and ushering him to a bench near the fire. She brought him a tankard of dark ale and, in his hearing, sent her boy to fetch Merewich and then see to the airing of a chamber.

When the old man came, he sat down across from Wandel and braced a hand under his chin. "So, harper. Tell me about Beresford."

Wandel shrugged. "The earthquake must have dammed the river and flooded the valley. There doesn't seem to be a Beresford anymore."

"Did you see any sign of the people?"

The harper shook his head. "No, but I think they'd have had enough time to get out. A valley that size would take a while to fill. Since they haven't shown up here, I guess they headed out to Auberg by some goat trail. It's impossible to tell for certain, since the King's Highway to Auberg is blocked."

"Ah." Merewich nodded and took a sip of the harper's ale. "There's an old trail over Hob's Mountain to Auberg. Kith knows it. I showed it to him myself when he was a lad and his father sent him to help with the sheep. He's not busy with farming, like most of the other men." *He paused, not mentioning Kith's missing arm—the reason Kith wasn't helping with the plowing. "It would do him good to take the trip."*

"Hob's Mountain?" said Wandel.

Merewich nodded. "No thornbush there. Only mountain in these parts that doesn't have it. There's a shorter trail between Carn and Harvest—they're the mountains just south and west of Silvertooth, but you can't take a horse through it."

"You think Kith would take me to Auberg?" Wandel's tone was reflective. "I'm not so certain."

Merewich sighed and shook his head. "Wandel, the folk here who aren't related to someone in Beresford are married to someone who is. Kith will take you over and bring us back news—regardless of what lies between you. Perhaps someone there will know what has happened to the Beresforders. All we ask is that you agree to come back next year and tell us what's happening."

I'd never known that there was something between Kith and Wandel. I would have spent more time wondering what it was, but the vision would no more let me waste time fretting over it than it would give me time to mourn for Beresford.

"You think there is something in the tale the girl told, then, that the earthquake was just a minor part of what has happened?" Wandel took his tankard back and drank deeply.

"Hmm." Merewich rubbed his hand on the table. "I know her grandmother was a witch. She saved my oldest boy. He'd fallen and hit his head on a rock. Four years old and the joy of my life. I took him to her, but I knew it was too late—there was a soft place on his temple that shouldn't have been there. She looked at him, then she looked at me. Without saying a word, she took him and set him on her dining table. She laid her hands on that soft spot and closed her eyes. When she took her hands away, his skull was whole again. Forty-two years ago, and you're the first soul I ever told that to. I'd thank you not to repeat it."

He drank from Wandel's tankard again. "Do I believe her to be mageborn? Yes. Do I think she believes what she says is true? Yes." He looked the harper in the eye. "Her grandmother showed me that mageblood doesn't make a person evil."

Wandel pursed his lips. "Today I saw a cobble knocked askew on the King's Highway."

"Eh?" said Merewich softly. "I'll tell Albrin we'll be borrowing Kith for a few days."

A DAY OR TWO AFTER THIS CONVERSATION I AWOKE stiff and sore from sleeping on the hard earth and stared into the darkness around me. Over the past few days, either I'd grown used to magic or the magic had faded, but I couldn't feel it humming in my bones anymore. The dirt in the cellar was just dirt, cool and dry. Best of all, no visions clouded my mind.

I hadn't changed clothes since I'd put on Caulem's tunic and trousers, and it struck me that he'd never have let them get this dirty. The cellar stank of sweat and sloth.

I bowed my head and bit my lip, wondering what Daryn would think if he could see me huddled in the corner of the basement. And I could almost see Gram, shaking her finger at me.

"You just get up now, Missy, and clean yourself. Then you start planning what you can do to help these people. For the fear and ignorance of a few, you will not let the rest suffer. They will need you soon, and you will be there for them, as I was and my father before me."

I couldn't be certain if it was my imagination or the *sight*, but Gram's words hit home. Cantier had carried me to rest in his house though he had no love of the bloodmages. Kith had been there for me when I needed him . . . as had the priest, for that matter, and I barely knew him—he'd been in the village less than a season.

"With this gift," I said, quoting Gram's favorite lecture out loud in a voice harsh with disuse, "comes great responsibility. We are caretakers. The bloodmages have forgotten that in their search for greater power. They don't care that they are destroying themselves and those around them by what they do. Death magic is evil, and no good can come of it."

"Responsibility," I grumped, but I got to my feet just the same. Without the incapacitating visions I lacked an excuse to cower in the darkness any longer.

I found a change of clothes (more of Caulem's), an old blanket partially torn up for rags and a bar of sweet-smelling soap before leaving the house.

Daylight almost blinded me; I had to stand on the

porch a moment before I could see. There were still a few chickens scratching in the dirt in front of the barn. Seeing the barn reminded me of the dead cow that had been rotting in there for the better part of a week. Somehow I was going to have to get her out.

Soul's Creek was icy cold, and I removed only my boots before stepping in. I scrubbed my face and hands first, while I still had the nerve, then set about washing clothes as quickly as I could. My hair took longer, but at last the dark strands were shiny and free of dirt and oil.

When I was clean and dry, I began tidying the cottage, setting right what I could and sorting through the rest. Some things were so damaged I broke them up for firewood. Others I set aside for repairs. When I finished, I got a bucket from the cellar and headed for the creek again to get water to wash the dirt off the floors.

Whether it was some fading of the long bottled-up magic, or merely the effect of working instead of sitting in the dark trying not to think of anything, I hadn't had a vision all day. It was enough to make me almost cheerful.

The afternoon sun was warm and the air was heavy with the scent of growing things. In the few days I'd spent in self-imposed exile, the world had bloomed. Yellowbells nodded in the gentle breeze where Ma and I had planted them around the house. Wildflowers were scattered shyly along the path to the barn and in the grass of the field where—Daryn's big sorrel gelding grazed.

He must have gotten free and come home.

I set down my bucket and walked past the barn to the field beyond. Daryn had left the gate open the morning he left. I closed it behind me as I stepped into the pasture, more out of habit than anything else. The sound of the hinges caught the horse's attention and he faced me, pricking his ears for a moment before trotting briskly to me, whickering.

He stopped a few feet away and snorted, tossing his head once before shoving it into my midsection and rubbing it against me. Since he was still wearing the remains of his working headstall, the rubbing hurt. I slapped him lightly on the neck.

"See here, sir," I said catching the shanks of the bit. "Stop that, Ducky." Daryn had originally called the horse Fire Hawk, or some such romantic name, but Caulem called him Duck instead, and that was the name which stuck.

I stripped the bridle off—from the looks of it, it hadn't been off since the raiders had stolen him. Sweat darkened his coat under the leather and there were several places where the hair had rubbed away, leaving small bare patches of pink skin. The reins, once long enough to drive him with, were a little shorter than my arms.

"Someone tied you by the reins, eh? Not too smart."

I continued to mutter soft nonsense to him as I opened his mouth to see if he'd hurt himself when he broke free. He put up with it for a moment, then stretched his nose in the air and forced me to release him. He forgave me for the indignity as soon as my hands were off his nose, and pushed his head forward to be scratched some more. Someone had pulled his shoes, perhaps to make it harder to track him.

"Well," I said, "I was wondering how I was going to get that cow out of the barn—now I just need something to use as a harness. Maybe Kith will loan me something."

The practical words didn't hide the tears, but I wiped them away briskly. Stupid to cry over a horse's return, but for some reason I didn't feel nearly as alone as I had this morning.

I left him in the pasture, set the bridle aside for mending, and continued with my chores. The cow could wait until tomorrow. I whistled a little tune as I scrubbed the cottage, but it echoed and made the house more empty, so I stopped. I'd done my weeping in the darkness of the cellar, and in Duck's mane; time to be done with it.

When the house was clean, I caught the five remaining chickens and put them in the coop, where they would be protected from predators. While I was measuring grain for the fowl, I heard the sound of hooves on hard-packed earth.

My heart leaped to my throat, but it was only one horse. It wasn't likely that a raider would ride out alone, at least I hoped not. Still, I stayed in the slight protection of the barn until Kith's red hair came into sight around the bend in the road.

He rode at a brisk trot, his back straight from years of military experience and Albrin's teaching—I rode that way myself. Torch, his yellow dun, was hammerheaded and thin-necked, but his strong legs were straight and heavy-boned. There was a spring to his step that would never let him be ugly while he was moving. He was big for a riding horse, though still a couple of handspans shorter than Duck.

There was no hesitation in Kith's movement as he swung off Torch and turned to face me, but I thought I glimpsed uncertainty in his eyes before he hid it behind the wall that kept him separate from others.

For an instant I *saw* a much younger Kith running at top speed with Quilliar tearing after him, wild glee lighting both of their faces. It hurt me afresh that the free-spirited boy I'd grown up with had turned into this reserved, dour stranger.

I smiled politely at him, glad he hadn't come the day before and caught me wallowing in self-pity or writhing madly under the effects of the *sight*. With the first humor I'd felt for a long time, I gave him the formality his demeanor asked for. "Greetings and well-seeming, Kith."

He gave me a suspicious glance, and I remembered his support when I stood before the elders. Softening my teasing with more warmth, I said, "What brings you here?"

His jaw clenched, causing his pale skin to flush under his cheekbones. "Beresford valley is flooded."

All humor left me, and I stepped forward to grip his arm—I had friends and kin there, too. "I know, I *saw*."

Kith nodded, as though it was something he expected, but then Moresh's bloodmage traveled with the army, so perhaps he was used to magic. "The harper rode up Wedding Pass yesterday; he says the whole valley is underwater. Nobody from Beresford has come this way, so we think they must have left for Auberg when they realized that the water was going to cover the village." He looked at me, and I shook my head. I hadn't seen the Beresforders, hadn't tried to see them.

He continued after a brief hesitation. "Wandel and I are going on the old trail over Hob's Mountain to see if any villagers made it out."

I kept my hand on his arm, knowing there must have been a reason he'd come to see me before they went.

"Aren?" He looked away from my gaze. "Would you see if you can tell what happened to Danci? If she's all right?"

"Danci?" I repeated. She was a widow living in Beresford who had begun a campaign of courting Kith that must have been rather more successful than anyone had suspected, if it had caused Kith to come to me.

"Do you know what happened to her?" he asked. "If she's not in Auberg, I'd like to have some idea of where she's gone."

I gave him a wry smile. "I can try, but you saw what happened when I tried to see Cantier's scar—all I got was faces of dead men, most of whom I didn't even know. I've been having visions like mad ever since Silvertooth fell, but I don't have any control over them."

He raised an eyebrow. "You don't remember? You grabbed Cantier and told him his dog had done it when it was hurt and afraid." He gave me a small smile. "Then you patted him on the cheek and said something to the effect that people and dogs had a lot in common. You were pretty frightening, Pest. If it hadn't been for the priest . . . It was a good day for you when Old Gifford died and Tolleck came to the village."

I nodded. "I remember the priest. Well enough. If I can find her for you, I will. Come into the house so I can sit down."

I did *not* want to do this. No visions all day—well, only that little one about Kith and Quilliar. But Danci had been—was—my friend, too.

Kith led his horse to a patch of grass and ground-tied him before following me into the cottage. I waited for him to shut the door, then took a seat on a stool set against a wall. As it was the only seat of any kind left in the house, Kith was forced to stand. Leaning back, I closed my eyes and let Danci's face form in my mind. If it had worked with Cantier, it might work for Danci.

Honey-brown hair, I thought, with a touch of curl. Gray eyes that glittered with fun and a stubborn jaw. Clear skin and a nose slightly too long for her face. Even as I cataloged Danci's features, her image faded into another face.

Predatory eyes, cinnamon-colored and slitted like a cat's, were startling, but his features were human. Merriment and laughter touched his face, which was a gray darker than night's shadow. His eyes met mine, and his brow lifted in mild inquiry. I was uneasily certain that he saw me, that perhaps the vision was as much his as it was mine. For an instant I glimpsed loneliness that matched mine, and I wondered what he had lost.

"Hob?" said Kith's voice in my ear. "You mean Hob's Mountain?"

I blinked stupidly at him for a moment, oddly startled by the color of his skin. "I don't know. Do I?"

"All you said was 'Hob.' "

Still half-caught in my vision, I shook my head, unable to answer him because I didn't remember saying anything. "You said you're going to Auberg by the old trail over the Hob?"

"Yes."

"Would you mind if I went with you? Duck's back, so I wouldn't need to borrow a horse." I started to get up, but a wave of dizziness caught me halfway up.

"Did you see something?" He pulled me to my feet and steadied me a moment.

I nodded. "Nothing to do with Danci. I have no idea what it means, but I think that I might find out on the trip over." It was something to do besides sit here and contend with memories and visions. Maybe, if I kept busy, the visions would go away. Even this one I'd had about the wildling with red-brown eyes wasn't as consuming as the ones I'd had earlier.

Kith nodded once, and stepped outside. "Fine, then. I'm meeting the harper at the inn just before dawn. Pack food to last at least four days."

I followed him to his horse. It took him a few moments to gather his reins, and I thought about how frustrating he must find it to have only one arm.

"If you take the ends of the reins in your teeth you could collect them faster and more evenly," I observed.

He smiled at me, surprising me with a glimpse of his old self. "I do, if no one is watching." Reins properly tightened, he stepped into the saddle.

"Kith?" I asked abruptly.

"Hmm?" His horse shifted its weight impatiently.

"Would you teach me how to use a knife? I can use a bow—Father taught me. But that wouldn't do me any good in close quarters. I've got one of Daryn's knives in the house." It was in the cellar, waiting for sharpening. I could do that tonight.

"Fighting?" He looked thoughtful. "I suppose I ought to, with you living out here alone." He wasn't stupid enough to tell me that I ought to move into town—the villagers might be more dangerous to me than the raiders.

"Fine. Bring your knife with you when you come, and we'll start tomorrow."

"Right."

"Aren?" he said.

"Yes?"

"Are you sure you want to bring Duck? No offense, but he's not really a riding horse. That trail is really rough, even dangerous in some places. I could borrow one of Father's mounts for you."

"Could you?" I said doubtfully, remembering Albrin's reaction on the long ride to the village. My memories must have been accurate, because Kith flushed.

"Never mind," I said. "Give him some time. Duck and I will do just fine. Remember, I've been over the trail before—with you, as I recall."

He looked blank for a moment, then grinned. "And wasn't your father fit to be tied about it, too? I'd forgotten that. Quill and I hiked up the Hob to spend our first night alone, feeling all grown-up and daring. Got to the place we were going to camp, and there was his skinny baby sister. Never did tell us how you got there ahead of us."

I laughed. "I was afraid to. I knew Quill would tell Father, and I'd never step out of the house again. I climbed the cliffs straight up rather than taking the route you did. It cut miles from the trip, but about halfway up, I wasn't sure I was going to make it."

He shook his head, and shifted his weight so Torch started back up the trail. "Always did have a fool's courage, I'll say that for you. See you in the morning."

"See you," I said, watching him ride away. With the suddenness of spring, the wind chose that moment to turn cool, sending a chill down my spine—a chill that somehow reminded me of dark skin and cinnamon eyes.

THREE

The streets were empty in the predawn hours. Duck's unshod hooves hit the dirt road quietly. A few dogs barked as I rode past their houses, but I didn't see any people until we neared the inn.

Merewich stood with Albrin. Even from a distance I could tell they were arguing fiercely, though in tones so hushed I didn't even catch the echoes of their voices. Beside them, isolated by the stone-grim expression on his face, Kith stood looking out at the darkened streets, absently rubbing his hand against the side of Torch's face. The gelding was the first to notice our approach.

Alerted by his horse's fixed attention, Kith said something to the other two men. By the time I rode into the inn's cobbled courtyard, both Merewich and Kith's father had subsided into silence.

Kith nodded in greeting. "Wandel is saddling his horse, then we'll leave."

I gave him a half-smile, but my attention was on Albrin, who turned his head aside as if he could not see me. I swallowed uncomfortably. Albrin had taught me how to ride and where the best strawberries grew in the spring.

Merewich patted my knee, talking as if Albrin couldn't hear him. "Give him time. I've talked with the priest, and he believes—as do I—that we haven't seen the worst of this. Brother Tolleck is something of a scriptural scholar. He says there'll be dark days ahead, and I find myself agreeing with him. Something rather worse than a few raiders. Mind that you keep your eyes open."

I nodded my head, turning away from Albrin to meet the old man's eyes. "I will."

Wandel came from the stable with his sweet-faced, creamy-white mare, and stepped into the saddle. He moved like a man several decades younger than he was— almost like Kith. I frowned, wondering why a harper moved like a soldier.

"My dear," he exclaimed, seeing Duck's bridle for the first time, "what *are* you using for a bridle? It looks like it's made of knotted rags."

I grinned at him, though the expression felt odd after so long. "It is—but it's a hackamore, no bit. Raiders took every scrap of leather in the barn. This was the best I was able to come up with. It's not as if Duck needs much more than a reminder now and again."

Duck stretched his nose toward the little mare. She let him in range, but then her small ears flattened and her eyes rolled wickedly as she snapped her teeth at him. Hurt and indignant, Duck pulled his muzzle out of harm's reach.

"The Lass doesn't like other horses," commented Wandel needlessly.

"Or children," said Merewich.

"Or dogs," added Kith with a faint smile.

"Or women," agreed the harper, who wasn't above us-ing his horse's peculiarities as fodder for song—or, I could see, to defuse tension. "I had the prettiest little wife once. . . ."

"Come on," said Kith. "If we don't start now, he'll be here telling stories until the sun goes down."

Wandel shook his head and handed his mare off to Albrin. "Aren can't ride bareback the whole way. Let me find a saddle for her to use in the stable."

He came out with a saddle, blanket, and saddlebags. While I saddled Duck, he mounted his gray mare. I divided my bundle evenly between the two saddlebags he'd brought out. I walked Duck out before checking the cinch. It was a little loose, so I tightened it before mounting. I took my time, refusing to give in to the awkward silence that hung over the courtyard by hurrying.

"Wandel, old friend," said Merewich, finally breaking the silence.

The harper smiled, and gripped the elder's hand firmly. "Until next season, then." He turned to Kith's father. "Albrin."

Albrin shook his hand, but when he turned to his son, Kith rode out without speaking.

WE USED THE TOWN BRIDGE TO CROSS ONTO THE LORD'S side of the river. The lord's fields were already tipped with green as the earliest of the crops sprouted, having been planted several weeks before the village's.

It took several miles for the horses to find a comfortable pace for traveling together. Kith's horse was used to traveling with large groups, but the harper's mare liked to choose her own pace. Then there was Duck. He had a ground-eating, syncopated walk that was too fast for either of the smaller horses: his alternative was the gait he used when plowing, which was too slow. Only when the animals decided that they had to travel together did things calm down.

There were serfs in the farther fields. The manor and lands were smallish for a lord's house, or so I'd been told. Lord Moresh had several much larger elsewhere. I didn't know how many serfs he had to work the land because they seldom came to the village and were discouraged from conversing with the freemen, but I supposed them to be fewer than fifty.

A work party of six men was clearing the irrigation ditches of winter's debris. None of them looked up, though I rode less than a long stride from several of them.

Farther on, a woman piled the burnable rubbish on a small donkey cart. She might have ignored our passage as well, if Wandel's mare hadn't decided to take exception to the beast.

Snorting and dancing, she skittered halfway across the road—startling the poor donkey rather badly. The woman dropped her bundle of dry sticks and ran to the donkey's head. Briefly her eyes met mine.

Wandel controlled his mount, then swept a flourishing bow. "My apologies, lady. My mare is overset by having such a large audience for her antics." The Lass snorted and shook her head, mouthing her bit impatiently.

Head bowed, the woman nodded, clearly waiting for us to move on so she could get back to her task. I noticed that her hands were shaking—in fear of Wandel? I looked at the minstrel, but, clad in his usual bright-colored foppery, he appeared no more dangerous to me than a hound pup.

I rode on, thinking about what I'd lost and what that woman would never have. I stored the sight of the other's lifeless eyes and trembling hands in my memory, to be brought out should the temptation to feel sorry for myself return. At least I'd had a family to lose—and I wasn't prey for any man who happened by.

BY MIDMORNING WE REACHED THE END OF THE CULTI-vated fields. Choosing a deer trail with seeming randomness, Kith led us into the dense, thorn-infested woods beyond. I hadn't been out this way since I was a child without the chores of adulthood. The trails tended to change a bit from year to year, but I didn't think this was the one I'd taken on the way to the Hob.

Kith, though, didn't hesitate. He'd obviously been riding up here lately, because he hadn't known the paths this well when Lord Moresh recruited him.

I frowned past Wandel at Kith's back. He was tense, like a hound on the trail. He was always looking to one side of the trail or the other, and I could swear he was testing the air for scent now and then. Torch seemed to be infected with the same restless urgency as his rider. He paced forward with his head up, nostrils flared, prancing ever so slightly.

Well, the forest felt different to me, too. As if there were something watching us. But the thornbushes made spying difficult. If anyone was crashing through the thick brush, we'd have heard them. Maybe it was an aftereffect of the magic's release that made me so unnerved. More likely it was watching Kith act like someone was watching us.

"Anything wrong, Kith?" I asked. "You're acting like a mouse in a fox's den."

"Nothing," he said. "But I feel . . ." He looked back at me. "If I say this, people are going to think I'm as weird as you."

I batted my eyelashes at him. "I'm not weird, I'm evil—the One God declares it so. Just ask Poul's mother."

He rolled his eyes, then turned his head so he could watch where he was going. "I feel like the forest is alive."

I thought about it a moment, and decided I felt the same way. Not that I'd say so. People might think I was weird.

"Me, too," admitted Wandel. "But forests always bother me. I can't see if there's anyone else around. Too easy for someone to set up ambushes."

"There's no one here," replied Kith shortly. "I'd smell them if there were."

Smell them? The trail narrowed, and I turned my attention to riding.

For the first time, I regretted not accepting Kith's offer of a riding horse. Trails that work for roe deer aren't built for a seventeen-hand draft horse—let alone for one with a rider on top. Finally, frustrated, I kicked my feet free from the stirrups and lay flat on his back, trusting him to follow the others without much fuss.

When Wandel pulled up suddenly, Duck got too close to the the Lass. She let fly with her heels, but Duck had gotten used to her tactics and pushed forward so she couldn't get room to put much force behind her kick. Infuriated, she spun on her hind legs, disregarding her rider and the dense flora, teeth flashing as she tried to bite poor Duck.

I grabbed the rolls on the front of the saddle and held on despite the branches that gripped and tore at me while Duck backed rapidly away from the charging she-demon.

Wandel leaned forward and sang softly to the mare. I didn't catch the words, but I happened to be sliding off in the right direction to get the full effect of the switch from enraged nightmare to child's docile mount. The surprise sent me slithering all the way to the ground.

The Lass stood still, eyes half-closed in ecstasy as Wandel sang a lullaby to her; only the speed of her breathing remained of the wild-eyed beast of a moment ago. The rare sound of Kith's laughter brought an answering grin to my face.

Wandel finished the chorus and patted his mare's white neck.

"I know," he said. "Oddest thing I've ever seen, too. Most of the Lass's antics are just flash and spit—I think she enjoys the attention."

The mare swiveled an ear toward the harper and cocked her hip, resting on three legs as if she were dozing—but the eye I could see was wickedly bright.

I found a place in the trail relatively clear of brush and remounted. "Why did you stop in the first place?"

"That," said the harper, pointing through the trees.

"The hob court," said Kith.

I maneuvered Duck until I could see the old stone foundation through the dense growth. Somewhere we must have joined up with the trail that I used to take, because the view was a familiar one.

The stones might have been the remains of some ancient farmer's storehouse, but by some trick of fancy or weather wear, they looked as if they were the remnants of a tiny castle, complete with curtain wall and battlements.

"Gram called it the sprite's court," I said, "but I suppose we'll never know. Grandpa trapped the high country in the winter; he said you could find unusual remains all over these parts—reminders of the wildlings who used to live here. He said he found a whole city once, nestled in a narrow ravine; but when he lost sight of it looking for a way down, he was never able to find it again." I wondered if it really was a sprite's castle.

"Your Grandpa liked to tell stories," said Kith repressively before starting off again.

I grinned at Wandel. "Yep, and about half of them were hog hooey. But deciding which ones were which was half the fun." More soberly, I said, "Lord Moresh's brother disappeared on Faran's Ridge. They hunted for him for weeks, but never found so much as a scrap of cloth."

The harper nodded. "There are many such tales here in the mountains. Too many to be dismissed as complete fiction." He set the Lass on the trail at a trot to catch Kith, and I brought up the rear.

THE GROUND BEGAN TO SLOPE GENTLY UPWARD AND the woods cleared a bit. The thornbush disappeared from the mix of underbrush. Overhanging branches no longer reached clear across the trail, so I could sit up, a position that I found much more comfortable.

Wandel brought his harp out. In keeping with the mood Kith had set earlier, he played a few tunes about the wild creatures who had held these mountains so long ago. I joined in with the ones I knew, ignoring Kith's exaggerated winces when I lost the pitch. Ever gracious, Wandel ignored my mistakes.

He switched at last to a tale of King Faran, the wizard-king who conceived of the highway. The ridge that formed the southwestern border of the valley was named after him because he was said to have won a battle there, though there was no real proof of it.

He had been, according to Gram and to Wandel's song, handsome and charismatic. He'd spent a long time as a warrior before taking up the additional robes of magery. Faran ruled wisely and well until the madness that inevitably twists bloodmages caught him—or so the stories said. I don't know how a bloodmage could be a good king, mad or not. The tower he'd thrown himself from was still standing (or so I'd heard).

I hadn't heard the story Wandel played, but it had a catchy tune and merry verses. Kith unbent enough to join in. He added a few verses himself, most of which were of the kind I'd have expected a soldier to know.

As we came out of the trees to the drier, grassy slopes of the foothill below the Hob, Kith stopped singing abruptly. Urging Duck beside the others, I saw what had brought on his silence.

Halfway up the foothill, below the first cliffs, was a boulder twice the size of my croft. It hadn't been there long. Looking up, I could see the raw places on the mountainside where it had broken loose and bounced. A shattered oak lay in aftermath of its passing, leaves still green with spring's promise.

I whistled. "I'd have hated to be here when it fell."

The sight of the boulder, a reminder that our world had come crashing down around our ears, cast a pall over our party. At least it dampened Wandel's mood, and without his steady cheer, Kith's grim nervousness infected us all.

We were silent as we climbed the gentle rise to the Hob. The mountain was the tallest of those surrounding Fallbrook, but we didn't need to go over the peak. The trail to Auberg twisted and turned over the mountain's shoulder, working its way along the only negotiable path through the cliffs. The route itself was about the same length as the one the King's Highway followed, though it looked shorter on a map. Maps, even good ones, didn't take into account the amount of a trail's climbing and descending.

The first part of the path was easy, just as I remembered it. The trail followed the bottom edge of the cliffs in a gentle rise that traversed the side of the mountain in the opposite direction from Auberg. The only alternative was to go straight up the cliffs. I smiled and followed the others.

It was several hours before the cliff gave way to a steep slope dotted with evergreens. The trail twisted back and forth among the trees until we reached the base of an enormous, steep, skree slope.

It looked as if a giant had taken a bucket of sand and poured it down the side of the mountain. The slope stretched from the very peak of the mountain to the bottom, now far below us. The trail narrowed to a goat's path that traversed the skree at a very steep angle. We'd be going up.

Wandel swore, looked at me, and flushed.

"That's why no one in their right mind would take a wagon through here," I said. "There's a lot of grazing up there." I nodded toward the top of the trail. "The shepherds bring their flocks up this during the height of summer to save the fields in the valley—and they lose a few sheep here every year. I haven't ever been all the way through to Auberg, but I've been told this is the worst of it—though there are some other rough spots."

Kith had already started up the slope ahead of us. It was obvious from the way his horse slipped and scrambled that the path didn't offer much better footing than the looser rock on either side. It was steep, too.

Wandel started his horse across. I waited until he was well on his way before setting Duck to it. On a trail like this, I wanted room to maneuver. Ideally I'd have waited until Wandel was at the top, but Duck was already starting to fret at being left behind. When we crossed, I wanted his mind on his footing, not on catching up the horses ahead of him.

Before we were a tenth of the way up, Duck was coated in sweat and gray dust. I could feel the subtle trembling of his overworked muscles as he hauled me slowly up the mountainside. I sat as still as I could, and crouched over his big shoulders to let the gelding find his own pace.

If the trail hadn't been so narrow, it might have been better to dismount. On my own, I probably would have done so. But since Kith had tackled it mounted, the rest of us manly warriors had to do the same. I smiled sourly to myself. I would have expected childhood competitions to die out with adulthood—but there was no way I was going to dismount if Kith was riding.

Wandel was about halfway to the far side when the Lass lost her footing where the trail crossed the smooth face of a large piece of unbroken shale. The little mare jumped and scrambled frantically but couldn't stop her downward slide even after reaching the end of the slick rock face and hitting the rougher surface of loose rock that made up most of the trail.

I stopped Duck foursquare in the trail. I had few seconds to worry before the Lass's rump hit Duck's chest with considerable force. My stout gelding grunted and rocked back on his haunches, but his weight and his shoeless, big feet gave him better traction than the mare had. He slid backward a pace or two before we all stopped.

"Bless you for bringing that horse," gasped Wandel, patting the Lass, who was blowing hard. "I thought that was going to be it. If he were any lighter, we'd have all been tumbling down to the bottom."

I was busy watching a rock the mare's feet had knocked loose finally hit the valley bottom. Duck shuffled back another step, then took advantage of my inattention to snatch a few strands of grass that poked out among the rocks, proof that horses have no imagination.

I shook my head in reply to Wandel's comment. "Nah, that would have been too easy. Surely all the tales that you've told will win you a more glorious and painful fate."

He laughed. "I'll keep that in mind while we try this again."

Kith was waiting for us at the top by the time Wandel urged the Lass forward. This time, I held Duck back until the Lass was on the far side of the rock sheet before letting him follow. When I reached the small meadow at the top, the others were already loosening their cinches. I dismounted and followed suit, slipping the bit so Duck could graze while he rested.

"The place I want to camp is about a league from here," said Kith. "That will give us an early night, but there aren't very many good places to camp past there. We'll make it to town by late afternoon anyway."

"Right," I agreed, not feeling all that fresh myself. Sitting in the dark for a week wasn't the best preparation for a trek through the mountains. Wiping the sweat from my forehead with the back of my sleeve, I looked around and tried to match what I saw with my last journey here.

"Hmm," I said, "this isn't too far from where we camped that time, is it?" I didn't wait for Kith's reply.

"Weren't there some runes or something on some rocks down there?"

"Runes?" inquired the harper.

"Mmm. Want to take a look while the horses rest?"

"I'll stay with the horses," Kith volunteered.

There was something in his voice that caused me to look sharply at him, but the expression on his face was simply reserved.

"I'd like to see them," replied Wandel, though he groaned as he stood up from the knee-high boulder he'd been sitting on.

"Walking will help keep you from stiffening up," I said, trying both to sound wise and not to look as stiff as I felt.

The harper raised his eyebrows with hauteur that would have done Lord Moresh proud. "My child," he intoned, "when you have traveled as many miles as I, you will understand that nothing—*nothing*—keeps you from stiffening up."

"If you don't come back by sunset, I'll come looking for you," Kith offered, watching as I searched for the right place to set off back down the mountain. He might have been amused, but it was hard to tell.

The path I chose wasn't the same one the three of us had taken almost twenty years ago. As I recalled, we'd been trying to find a way down that would allow us to avoid the skree slope (that the boys had already been across once). We'd run into thorn thickets at the very base of the mountain and had had to climb all the way back to our starting point, but scrambling around had led us to . . .

"There," I said pointing to a large, reddish rock balanced against another, both easily taller than three men standing one atop another.

I had led us too far down, so we had to scramble back up to the site.

"Here," I said, panting. "On the underside, where the weather couldn't wash them away."

They weren't as impressive as I'd remembered them. Merely worn black lines on stone, almost pictures but not quite. Wandel didn't seem to mind.

He scrambled close to the faint marks and crouched on his heels with an ease that gave lie to the stiffness he'd been complaining about. He frowned a moment, then opened his purse and unwrapped a bit of char. With a delicate touch he added a mark here and there, sometimes merely darkening what was already there, but once he added a whole series of the little symbols.

"Can you read it?" I asked in unfeigned awe. I could read a little, thanks to Gram—but that was the king's tongue. Only noblemen knew how to write anything else, noblemen and scholars.

The harper nodded. "A bit. I think. Some of the runes are different." He pointed at one. "I've never seen anything like that. And here, see, this didn't have this tail— but it makes sense if I change it so."

"So what does it say? Do you know who wrote it? How old it is?"

"Well," he said dryly, "it's older than the last time you saw this. Any scholar could have written this. It's an ancestor of Manishe—a common tongue among scholars, though it hasn't been in everyday use for four hundred years or so."

He said "four hundred years" as if it were a few days. Harpers were strange that way.

"The mercenary patois has its roots here." He tapped the rock with the hand that still held the char, leaving a dark blotch on the stone. "But of course they have altered it almost beyond recognition—simplifying it to three or four hundred code words that even the stupidest man can command in a short period of time with the proper instruction. That way it doesn't matter what country a man comes from."

He paused, happily surveying the black marks. "But this, this is very old. Legend says that mankind stole writing from another race—the dwarves. There's some of their work in the museum at the king's castle of state. A goblet, three plates, and a sword. The sword has runes on it, one of which looks just like this." He pointed to a faded mark, one that looked to me just like the one next to it—or the one above it, for that matter.

"That's a mark we don't have in our Manishe, though it's supposed to be read as if it were two other glyphs combined. Now a scholar who wanted you to think this was a message written by dwarves would probably write something that looked like this, but—" he said intensely, "—but how many scholars do you think would have climbed down the backside of this infernal mountain to do that?" He didn't wait for an answer. "Right. That's how many of them I think came here, too."

His enthusiasm was infectious—I had obviously happened upon a hobby of his.

"So you think it was written by dwarves?" I asked. The dwarfs had died out a long time ago, victims of plague, war, or the same thing that had killed the rest of the wildlings.

"Perhaps, but we weren't the only ones to steal dwarf runes. This says . . ." He continued speaking in a language that was harsh and nasal.

HIDDEN FROM THEIR SIGHT, THE HOB WINCED, FLATTEN-ing his ears against his head. His spells allowed him to interpret what they were saying, but he *knew* the language the musician was butchering. Manlings had little enough appreciation of beauty in their souls, but this was extreme. Never had he heard such an accent, though he supposed after—how long *had* he been asleep?—things could have changed.

The girl, the one he'd seen in that brief seeking vision yesterday, spoke again. "What, exactly, does that mean?"

The older man smiled, his face lit with the joy all scholars share in new discoveries. Some things had not changed. "It says, 'Be welcomed here, fair travelers of good heart: benevolent souls have always been welcome on the mountains of the hob.' "

Close enough, thought the hob.

"Hob's Mountain," she said touching the stone.

The hob drew in his breath at the magic that pulsed wildly around the girl. Didn't they teach their younglings better than that? Such a signature would attract all sorts of nasties.

I TOUCHED THE ROCK. IT WAS OLD, SO OLD THAT ONLY bits and pieces came to me.

A dark-skinned hand, twisted with hoary years, held a brush that he carefully dipped in a clay pot of dark ink . . . a sense of mischief, for hiding the message would allow them to torment the wicked without warning them off.

Foul weather, I thought—or maybe it was that long ago artist—*mud and rust and broken swords*. I looked at Wandel, but he was still examining the rock. I don't think he would have noticed if I had fallen on my back and foamed at the mouth.

"Unless they were known by another name," he said, "I've only heard of hobs in two contexts. The first one is the name of this mountain. When I first came here . . . oh, thirty years ago now, I thought it was named for a man, like Faran's Ridge. The headman before Merewich, Ivn, said not. Said that the mountain was supposed to belong to a hob. No one in Fallbrook, Auberg, or Beresford knew exactly what a hob was, except that it was a wildling and relatively benevolent, and it owned this mountain, or belonged to it. The other is in an old song that I heard far south of here—I'll sing it for you after we make camp."

• • •

THE HOB SAT IN THE SHADOWS AND WATCHED THEM leave. Loneliness and fear ate at him, a loner by choice who had prided himself on his daring and courage.

The last, he thought. *I am the last one left.* The thought left ashes of sorrow in his mouth, and he lowered his head and wept for his people, who had only a mountain to remember them.

WHEN WE FINALLY GOT BACK TO WHERE THE HORSES waited, Kith had them ready to go. He led the Lass to Wandel.

"Mount and ride," he said, biting off the words.

It was hard to tell if he was still twitchy from the same unease that had gripped him earlier, or if there was something else worrying him. I hurried to Duck and, after a quick check to see if Kith had tightened the cinch (he had), I mounted, falling back into my usual place behind Wandel.

The area was relatively level, one of the shoulders of the mountain, almost a hanging valley except that the far side fell rather than rising in a peak. Kith led us into the grassy land at a brisk trot. Despite the rest, the horses were too tired to move quickly for long. As soon as we were on open ground, he slowed his horse and waved us forward.

I could see a slight tic by his eye. Torch was collected and ready to sprint, though Kith was holding the reins loosely.

"Sorry," he said. "I thought I saw something up above us. Might have been an animal . . . but it didn't smell right."

"Didn't smell right," I said neutrally.

"If you're on the trail for very long, you learn to use your nose as well as your ears and eyes," replied Kith a shade too easily.

I happened to glance at Wandel at just that moment. He looked sad.

"Better to be safe than sorry," the harper said after a moment. "With the magic free, things could change, no knowing how quickly. Old Merewich and our lass here"—I assumed from the context that he was talking about me and not his horse—"sound pretty certain that it will be sooner rather than later."

Kith met the harper's eyes and said, "Yes, well, I've learned to trust . . . my instincts."

I saw something pass between the two men that left Kith cold-eyed and stone-faced while the sorrow on the harper's face remained unchanged. I wondered what it was that I had missed. There would be time to extract it from them after we set up camp.

Kith fussed around for a while before he let us dismount at the place he'd originally planned on, a flat, rockless stretch of ground not far from a stream but a little farther from the wooded area. I couldn't tell if it was the place where we'd camped the time we'd come here. If it wasn't, it was very similar.

He'd reluctantly decided it was better to keep an eye out than to try to find cover where we'd not be seen. Muttering something about being so leery that his mother's womb wouldn't feel safe to him for a day or so, he stomped into the trees to find wood for a fire.

We hadn't brought tents, but Wandel and I laid down oiled cloth before we put out the bedrolls, and each of us had another piece to lay on top of ourselves if the rain held by the gathering afternoon clouds fell.

Having laid out my own bedroll, I took Kith's off Torch's back. War-trained he might be, but he knew me well enough not to object to my fiddling—I'd helped train him. I patted his hip as I left.

Now, I thought, *try it first while you have Wandel alone*. If Kith decided not to talk about something, it was almost impossible to get it out of him. The harper, on the other hand, liked to talk. "Why does Kith's woodsmanship cause you to exchange sorrowful glances?"

He looked up from digging the fire pit and waggled his eyebrows at me. "Ask Kith. It's his story, not mine. I'd not last long as a bard if I were to tell other people's secrets to anyone who thought to ask, now would I?"

"Ha," I said. "You'd tell the world what your best friend wore to sleep if you thought it made a good enough story."

"Tell her," said Kith flatly.

I started, not having heard him come back. He dropped a large pile of wood an arm's length from the fire pit and unfolded one of the smaller oilskins with a snap. He tucked it carefully around the pile.

He was all I had left of my brother . . . of my family, really, though we were not blood kin (at least not close kin). I wouldn't have hurt him for the world. This had all started as mere curiosity. As I looked at Kith, I realized that this was not a little secret, and Kith was already hurt by it.

I turned back to Wandel. "Tell me."

"After we finish camp," he said.

I TOOK THE DIRT WANDEL REMOVED FROM THE FIRE PIT and mounded it in a circle around the pit, a further barrier against the flames spreading to the surrounding grass.

Wandel stacked the grass-sod he'd cut and set it near the pile of wood. When we left in the morning, we'd shovel the dirt back in the hole and cover it with the sod—after a season the place would look as if we'd never been there. Kith unsaddled the horses, hobbled them, and let them free to graze.

I washed the dirt from my hands at the stream. By the time I returned, the men were seated at the edge of the fire pit. Wandel struck flint to steel a few times, setting the small pile of tinder alight. Then he fanned and fed the growing flames. When at last the fire blazed merrily, the harper took up his harp and sat cross-legged on the end of his blankets.

He fingered the strings lightly, then set the harp aside, politely waiting for his audience to settle itself. I sat rather gingerly at the end of my bedroll. Duck was too wide in the barrel to be an easy mount. Once Kith, too, was sitting on his bed for the night, the harper began.

"Lord Moresh inherited his bloodmage from his uncle, his mother's brother. Moresh's uncle was the king's high marshal before the king had him beheaded for unnamed crimes. He stood off the whole of the king's army at a crofter's hut with nothing but fifteen bodyguards— bodyguards that his bloodmage had created for him. They all died there, along with fourscore of the king's men. If he could have, the king would have killed the bloodmage as well, but without a specified charge against the marshal he could not nullify his will. Jealousy is not a charge that can be lodged in the court, so the bloodmage went to Moresh"—Wandel looked at Kith—"where he continued to make warriors for Moresh's use."

"Never too many, you understand, because the king limited the number he allowed Moresh, not wanting Moresh to gain too much power. The berserkers are scouts and Moresh's personal guard. One of the old marshal's men told me they can track like a hound and hear a bee sneeze in the next room. They fight as the old legends say berserkers did, not bleeding from their wounds until after the battle is over. Those who are maimed or sorely wounded are killed." He looked at Kith. "Since Moresh can have only a few of them, he wants them whole."

Kith laughed without amusement. "Moresh owed my father a life." He looked at me. "Remember, it was my father who found our lord's heir when the boy got lost in the fog. So he sent me home last fall. Before the war turned so bloody, Moresh planned on being here for spring planting. Three months, he said, a fair payment for his son."

He turned his gaze to the darkening sky. "It's not as

if I can run: Nahag has his mark on me. One of us ran once. Silly fool fell in love."

Nahag wasn't Moresh's bloodmage's real name, though I couldn't recall what it was offhand. A nahag was a night demon who consumed children while they slept. It said a lot about the mage that he'd been given such a nickname.

Kith turned to me with eyes lit with self-mockery and a message. "Nahag got to play with him, brought him out for our enlightenment every evening for two weeks. The bloodmage is as old as my father, and he's been a mage since his parents abandoned him to the mage guild when he was a child—whoever he was once, the madness has taken him now. The runner died—I think, I hope—at the end of the first week, but it was a little hard to tell. I didn't know until then that bloodmages eat their victims. Lord Moresh knew I wouldn't run when they came for me."

For the first time I felt something about Lord Moresh's death other than the vague fear of a sheep whose shepherd is lost—satisfaction. Such a man should be dead.

I could feel my lips peel back from my teeth. "If," I said softly, in a gentle voice, "he were not dead, I'd curse him that his kith and kin would know him not for the ague that would twist his bones. I would curse him that pain would make of him something neither human nor animal. I'd see to it that he lived forever knowing nothing, neither darkness nor light, for the agony of his transgressions."

Wandel looked at me as if he'd never seen me before.

Kith gave a rusty chuckle. "That took me back. I haven't heard that curse since the last time your brother and I raided your grandmother's garden. Scared us silly." He pulled up a blade of grass and played with it in his hand.

"Anyway, now you know." Kith stopped playing with the grass and met my eyes again. "And if we find Danci, you can tell her why I'm not a suitable candidate for a husband and father."

So that's why he told me. My eyebrows shot up. "Why? Because a bloodmage, who is now dead, was searching for you?"

"Because I'm dangerous enough to need him to do so."

"Dangerous to whom?" I sputtered. "No one at the village seems to be suffering from your presence."

He shook his head, the stubborn mule. "It doesn't matter. Just tell her what the harper and I told you."

FOUR

Crouched in the gathering shadows, the hob held very still as he watched over the party. He'd always avoided the traditional task of following well-meaning folk whenever he could—his talents and interests lay in tormenting the wicked. But here he was. No wine to sour, or horses to loose, just the soft sounds of the humans' voices to drive away the loneliness. He hunkered down further and let the warmth of their camp wash over him.

KITH JUMPED TO HIS FEET, STARTLING ME. "COME ON, then," he said. "We've got some time now. Why don't you get your knife, and I'll see what I can teach you."

Grateful for a chance to put the last few revelations behind me, I took Daryn's knife from my borrowed saddlebags and scurried back to present it nervously to Kith. I'd spent a good bit of time yesterday sharpening it, but Kith was particular about things like that.

He took it and turned it over in his hand. "Good thing

it's got an edge on it. I'm not much of a hand at sharpening things anymore." He grinned at me unexpectedly. "Father's been putting the edge on my stuff, but it's not like doing it yourself."

I smiled back. "I'd guess not."

"Right." He gave me back my knife and watched how I held it. His frown made me shift my grip several times, but the disapproving expression didn't change.

"The first thing to remember is that the knife is sharp," he said.

I rolled my eyes. "And I haven't been butchering pigs and cattle since I was old enough to crawl."

He smiled, and, drawing his own knife, he continued talking. "It can cut you as easily as it will cut your opponent: keep it away from your fingers. The second thing to remember is that you can do a lot of damage with it by just holding it in your hand and punching."

He closed his hand into a fist and demonstrated with an imaginary opponent. He moved with swift efficiency, and his imaginary foe's instant death was obvious.

"For now, forget you even have a knife," he advised. "It will take care of itself—at least until you have more experience. You're at a disadvantage because you're a woman. A man will back off from another man with a knife, but he'll not do the same for a woman." He watched me try to imitate his move several times. I couldn't tell if I'd done anything right or not. Probably not.

"Put that away for now," he said, in sudden decision. "We'll practice with something else."

When I got back from storing the knife, Kith was waiting with three sticks a little longer than his forearm. They were green wood, and very nearly equal in diameter.

He motioned for me to follow him to a flat area a little way from camp, then handed me two of the sticks and tucked the third under his arm.

He adjusted my grip, then took up his own stick with

a clever little toss. "The sticks will teach you the moves without either of us chancing a cut. The additional benefit is that the sticks are a decent weapon in their own right. Around here, there are always sticks of some sort."

Then he proceeded to teach me how to fight—at least that's what he said he was doing. I thought he was beating me with his stick. Shows what I know.

By the time he said "Enough," I was so tired that I stumbled while walking back to the fire. I knew if I just sat down, I was going to have some really stiff muscles in the morning. Maybe if I walked it out, they'd only be very stiff.

"I'll get some more firewood," I said, turning away from the fire. "What we have won't last the night."

"Best do that, I think," Kith said. "Wandel and I'll see about dinner."

"I thought the woman should do the cooking," said Wandel, teasing but still half-serious. He hadn't eaten what I could cook over an open fire.

"We'll cook," replied Kith, who had.

As soon as I was out of sight, I stopped to tie my boots. I could hear them talking . . . about me. A well brought-up person would have left.

"She startled me when she spoke to your elders," commented Wandel. "I've never seen her as a forceful sort of person. She's always in the back of the room, never speaking unless someone asks her something."

"Not talking when the men talk," agreed Kith. Was that sarcasm I heard in his voice? "Like a good little village woman." Yes, it was sarcasm.

"I've seen your village women. Most of them don't act like that." Wandel half-laughed, no doubt picturing Melly or the smith's wife.

"Hmm," grunted Kith. "Let's say her father's idea of a good village woman. Or her mother's. I'd guess it goes back to when Quilliar died—her brother."

"When you killed him," said Wandel. It surprised me

that he knew that; he hadn't been in the village then.

"He was my best friend," replied Kith obliquely.

"I wondered about that." The harper grunted, and I pictured him tossing a chunk of wood into the fire. "From what I know of Moresh's berserkers, I wouldn't have thought you could act against orders."

"Neither did Nahag, or else I'd have been executed in Quill's place."

"So you think Aren's been trying to hide what she is so she doesn't get singled out by the bloodmage or the villagers?"

Yes, I thought, *it had been hide or die.*

"Hide from herself most of all, I think. It is hard to accept being different, hard to have people avoid looking at you, and still believe in yourself."

Yes, you'd know about that, wouldn't you Kith? I thought.

His voice changed a bit, becoming almost playful. "I *do* know that every time I saw her playing the grateful, submissive wife to that arrogant pup she married—"

Arrogant? I tried the word on Daryn. It didn't fit.

"I wanted to shake her. I kept waiting for her to wake up and put him in his place the way she always did Quill and me when we ganged up on her."

Perhaps it was Kith's voice that told me. It was just a shade louder than it needed to be. Perhaps it was the "arrogant"—Kith had liked Daryn as well as the next man. Kith knew I was listening.

"Daryn was just nicer than you two were," I said.

"If you'd waited on us hand and foot, we'd have been nicer, too," called Kith without pause. I heard Wandel's snort of surprise.

I laughed and set off, pushing the moment of self-examination behind me. When I'd traveled a bit, I stripped off my clothes and washed off the trail sweat in the shallow water of the stream. I used my tunic to wipe off, then dressed again. I pulled the tunic over my shirt, disregarding the dampness. It would dry before I got back to camp.

I walked for a while without collecting any wood. The way back would be soon enough—no sense carrying it any farther than I had to. The late afternoon had the peculiar yellow tint that happens only in the spring when the afternoon clouds gather threateningly in the sky. The shadows were deep, but where the light touched down, the colors were dazzling.

For the first time since Daryn died, I felt at peace. I knew Moresh wouldn't be back to kill Kith. Time would heal him. With aid from Auberg, the raiders would be driven away.

I stopped in a small clearing and decided that if I went any farther, Kith and Wandel were likely to come looking for me. I turned around and stopped abruptly. Standing on a downed tree, only a horse length from me, was a . . . well, a creature.

I felt no fear, only a surprised kind of delight. If he had been standing on the ground, he would have come up to my shoulder. The wildling was a fragile-seeming thing, his feyness blending into the odd light as if he, not I, really belonged to this world. His arms and legs were slender, almost spindly. The bones of his ribs and shoulders were clearly visible, though his belly was round.

He had the proportions of a child, his head too large for his small body. His skin was the warm brown of stained oak. If there were claws on the ends of his fingers, those fingers were long and slender like those of a great lady.

He wore only a pair of roughly made hide shoes and a loincloth. His pale, ash-gray hair was braided in complex patterns with colorful beads woven here and there.

His eyes were large, even in the oversized, inhumanly round face. Wide gray irises gave a strange beauty to something that might have been grotesque. His mouth balanced his eyes, being wider than any I'd seen on a human face. As I watched, a smile lit his eyes and touched the corner of his mouth.

"Hob?" I asked softly, half raising my hand to him.

His smiled widened, exposing the sharp, interlocking teeth of a predator. Before the significance of that registered, he launched himself at me. His arms closed with viselike strength on my shoulders as his head darted for my throat.

Somehow I managed to get the arm I'd been lifting between his face and my neck. His jaws locked on my arm with vicious force. I heard the crack of bone, shock momentarily protecting me from the pain. I noticed that the corners of his mouth were still tilted up in a smile.

He smelled of musty leaves and damp earth. I tried to dislodge him, but for all his lack of size he was much stronger than I was. I'd left my knife back at camp, and there were no sticks within reach.

He wrenched his head, twisting my forearm to an impossible angle. I remember hearing a loud ringing in my ears—then nothing.

THEY TOLD ME LATER IT WAS WANDEL WHO FOUND ME. Kith had come across the creature's spoor and was tracking it when he heard the harper's shrill whistles. By the time I woke up, my head was propped on Wandel's leg and he was mopping my face with a wet cloth. I was quiet for a moment, more out of sheer surprise than anything else. I hadn't expected to wake up at all.

When a cold drop of water hit my ear, I batted at Wandel with my unhurt arm and struggled to sit up. Upright, I was lightheaded and dizzy.

"Who'd you meet out here, Aren?" called Kith from somewhere a fair distance to my right.

I opened my eyes, but it was nearing dark and my vision kept trying to black out, so it took me a while to find Kith. He was kneeling beside something a short distance away. After a moment I decided it was a dead body.

"Don't know," I croaked, closing my eyes again. "What's it look like?"

"*This* looks like some malformed human child with teeth like a shark," he replied. "But you met something else, too. No way you could break its neck like this. Whatever did this is stronger than I am—came near to ripping the head off while he was about it."

"Whoever it was, they bandaged her arm," added Wandel.

I'd been trying to ignore my arm. I had a clear memory of bone showing through flesh. I looked down and saw that someone had wrapped it with strips of my tunic. It still looked like an arm ought to, and I didn't think it should. It also hurt.

Kith swore softly. I raised my eyes from my arm and watched him pace back and forth, stopping here and there to examine the ground. My vision was better, but I was still dizzy.

"Look at the bruises. He snapped that thing's neck with one hand," Kith muttered. "Then he used a stick to pry its jaw open. He tossed it from here"—he stood, as far as I could tell, where the creature had attacked me— "to there." He pointed to where the body lay, some distance away. "Now it's not huge, but it weighs a good seventy or eighty pounds, and I don't know a man alive who could toss it that far—not even a magicked one like me." He said some more, but I started seeing black again and only caught something about soft-soled boots.

"A Beresforder?" guessed Wandel. "Some of those mountain folk are big enough to take a bear and toss it into the next valley. But then why didn't he stay to meet us?"

"Not a Beresforder," refuted Kith. "I don't think a human could do this. Certainly no one *I* know from Beresford." He went on mumbling to himself about wildlings, but I was paying more attention to my arm than to what he said.

After a moment Kith stopped speaking and knelt beside me. "How badly are you hurt?"

"I don't know," I replied, breathing through my nose like a winded horse. "I'm afraid to look."

"So someone killed that thing and dressed Aren's wounds," said Wandel, sounding fascinated—but then it wasn't his arm he was talking about. "I wonder who he was and why he didn't stay."

Kith shook his head. "I think we ought to get back to camp. Where there is one of those things, there might be more. If you'll help me get her over my shoulder, I'll carry her, and you can collect the wood we'll need on the way back."

"It'll be easier if I carry . . . ," began Wandel. I had my eyes closed again, and I didn't get them open fast enough to see what caused him to stop talking.

"I can walk," I offered, squinting up at Kith.

Maybe the look that Wandel had gotten was similar to the one I received. It shut me up, too.

With considerable help from Wandel, I managed to get to my feet. Kith shoved his left shoulder into my midriff and heaved me up. The sudden change in position put me out faster than a candle in water.

WHEN I AWOKE, A FAMILIAR TUNIC WAS BOUNCING around under my face.

"I can walk," I said groggily.

"No," Kith replied firmly. "From the amount of blood you left behind, I'm surprised you awoke before morning. If I set you down and you pass out, it'll be twice the work to get you back up. We're not far from camp, Pest. Just keep quiet 'til we get there."

Of the rest of the trip back I have a hazy memory of watching the back of Kith's calves gray in and out of my shaky vision. I really only recovered consciousness when the steady jolt of Kith's shoulder in my stomach stopped, and I started to slip off.

He muttered a word I'd never heard him use before and made an attempt to forestall my fall. I ended up on my blankets beside the small fire pit. My arm throbbed, my rump ached where it had landed on a rock, my head hurt; but overall, I decided, I would survive.

He left me and fumbled a bit through my saddlebags until he came up with my extra sweater, which he dropped over my head. The additional warmth was welcome—with the sun down, it was a lot colder. The warm tunic I'd worn into the woods was less warm when it was missing the bottom third of its length.

"Kith . . . ," I began, feeling much better right side up, but he stopped me with a gesture.

"Rest a bit, Pest. We need to wait for Wandel, and I need to catch my breath." He settled down beside me and handed me a small flask. "Take a drink of this."

I don't know what I expected—some sort of alcohol, I suppose, even though I knew Kith didn't drink strong spirits. What I sipped wasn't alcohol, but some kind of herb-laden apple cider. That and the stew they'd concocted for dinner had me feeling almost myself by the time Wandel made it back to camp with his load of firewood.

The men ate and I half-dozed by the fire. I should have gotten up and washed my bowl, but it was too much effort. When he was done eating, Kith took my bowl with him to the stream. Maybe I'd have to make sure I was wounded every time I traveled. It sure got me out of a lot of work.

When Kith returned, he sat cross-legged next to me, on the other side of the fire from Wandel. "Now tell me what happened."

I sighed. "You already know most of it. I looked up, and there he was, the creature you found dead. I was so busy wondering what he was, that his attack took me completely by surprise." I thought a moment. There was something odd about the fascination I'd felt for him, but it was too hard to describe, so I let it go. "He was aiming for my throat, but I got my hand in front. He bit it and shook his head like a dog killing a rat, and that's all I remember."

"You don't remember anything about the . . ." Kith's voice trailed off for a moment. "About whatever it was that killed that thing?"

I shook my head. "I don't even know how badly I'm hurt. I could have sworn it nearly tore my—well, at least it did a lot more damage than it looks like." I snatched Kith's knife from his boot sheath and slid it under the strips of cloth that wrapped my arm.

It was a mess. On either side was a deep slice that ran the length of my forearm, but the splinters of bone weren't there. It hurt when I closed my hand and started bleeding sluggishly—all right, it hurt *more* when I closed my hand, but that was all.

I'd butchered enough animals to know there was a lot more odd about my arm than the fact I knew the bones had been broken. For one thing, there should have been more blood. There were arteries close to the surface that should have been severed with cuts that deep. Without a pressure bandage, blood should be pouring out.

"When it bit down," I said distinctly, as much to convince myself as anyone else, "it broke my arm; I heard the bones go. When it twisted its head, my arm bent here." I didn't quite touch the wound just below my elbow.

Kith held my arm still and examined it. When he was through, he shook his head. "I can't tell that the bone's ever been broken—and right here it should have cut through an artery"—he ran his fingers over one of the cuts—"and again here. I'd say he can work magic I've never seen a bloodmage do."

"Not that they would feel inspired to help anyone," I said. Kith smiled at me tiredly.

Wandel opened a pouch on his belt and took out a tin

before rounding the fire to my side. He took the bandaging I'd cut off and spread a layer of salve from the container on part of it.

"Put this back around your arm," he said, fitting the bandage back around the wound.

With my assistance, he tore another strip from my poor tunic and used it to hold the bandaging in place. "From all appearances, your wounds have already been cleaned—so there's no use putting you through it again tonight. I have some brandy in my bags, and I'll clean it again in the morning. Bite wounds are always difficult to get to heal if you don't keep them clean."

When he was finished with me, I stretched out on my blanket, staring up into the night sky. "Wandel," I asked, "do you think that thing that rescued me was a hob? Like the runes we found?"

Wandel took up his harp and plucked a string delicately. "I don't know. I told you, I only know a song about them." He began to play a sprightly tune on his harp, one of the kind that's difficult not to hum along with. By the third verse I was singing with the chorus. Kith didn't join in.

The gist of the song was that there was a rich farmer who owed his success to the hob living in his barn. The farmer, due to his wealth, found himself a wife from a well-to-do town family. They lived happily enough until the hob surprised her in the barn. They disliked each other on sight; she tried to rid the barn of the hob, and the hob tried to rid the farmer of his wife. The wife was clever, but the hob was more clever still: everything she tried to do to him, he turned back on her. At last the farmer stepped in, kept the hob, and got rid of his wife. With the help of the hob he found a farm-bred wife who put out milk and bread every night for the fey folk, and they all lived happily ever after.

The most interesting feature of the song, as far as I was concerned, was the detailed description of the hob:

a little man with skin like old oak, eyes blue as the sky, and a head too big for its body. It sounded like my attacker, but. . . .

"So," said Wandel, finishing the last chord with a flourish, "the creature who attacked you could have been a hob."

"No," I said, suddenly remembering something. "I named the wildling that, just before it attacked me. Then after . . . someone"—I remembered the dark gray skin and red eyes of my vision yesterday and a tone of dry disgust—"someone said, 'That's not a hob, Lady.' "

MY ARM WAS STIFF AND SORE THE NEXT MORNING. When Wandel offered to saddle Duck as well as Torch and the Lass, I let him do it and helped Kith pack camp— or at least watched while Kith did all the work, offering unsolicited advice until he threatened to toss his shovelful of dirt on me rather than the fire pit.

By the time Wandel had tied the small shovel behind Torch's saddle, I was starting to feel better. Mounting was awkward, and Kith gave me a sympathetic glance.

"Well, at least it doesn't hurt you when you do this," I groused as I found my stirrups.

"Yours will pass," he replied softly.

"You're not going to make me feel guilty when I feel so bad are you?" I whined.

He laughed. "Let's go."

After the first few miles, my arm subsided to a dull ache that I could ignore. I noticed Kith wasn't nearly as nervous today, and I wondered if the thing that had attacked me had been following us. With it gone, there would be nothing to set off his magicked senses. Maybe, I thought, but it was more likely that the day had relaxed him as much as it had me. It was hard to worry about wildlings with sharp teeth with the sun shining on your back.

It was warmer today than yesterday, and the scents of

the early spring wildflowers were almost erotic in their fullness. The horses were feeling it, too; the Lass had managed to bite poor old Duck twice. He, for his part, seemed to take a masochistic interest in her. He kept trying to sneak closer to her when I wasn't paying attention. If he hadn't been a gelding, I would have thought he was courting the mare. Even Torch, the old campaigner, was dancing a bit more than usual.

It was late afternoon when we started down the slopes of the Hob into the valley where Auberg lay, about the same time that we'd made camp yesterday. From our vantage point, the town didn't look nearly as large as I remembered it—but it had been several years since I'd been there. As we started down the side of the mountain, I saw the bones of a winter-killed wolf stretched under the green foliage of a wild lilac. The climate was warmer here than it was in Fallbrook, and the lilacs were in full bloom.

The pastureland crept up the sides of the foothills of the Hob, and soon we were traveling along a shepherds' track between the rock walls that fenced the pastures. Generations of farmers had combed the rocks from the land and used them for fences and buildings, leaving behind land well-fenced and less rocky. Land that once had been poor had become, over centuries of management, rich and fertile.

The grass in the pastures here were already three times as long as the grasses in Fallbrook's fields. Even the pastures that had been recently grazed were longer than . . .

Torch halted, giving the Lass time to aim a nip at his rump—though even she wasn't so bold as to actually bite him.

"What's wrong?" asked Wandel before I could.

"You tell me," answered Kith, his gaze drifting around the valley spread below us.

I followed his gaze, looking for something—but there was nothing to be seen.

"Faran's breath!" I swore, standing in my stirrups for a better view. There *was* nothing to be seen.

"Where are the cattle?" asked Wandel. "These are cattle fields, you can see where they've grazed—but they're all gone."

"No sheep either," added Kith softly. "Nor any people. We should be able to see the men in the fields and the people going in and out of town. Look down by that little croft. There's laundry hung to dry and half of it swept loose from the pins."

I knew the others were thinking *raiders*. It was possible the group harassing Fallbrook was part of a larger raiding party or even an enemy army—but a feeling that chilled me down to the bone told me the answer was worse than an army. A feeling and the memory of a vision of men dissolving into ash didn't allow for so mundane an answer.

The quick glimpse I'd had of the wolf bones became more sinister. I didn't say anything, though, merely sent Duck after the other two horses as they headed down the trail to Auberg. What could I have said?

We passed the croft with the hanging laundry first. There were a few chickens in the yard: small and scrawny, half-grown chicks. The men rode past the trail to the house but, on impulse, I turned in. Kith and Wandel stopped to wait for me.

The grass was knee-deep, so it wasn't until something crunched under Duck's feet that I realized there were bones scattered here and there throughout the yard. I dismounted and kicked some of them out from under the grass.

They were clean as if someone had boiled the flesh from them—chicken mostly, though some of them might have been goose. Nearer the clothesline I saw the bones of a dog. A basket sat nearby, half full of washing.

I led Duck around the fluttering clothes. A brightly

striped kerchief was still wrapped around the skull of the woman who had been hanging laundry.

Not raiders, I thought. There was no sign the woman had met an untimely end by ax or knife. It might have been a plague that killed her. There were some that swept through towns, killing entire populations. Most of those were mageborn, but some of the natural diseases could do it, too.

If this were a plague, we shouldn't go into town. If this were plague, it couldn't have happened very long ago. The bones were yellowish, almost greasy looking, with dark spots on the long bones of her arm. Newly stripped bones that had lain there for no more than a month.

I'd *seen* an army turned to bone, then ash: it hadn't been a plague. But what madman would have loosed such a spell here? Auberg was no threat to anyone.

I sat beside the skeleton and touched her wrist gently. The bones were dry against my fingers. I wondered what the unknown mage who'd stripped the land of magic bindings had done with the power he'd acquired. Duck touched the top of my head with his nose, worried about my unaccustomed place at his feet.

I closed my eyes and tried to *see* what had happened to the woman. I tried to put aside all of my speculations. For a long time, nothing came to me. Visions all the time when I didn't want them, but they were harder to call on purpose. My right leg started to go to sleep.

I heard hoofbeats approaching. Kith and Wandel must have gotten tired of waiting. I opened my eyes and turned to look. . . .

A bloodmage clad in black and red with arcane symbols climbing his sleeves stood alone in a gray tower that looked out over the city. Some of the runes worked into his clothing I knew from Gram—calls for health and well-being.

The man turned, letting his face touch the lamplight.

It was the face of a man eaten from inside by his magic. I knew what it was because Moresh's mage was showing signs of it. Father said it was because bloodmagic made the bones go soft. What this man's original features might have been was impossible to tell.

"I told you that we would lose this fight, my lord," he said. His voice was only a harsh whisper, but it carried power.

Someone made an answer, inaudible—but the effect on the mage was electrifying. "I have done all I could. Do you accuse me of treachery?" He listened, then replied even more softly. "A truce? What would he take in return for truce when he knows we have already lost?"

Madness lit his face briefly, then he closed his eyes, rubbing one of the black runes with his left hand. When his eyes opened, there was something sane dwelling there, but his left hand still moved on the runes, which glittered with an eerie yellow light.

In the manner of a man overtired by work, he repeated himself, but the dangerous edge to his voice was gone. "What have you offered him?"

This time I could hear the other man. "I sent your son to him with a sealed message which he has read several hours since. I told him the boy was his to do with as he pleased—like you, he is a bloodmage. What strength would he get from a mage as powerful as your son? But perhaps the boy was able to defeat him as you never have? The rituals you go through take so much time—perhaps you can do something about him before your son dies? Perhaps the war is not so hopeless after all?"

The bloodmage closed his eyes again and moved his right hand, the left one still tracing the runes on his sleeve. When he opened his eyes, he appeared calm and his left hand dropped to his side—but there was nothing sane about him. "You are correct. There is something I can do to defeat him—I discovered it a month ago. Who could have told you? Ah, no matter. All the reason I had

*for not doing it is dead with my son. For your part in
this you shall not die here."*

*The mage spread his hands and closed his eyes again.
An aura surrounded him, growing gradually, making first
him, then the room, and last the tower glow red with the
power he called to him. It took a long time to gather and
barely an instant to send on its way, taking with it the
mage himself.*

*My vision fell away from the tower and the king who
sat there alone. I traveled some great distance outside
the city before so much as a blade of grass survived the
bloodmage's wrath. Far from the city, empty battlefields
were covered with bits and pieces of metal scattered here
and there across fields of yellow flowers where butterflies
danced. . . .*

THE BUTTERFLIES WERE RATHER ABRUPTLY OBSCURED
by Wandel's mustached face. I blinked at the harper stupidly for a bit while I slowly realized that Kith was standing beside me. My arm ached. When I looked down,
fresh blood spotted the bandages.

"I'm fine," I said, surprised at how steady my voice
was.

"What did you see?" asked Kith.

I stood up stiffly, then swung my uninjured arm to
indicate the dress-clad bones. "She was killed by the
same thing that killed all the cattle in the fields—I'll
wager we could find their bones under all that grass. It
killed everything here larger than these chickens. The
king's bloodmage pulled the bindings from the land to
destroy everything he could reach. And he reached as far
as Auberg."

Alarm flooded Wandel's expression. "Why would he
do that? The nearest fighting is close to thirty leagues
from Auberg."

"He set the spell from the capital—at least I think
that's where they were," I said. "I don't think anything

closer to the king's castle than Fallbrook survived."

Kith whistled sharply, and Torch trotted over from his grazing. The one-armed warrior swung gracefully to his saddle, collecting his reins by using his hand and his teeth. "Let's see what remains of Auberg. We'll go home with a report, and then perhaps we can send a party from here back to Beresford over some of the old trails if the raiders give us time."

THE STREETS OF AUBERG WERE SILENT, BUT I HADN'T expected them to be otherwise. We rode around piles of cloth and bone lying here and there on the streets. At the well in the center of town, Wandel pulled his mare to a halt. He'd been uncharacteristically silent since I'd told them what I'd *seen*.

"This will get us nowhere. If Aren's right, and I have seen nothing to disprove it, no one who was here when the spell hit has survived. Since we're looking for refugees from Beresford who might have come here, we ought to try and find somewhere they'd gather. The innkeeper of the Pale Grouse was from Beresford, so I suggest we check there."

Kith nodded and turned Torch to the left. I had never stayed at either of Auberg's two inns, real inns with six or eight rooms for travelers. Auberg was at the northernmost point of the river that was navigable and had several trading fairs throughout the year. Father took—used to take—the surplus harvest to the fall market, and got more for it than if he'd sold it at the market in Fallbrook. But when we came, Father usually found a family who would take us in for a few measures of grain. I didn't even know where the Pale Grouse was. Kith and Wandel seemed to, though. After a short ride we came upon an inn. The bird painted on the sign might have been a grouse twenty years ago.

When I saw the horses in the paddock in front of the inn, I turned to say something to Kith, but held my tongue when I saw that he searched for a specific animal. Danci's horse was sired by the same stallion that had sired Torch, and shared their father's yellow coat. There were no duns in the small enclosure.

As we rode into the yard, several men came out of the inn and looked at us suspiciously. Their faces held the same despair that had begun growing in my heart since we rode down off the Hob.

"Who are you?" asked the smallest of the four men who blocked the way into the inn.

"We're from Fallbrook, looking for refugees out of Beresford," replied Kith slowly. "And you are?"

"Folks call me Ice. Don't know you," replied the man, narrowing his ice-blue eyes. "Been some strange goings-on here. Heard things walking the streets at night. Most of them things my grandfather used to tell us about when my grandmother wasn't around to stop him. How do we know you are who you say you are, and not some haunt looking for a way in?"

I hadn't expected to meet with such suspicion. I didn't know any of the faces I saw, and I knew any number of people from Beresford. I glanced at Wandel, and he shook his head—he didn't know any of them either. Kith, though, narrowed his eyes and nodded his head slowly.

"I see your point. I'm Albrin's son, Kith, and in the field there's a bay gelding I trained eleven summers gone for a man named Falkin from Beresford. If he's here, he'll vouch for me." He nodded toward Wandel. "This is Wandel Silver-Tongue. If there's some of you mountain folk who spend time in town in the late spring, they'll recognize him."

Ah, I thought, *that's why I don't know any of them.* There were several clans of trappers living in the mountains above Beresford. They were loners for the most part, staying to themselves except when they traded fur and meat for other goods in town. Obviously they'd been in a better position to survive the flooding than the towns-folk had been.

"And the woman?"

I answered for myself. "I was married to Daryn of Beresford less than a fortnight ago. He died at the hands of raiders the same day the mountains fell." I patted my horse's neck. "He left me Duck, here, and an obligation to his home village."

A tall, thin man with haunted eyes shook his head. "Be careful, brother mine, the wraith that knocked on my window last night bore the face of a man I knew. If my window weren't on the third floor with nothing for a man to climb up, I might have let him in."

"Ah, stuff and nonsense, Manta. If Kith died, he'd be a demon full-grown, and not some pathetic haunt reduced to aping the living!" scolded a voice I knew full well.

Danci pushed past the men as if they were cattle, though she didn't reach the shoulders of the smallest of them. "It's no use hiding that smile, Kith, I know you're glad to see me—and it's about time you got here."

If Kith smiled, I missed it. I swung off Duck's back, but before I could find somewhere to put him, one of the young men on the porch took the reins from me.

"I'll loose him with the others," he said, softly enough that he didn't interrupt any of the questions going on around us.

I caught his arm and shook my head. "No," I said before I knew I was going to. I projected my voice over the general conversations. "We have to leave before nightfall." A deepening dread was growing upon me, as it had the day Daryn had died.

Kith turned toward me. I shook my head again, ignoring the others. "I don't know why, but it's important."

It had something to do with the defeat clinging to the faces of all of the people in the inn yard, even Danci; the weariness that left the children creeping slowly out the inn door instead of running to see the strangers. Even the wariness of the men seemed to be unnatural. Then, again, I was still spooked from the vision of the king's bloodmage—and maybe from yesterday's attack.

Wandel grinned reassuringly. "We've learned to listen to Aren's hunches. If you don't have a pressing reason for staying, I would urge you to come with us to Fallbrook—though that might be jumping out of the pot into the pit. Fallbrook's been invaded by a band of raiders."

"If we're outside at night, the haunts will get us like they did Leheigh the first night we were here," said the man Danci had called Manta.

"My brother's right," agreed Ice, who seemed to be the leader. "At least something killed Leheigh, and what it left behind didn't look like the work of anything I've ever seen before. It's going to take more than a woman's hunch to make me travel at night."

Kith pursed his lips thoughtfully, but when he spoke, his voice was dangerously soft. "I'm going. If you're wise, you will come, too. Aren's got the *sight*, and she knows things that we cannot."

"Tier, go get Chatim and Falkin," commanded Danci briskly. "I'm going with Kith. Anyone who wants to come with us, can." No one argued with her. Not that I was surprised; I'd never been able to argue with her.

The young man who held Duck's reins gave them back to me and ran to do Danci's bidding.

Danci turned back to Kith. "They left to check out the other inn and to pick some vegetables. It may take a little while to find them. We've run low on supplies."

"Have you raided the houses for food?" Kith pointedly addressed Danci rather than the men.

"No one wanted to," she replied, a little sheepishly.

Kith nodded once. "Then the three of us"—he indicated Wandel, himself, and me—"will scavenge food for the ride back from the houses nearby while you pack."

Wandel looked at the disgruntled faces of the Beresforders and shook his head. "You two go scavenge—I think I'm needed here. I'll tell them why we're so quick to take Aren's suggestions."

I TOOK THE LEFT-HAND SIDE OF THE ROAD, LEAVING Duck ground-tied next to Torch and the Lass in front of the inn.

If it had been anyone else who suggested exploring the houses, I would have danced naked in the winter snow before I stepped foot inside any of the buildings in Auberg. But it had been Kith, and anything he could do, I could do—especially when the alternative was to watch all the Beresforders' faces while Wandel explained what kind of freak I was. Besides, after Manta objected to a woman going through the houses of the dead, I was left with no choice at all.

The first house wasn't bad. I located the larder immediately, just off the kitchen. I found a tablecloth and loaded it with what food would travel—cheese and unleavened bread mostly. After tying the bundle, I set it on the street in front of the house, where I could pick it up on the way back to the inn.

The next house was smaller than the first, made of stones set one on top of the other with no need of mortar to hold it together. As I stepped over the threshold, I came face to skull with the master of the hearth.

Except for the woman on the farm, I'd tried not to look at the heaps of bones we'd passed in Auberg. I hadn't let them be people, only piles of rubbish. But, even dead, this man wouldn't let me do that.

He must have been resting in front of the fire, for his remains were still settled in a chair before the blackened grating. His trousers were patched neatly, though without the ornamentation a woman would have given them. His shirt was made of fine cotton cloth and showed no such wear.

He'd been a big man, a hand or so larger than Daryn.

I couldn't repress the feeling that he watched me as I walked past him to the room beyond.

His larder was small, but stocked with the sorts of food a traveler would need: rice cakes, sweet oatcakes, and salted, dried beef. I took all I could carry in a tablecloth I'd brought from the first house. And all the time I stacked the food, I had the twitchy feeling that someone was observing me. Just before I tied the bundle together, I took an oatcake and a piece of the beef and set it aside.

I walked into the front room and set the bits of food I'd kept out on the floor before the dead man in the chair. Remembering what the Beresforders had said about the unrestful dead and stories learned at Gram's knee, I knelt before him as if he were a king on a throne.

"Good sir," I said, in as formal a manner as I could muster, "I take this food to ensure the safety of others, not for personal gain. Accept this offering as my good faith and hear my prayer for your rest. Be at peace."

If there had been someone with me, I wouldn't have done it, but it made me feel better. Coming to my feet, I brushed against something hanging on the stone wall. It fell to the floor with a clatter and a thunk.

A glance showed it to be a crossbow, oiled so dark it was black. I picked it up and took the quiver of arrows that hung next to the space where it had been. Then I nodded respectfully to the man who had owned them, and began to leave.

A chill touched my shoulder, stopping me where I was. I turned back to the skeleton who brooded in his chair, staring not, I saw finally, at the door but at the wall where the crossbow had hung. I, too, looked again. A black leather bag rested on the same peg the crossbow had hung on. I'd left it there. Now, after a careful look at the resting warrior, I lifted it down, too. Inside was an odd metal contraption, the same color as the crossbow—tarnished silver, I thought.

"For the crossbow?" I asked.

It almost surprised me that there was no answer. I took the bag with me. When I set the bag of food outside the door, I kept the crossbow and slung the quiver into its proper place across my shoulders. The leather bag I attached to my belt.

My last experience made me wary as I opened the door to the next house. Nothing greeted me but the faint scent of lemon verbena.

The first room was so prosaic it seemed to disallow a world in which a warrior could guard his domain after death. Ruffled curtains framed the windows covered only by a screen of creamy linen to keep out insects and dirt.

The next room was a bedroom, and I walked quickly through it. There were two doorways on the side of the room. I opened the first and walked into another bedroom, much smaller than the first. A cradle creaked back and forth as the breeze swept through the window where the protective screen had been torn loose.

Almost involuntarily, I stepped farther into the room and looked at the tiny bones lying clothed in a soft gown embroidered with yellow and orange flowers. A rose-colored quilt had been tucked lovingly around the baby. I tightened my hand around the crossbow until it hurt, but the pain didn't help.

A soft lullaby filled my head. The breeze died, but the cradle still rocked. I watched as a mother sang her babe to sleep. The dead woman looked up at me and smiled— a simple, uncomplicated smile—and raised a finger to her lips, protecting the sleep of a child who would never awaken.

I walked out of the house and shut the door gently behind me with a hand that shook. It hadn't felt like a vision.

Sweat gathered on the small of my back. I knew I should have gone on and searched for the larder, but it was beyond me. Perhaps Kith could have done it, but not even the power of old taunts was going to make me go into another house.

Kith came out of a house on the other side of the narrow lane, and looked at me. Something in my face must have shown how I felt, because he crossed the street and frowned.

"What?" he asked.

"Well," I answered, smiling grimly, "at least we know we don't have to search for babies left unattended. The one in there was only a few days old, and the spell took it as surely as it took larger creatures." I decided not to mention the ghost.

Kith closed his eyes briefly and nodded. "I have enough food for the journey if there aren't many more people than it appears. What you have should fill in the gaps." He gave me a look that told me what he had found hadn't been much better, then he chose to change the subject. Soldiers were probably good at avoiding unbearable things. "I see you found a crossbow."

I gave it to him, and he looked it over closely before returning it. "Steel bow," he said. "They're expensive. My own is a composite, easier to draw but less range. Most of the weapons like this belong to noblemen—Moresh has one. I wouldn't have thought a town this size would have a weapon of such quality. It's too bad we can't use it."

"What do you mean?"

He set the bow on the ground, holding onto the stock first, then bracing it against his shoulder. He ran a finger down the stock and showed me two black metal pegs, one on each side.

"This was meant for a goatsfoot. You'll not be able to draw it by hand."

"A what?" I asked, trying to picture how a goat's foot would help to draw a bow.

"Goatsfoot," he repeated. "It's a device that you hook under the string and over the pins." He fingered the pegs he'd shown me. They didn't look like pins to me. "Then you pull it back. The extra leverage allows you to draw the bow."

I opened the leather bag and pulled out the contraption it held. "Is this one?"

He took it from me. "*That* makes this bow a lot more useful." Kneeling, he pressed the toe of his boot to the bow, holding it steady as he showed me how the goats-foot cocked the bow.

The back of my neck crawled suddenly, and I glanced behind me. But the houses all stood empty.

THE SUN WAS LOW IN THE SKY WHEN WE FINALLY SET out from Auberg. It had taken longer than I'd expected to collect the two men who were out. Then the Beres-forders had a bunch of livestock—cattle, sheep, pigs, mules, and a few horses (including Danci's dun)—in a larger paddock behind the inn. At least Wandel had worked the magic of his charm on the Beresforders: there wasn't a grumble among them at the hurry. And everyone except Danci avoided me as if I had the pox.

Once we set out on the road, the animals gave us little trouble, seeming almost as relieved as I to leave Auberg's shadows behind them. By the time we reached the lower slopes of the Hob, the children began to play and laugh.

Danci deposited her youngest in Kith's lap without asking and rode her horse to me.

"I hadn't realized what it was doing to us, staying there among the dead," she said.

I watched Kith struggle to hold the squirming toddler in front of him and guide Torch at the same time. But, interestingly enough, he didn't try to give the boy back.

"It would be enough to give anyone the creeps," I agreed with a smile.

I'd noticed the lift in my own spirits when we rode out of the valley. Comparing the rascal who held Torch's reins while Kith held him with the mopey, whiny child at the inn, I thought it was more than just the silent town that held us in thrall.

"Gram always said death magic leaves its mark on the land."

"Death magic?" asked Danci softly.

I nodded. "I don't think Auberg is a healthy place to be."

THE HOB HEARD THEM BEFORE HE SAW THEM. *REFUGEES*, he thought, watching the ragtag bunch climb out of the shadow-shrouded valley. Looking past them, he wondered what had caused the fog of ill that grew thicker as it stretched away from the mountain. Bits and pieces still clung stubbornly to the party riding onto his mountain.

He was exhilarated from the chase he'd given the pack of grims—they wouldn't be coming back to his mountain anytime soon. He rather regretted that; truth be told, they made great sport. He wished there were another pack around—he was in the mood to play.

The big horse the woman called Aren rode saw him and whickered a greeting, though the one-armed man's dun gelding, who saw him as well, chose to ignore him. Aren looked hollow-eyed and tired.

As suddenly as that, he decided to give her something to think about that might take the shadows from her eyes. He skittered down the tree and wandered among the riders. The knowledge that either Aren or the warrior—both touched by magic—might detect him added to the fun.

Just yesterday he wouldn't have been able to hide himself from any of them in the bright light of day, but the mountain was waking up from its long sleep.

The hob rubbed the red gelding's chest and slapped him lightly on the haunch as he passed, sending him bouncing forward a few steps. Half-fey herself, the minstrel's white mare cast a merry glance and snorted at him. He grinned back. Mischief that mare was, much like himself.

Toward the back of the party, an aging herd dog limped soberly at the side of an old man on a mule. The old man kept up a constant reassuring murmur that belied the worry on his face. Worry he should, for the hob could see the shadow that clung to the dog's tail and hindquarters. The dark of the valley beyond had used the animal's age and infirmities to attach itself like a burr.

The hob stooped and ruffled the dog's fur, washing it free of shadow—and managed to clear a bit of the age-related problems as well. The dog whined his appreciation and rolled in the hob's embrace, licking his face with frantic gratitude. Dogs were like that.

"Here, now, Cary, what's up with you?" The man stopped his mule.

At the sound of his master's voice the dog threw himself out of the hob's care and leaped up to lick at the mounted man's hands before taking off to run a frantic circle around the entire group—for all the world as if he'd not been a trained cattle dog for a decade. The hob laughed, and one of the two spotted milk cows answered him.

Grinning, the hob turned to see the one-armed one approach him as surely as if he could see him. The child who rode in front of the grim warrior saw the hob quite clearly, of course. The babe clapped his hands and caroled encouragements so clearly that the hob's smile widened in answer. Here was a child after his own heart. He did a couple of back flips for his audience of one, then turned his attention to the soldier.

This close he could see the workings of the bloodmage the harper had spoken of yesterday while the hob spied upon them—though he couldn't tell how deeply the damage went. Whatever had been done to the man made him aware that the hob was there. The taint of the bloodmage made the hob more wary than he might otherwise have been. He'd never feared humans, but the bloodmages had taught him a bitter lesson in caution.

The one-armed man set the child with gentle firmness in the arms of a nearby rider. One of the cows, deciding this halt might last a while, began grazing. The blood-mage's warrior approached warily, drawing his iron sword—as if even cold iron could hurt a son of the mountain here.

Experimentally, the hob crouched, and the dun's ears followed his descent—a moment later the soldier's attention focused downward.

If a child of five or six hadn't begun to cry—soft, tired sounds of a soul pushed beyond enduring—the hob might have gotten caught up in the fun. Wariness only added spice to the play. But these were good folk, enti-tled to the mountain's protection. He darted silently to the sobbing girl, who was riding by herself on a pony led by a man who might have been her father.

The shadow upon her wasn't strong enough to do her harm; likely it would leave as soon as she'd spent a night on the mountain. Still, it was easy enough to banish it.

He couldn't resist a last dash through the middle of the group, tugging gently on the dun's tail as he swept by. If the war-bred gelding's feet were quicker than most—well, then he had only to dodge a little quicker yet. Aren's big horse stretched his nose out for a pat before he left.

"WHAT IN FARAN'S NAME IS GOING ON?" EXCLAIMED one of the old men, the worry in his voice finding its echo in the shivers that crept up my spine. "I've never seen animals act like that."

Kith watched his horse's ears a moment, then sheathed his sword and said thoughtfully, "It must have been a wildling of some kind. It didn't smell of bloodmagic, but no natural creature runs about invisible. I don't think it did any harm."

The old herdsman had dismounted from his mule and was rubbing his dog, to the dog's great delight. After

Kith spoke, he nodded. "The opposite, I would think. I haven't seen Cary look so well since he caught cold last winter. I was worried I'd have to put him down before we reached Fallbrook—now look at him."

To demonstrate, he threw his arm out and gave three sharp whistles. The black and white dog took off at a dead run, aiming for a pig that had taken advantage of the stop to ease away from the rest and root at the base of an old ash tree. The dog drove the protesting pig back with the bunch.

I watched, and felt something I'd taken from Auberg—fear, perhaps, but more atavistic than that—lose its fell grip on my shoulders. Melodramatic, but that's what it felt like.

"Shall we go on?" asked Ice. "Or do you think we should go back to Auberg?"

The old herdsman coughed and spat, then said, "On-ward. Wish whatever it was had given me a bit of what he gave that old dog." He glanced around at the rest of us. "I'd almost forgotten it, but my great-aunt was from Fallbrook. When I was just a tadpole, she used to tell me stories of this mountain. Said that if you left a bit of food out for the wild folk, they'd keep the creepy-crawlies away."

He shrugged and started his mule in the direction we'd been headed. One by one the others followed him.

As he passed me, he doffed his cap. "It's good to re-member there is magic that heals as well as the wraiths and whatnot we've been fighting for the past few days."

He meant me. When I smiled at him, he smiled back.

After the rest had gone on, Kith rode to my side. "It's still here," he said.

I nodded, watching Duck stare at an oak tree not too far from where we stood. "Do you think we should we be worried?"

Kith shrugged. "If it healed that dog, it stands to reason

that it could have hurt any of us equally well. I suspect we're safe enough."

"But we'll leave some food out for it tonight," I said, thinking about the bit of meat and bread I'd left at the house in Auberg.

He squinted at the shadows under the oak. "I suspect we will."

SUMMER
THE GROWING SEASON

FIVE

Sticks clattered together like an odd sort of music, much faster than I'd have thought possible when I started this a couple of months ago. *Ah, missed one—this was going to hurt.*

"Ouch," I said, stumbling backward out of further harm's way. I *would* miss the one aimed at my jaw.

Manta stepped closer to see the damage. "I mistimed my pattern," he apologized. "Are you all right, luv?"

"She's fine," said Ice, his brother, coming up behind me. "Raiders don't fight in patterns, anyway. If all you learn is patterns, you might as well be dancing." Despite his brisk words, he pulled my hand away from my face so he could inspect the welt. "Time to put the sticks up anyway. Practice is over."

I glanced around. Sure enough, Koret was stepping up to the upturned manger that served as a podium in the barn. I set my sticks in the open-ended barrel with a dozen others.

My knapsack was nearby with the crossbow next to it.

I was still a beginner with the sticks, but at least I'd been a natural with the crossbow. Though, as Kith observed dryly, it wasn't that hard, just point and shoot. I just pointed better than others. It didn't hurt that the steel bow shot farther than any of the village crossbows, almost as far as Koret's longbow.

By the time I came to the podium, practice had pretty much ended; Ice hadn't been the only one who'd noticed Koret. We were a scruffy-looking lot gathered around the front of the barn.

There were four Beresforders in our group, including Manta and his blue-eyed brother, Ice—whose real name, I had learned, was Eannise. Ice had been made an elder to represent Beresford, though I'm not certain I wasn't older than he was. Manta was older, I knew—but there was something about Ice that made him a man others would follow.

The Beresforders were easy to pick out because, other than Kith and me, the Fallbrook patrollers were boys— the ones who were too old to be content shuffling around town with the women and children, yet not old enough to guard the lands against the raiders.

The far fields had been abandoned more than a month ago; they were too vulnerable to the bandits' attack. We'd fallen back to protecting just the near fields, most of which were grazing lands and vegetable gardens. There wasn't enough grain produced on the land that was left to feed the village through the winter.

A month ago Merewich ordered the two bridges across the river guarded day and night, without actually saying he intended to claim the lord's fields for the village. Hard on his announcement, Albrin—whose lands had been among those abandoned—took over guarding the eastern bridge by Fell Lake, relocating his horses to the lord's grazing fields bordering the swamps. He, his hirelings, and a number of newly homeless men moved into a hay storage barn over the objections of the steward.

"All right now, lads," said Koret in a voice that would have carried over ocean waves. "You know there's been a movement afoot to restrict our patrols to the near fields we are actually guarding. I've talked to Merewich, and we've come up with a few alternatives, so for now your routes are the same. New orders are that if you see a group larger than five raiders, come in directly to report."

"What if they try to hit the town?" Someday I needed to learn how Ice could make his soft voice heard so easily over the shuffling noises of the group. "We lost ten men in that raid on Lyntle's—"

"Eleven," someone added, "Lyntle's son died this afternoon."

Ice nodded but continued without pause. "And at least that many more are injured. That leaves us with less than sixty fighting men in town if the patrols stay as they are."

Koret nodded his agreement. "We've talked to the steward, and the remnants of Lord Moresh's fighting men—there are twenty of them—are staying in the village as of today. They're being mixed with the teams of guards we already have, so there'll be someone with experience fighting in each team. I've pulled Kith from patrol to train them. I don't have time now. As you might have heard, I've begun an afternoon training session to teach some of our women how to defend themselves." He grinned, adding, "Some of the nastiest pirates I've ever known have been women. Look at Aren."

I stuck out my tongue at Ice when he cowered away from me.

"There's a couple of those old beldams I wouldn't want to tangle with," commented someone fervently.

"Women are sneaky," added another.

"Can we defend ourselves against them?" asked a boy.

"I've never managed to," admitted Manta. "But I've never minded losing, much."

The boy puzzled it out, then flushed. "I mean, can we defend ourselves against the bandits?" He blushed again when his untrustworthy voice cracked on the last word.

The people shifted uncomfortably. No one else would have asked the question, but we all waited to hear Koret's answer. Koret knew these things. He had experience.

The old pirate smiled serenely. "Of course." His eyes, I noticed, were very tired. "Aren, stay a moment. The rest of you to your patrols."

He waited until the others had left the barn before he said anything. "Touched Banar was killed last night."

"I know," I said. The smith's brother had been a gentle soul, if simple. I hadn't spoken to him much, but he'd been a fixture at the smithy.

"The official story is that the raiders caught him. Kith found him. He and Merewich brought the body back to the smith. Then Kith came to me and asked me to tell you to stay out of town as much as possible."

"Me?" I asked, surprised.

"You haven't been around town much anyway," Koret said, scuffing a bit of loose straw with the side of his boot. "You might not have heard. . . . There's a group, the last priest's staunchest followers for the most part, who are becoming rabid about anything smelling of magic. They claim it's the village's wickedness that caused the One God's anger and shook the world."

I smiled without amusement, then stopped when it hurt my jaw. I'd forgotten Manta'd hit me. "I know about them. My brother by marriage is one of them. Kith thinks they're responsible for Banar's death? Because of the old tales about changelings?"

Koret met my eyes, not speaking a word.

"I'll stay out of town."

THE SUMMER NIGHT WAS RICH WITH THE SOUNDS OF THE creatures who haunted the dark. Crickets sang from the fields, answered by the frogs in the nearby creek.

I stood in the sheltering shadow of my barn and watched the raiders poke around the empty cottage. I had stopped here deliberately, though the route Koret had assigned me actually passed a mile or so below this.

It had been several months since it had been safe to live here—not since we got back from the Hob, as a matter of fact. I'd come back and found traces of the raiders all over. So I lived in a camp just outside of town.

It wasn't the visions that kept me from moving into town. I no longer had to worry about going into visionary fits every time someone asked me a question, not since the trip to Auberg. The visions weren't gone, but the force of them had eased, much as the earth tremors that followed the big one had subsided.

I thought the cause of both was the gradual decreasing of magic to the level it must have been at before the bloodmages locked it away. The magic, it seemed to me, was like the steam trapped under the lid of a pot of boiling water. When the lid was removed, steam billowed out, then subsided to a steady mist.

What kept me out of town was the looks I received whenever I walked down the street. Melly, Wandel, and Kith were the only ones who treated me as they always had. Crusty old Cantier treated me like a long-lost daughter while his wife hung protective charms around her neck and glared when he wasn't looking. Merewich and Koret wanted me to find out what the raiders were doing, but I couldn't *see* the bandit's camp, no matter how hard I tried. I didn't know why that was. Kith suggested they might have a bloodmage's spell blocking my *sight*.

Some people just avoided me, sending nervous glances my way when they thought I might not be looking. It was the others I minded most: the ones who crossed the street to get away, then watched me with fear or hatred. People like Poul, my brother by marriage, and Albrin, Kith's father.

I'd thought it was getting worse lately, but I hadn't thought it would go so far as murder. Deliberately, I turned my attention to my former home.

The croft was already showing the lack of care. The first earthquake had pulled a shutter loose from a window; it had fallen to the ground since the last time I'd been here a few weeks ago. The garden fence had developed a decided lean, and I could smell the polecat who'd taken possession of the barn. The farm had kept me sane after my family had died; it hurt to reward it with such neglect. The raiders' presence tonight was a further indignity.

In the months since I'd come back from Auberg, I'd gathered quite a bit of experience watching raiders from the shadows, but it wasn't the same as seeing them here, in my home. I leaned into the roughness of the barn wood. Having something solid against my back helped me stay still. Daisy the cow no longer smelled bad—something had come up here a couple of weeks ago and eaten most of her.

The group of raiders I'd come upon was small—only three that I could see—though I suspected there was another one hidden near the thicket just east of the house. Something had frightened a sleeping bird out of the gorse bush anyway. If I'd seen them before they were so close, I would have avoided them. But they'd come just as I was leaving. There was no sense risking their seeing me by moving about, so I settled down to wait.

There weren't enough men to make a real raiding party—this bunch was probably out scavenging. Since they were doing it at night, they were probably scrounging without permission. Two of the men entered the cottage with a torch, leaving the third on guard just outside the door. I don't know what the one by the gorse bush was doing.

The men were on foot, so their camp might not be too far away—something that would interest Koret. Although we'd found the remains of a number of overnight camping places, no one had been able to pinpoint their main camp. If they had a camp outside the range of our usual patrols, it would explain why we hadn't been able to find them. Kith felt their camp would be some distance from where they attacked, so we'd concentrated our searches in the western slopes. Maybe they weren't as smart as Kith thought they were.

As I sat musing over possible nearby camping sights, I noticed movement in the darkness. It wasn't in the gorse bush, but I thought it might be the same man. I resisted the urge to move to a better location, knowing any movement might give my position away as easily as it had let me see the fourth raider.

A shadow moved near the cottage, and the man on guard disappeared into it without a sound. I stiffened at my post. Whoever it was had moved with amazing swiftness.

One of the men in the cottage cried out, and then the peace of the night dissolved in wild cries and . . . the sounds of an animal feeding.

It wasn't any of their fellow raiders attacking them, not unless they'd taken to cannibalism. I thought of the thing that had attacked me on the Hob. I'd told Merewich about it, and Koret as well, but no one had seen anything out of the ordinary since.

Well, maybe they'd take out the raiders and leave us alone. My caution increased by the ache that still troubled my arm, I concentrated on being very quiet and stayed in my place until long after the sounds had died away, leaving only crickets and frogs in their wake. Dawn crept out slowly, and in the early morning light, I walked to the cottage and surveyed the area.

The ground, dark with blood, was torn up in front of the door. A few paces away a sword lay in its sheath. Inside the house there was little more: enough blood to prove both men had died, their weapons, and a well-chewed shoe. I wondered if it had tasted bad.

I started up the trail to the upper field, passing a dark stain where the fourth man had stood lookout. As I came to a switch in the trail, I heard a man cough. Quietly, heart pounding, I darted under the boughs of an evergreen, realizing only after I was there that it was the same tree I'd hidden in the day Daryn died.

I crouched motionless in Caulem's trousers and tunic, staring at a hole that was developing in the trousers' knee. It seemed to take a lifetime for the two raiders to move past my hiding place. As soon as they were gone, I dusted off my hands and set off parallel to the trail at a steady trot.

When I reached the field where Daryn and Father had been killed, I slowed to a walk. I hadn't actually seen it since that day. The plow was gone, but even without it I could tell where they had been cut down. The dirt hadn't been harrowed behind them, and short tufts of wild grass grew awkwardly around the big clumps of dirt.

There was a bench at the far end of the field, a short, sharp rise with a flat area beyond it. It caught my attention because we'd cut a stand of trees there to build the cottage, and the bare area we'd left seemed to be full of trees again.

I walked on, careful to blend in with the woods. After I'd walked to the cornerstone that marked the end of cultivated land, I looked across the field at the bench. From my new vantage point I could see that what had appeared to be trees were tents painted to match the colors of the forest. I'd found the raiders' camp.

I headed back to the village as fast as I could, wishing I were as conditioned as some of the boys (and all of the Beresforders, hillfolk that they were), who could run miles without stopping. The harsh months had toughened me, as they had everyone, but I still could only run a league before stopping.

The path I took brought me behind my parents' house, but I'd been by it so often on patrol that I could pass it with no more than a nod of respect for any unquiet spirit lingering nearby.

I needed to get to the village with my information. There was a bare chance that we could take their camp by surprise and bring the battle to them for once.

Because of the long time I'd spent waiting for dawn to come, I missed my rendezvous with the patroller scheduled to make the next tour of this part of the valley. Since daylight patrols were always on horseback, I'd hoped he might have waited for me, so I could use his horse to get back to the village sooner with my news.

Mindful of Touched Banar's death, I cut through the pastureland, coming into the village by the back way. I had to climb over the shoulder-high wall that gave Fallbrook what little protection it could. Koret's house was not far from the wall, so it was only a moment before I knocked lightly at the door.

Narania, Koret's wife, opened the door looking upset, but when she saw me, she smiled. "Ah, child, you're late in. I'm glad to see you're still in one piece."

I returned her smile, and wiped the sweat from my eyes. "Me, too. Is Koret here? I have some information for him—I found the raiders' camp."

"He was called to a meeting of the elders just a short time ago. For news like that I would think that they'd all be glad to hear from you. Why don't you go to the inn and find him?"

I hesitated. Koret's warning still rang in my ears. I had no desire to head through town in broad daylight. But the raiders' camp was important, and I should tell someone about the creature that had fed at my home. "I suppose I'd better."

I SLIPPED IN THROUGH THE BACK OF THE INN. MELLY was slicing pork for stew, but she took time to give me a friendly nod. There was no crowd here today. When I walked into the room where the elders were, there were few people there who were not on the council.

Whatever it was that sparked this meeting, it must have

been bad, from the looks on their faces. Merewich had the acorn, but he stopped speaking when I stepped through the door to stand before the council in the traditional place for a request to address the group.

"Aren," he said, as if women interrupted his meetings every day. Most of the rest of the council looked as if they were too disturbed to object—not a good sign. "Is this important?"

I nodded.

"Speak."

"I found the raiders' camp. It's on the hill overlooking my father's field above my cottage."

Merewich ran a hand over his face, then turned to Koret. "Do we have the manpower to take it now?"

Koret thought a moment, then shook his head. "No. They'll have it moved soon enough anyway. The manor is much more defensible." The weariness on his face went all the way to the bone.

"What happened?" I asked. Their reaction wasn't what I expected for the first chance we'd had to strike back at the bandits. Alarm and fatigue combined to let me speak out of turn. When I had left last night, there would have been plenty of fighters to launch some sort of attack.

"The raiders took the Fell bridge last night," replied Merewich without chiding me. He looked a decade older than he had this spring. "And the manor house as well. As far as we can tell, Albrin and his men were all killed outright. We wouldn't know that much, but one of the manor serfs escaped."

He nodded toward the corner of the room, and I saw a boy of about fourteen, thin and ragged, who was curled in a tight knot against the wall. His eyes were open, shifting from one side to the other. The tautness of his stillness reminded me of last night, when I, too, had sat very still so no one would notice me.

"Has someone told Kith?" I asked. *Albrin*, I thought, *not Albrin*.

"I did," said Merewich. "It's hard to tell how he took it."

I nodded and fought tears. If this last spring had taught me anything, it was that I could do nothing about past events. *But I can make the present worse*, I thought sourly. Well, best to get it over with at once. "Koret, for your count—four of the raiders died last night on my rounds."

"Did you . . . ," began Merewich. He stopped when I shook my head.

"No, it wasn't me. Kith's the only one who can take them out in multiples. I came upon a group of raiders unexpectedly. There were only the four of them, so I took cover instead of sounding the alarm. It was dark, but I heard something attack and eat them." A few of the elders blanched at my bald telling. "I'm not sure what it was. When it was quiet, I came out and looked the area over. I'm not much of a tracker, next to useless in the dark. If you want to send Kith or Red Toam out to my cottage to read the dirt, they might be able to tell you more. If I were to guess, I'd say it was something— something like that thing that attacked me on the Hob."

They didn't like that, but neither did I. We'd all been hoping it had been the only one. No one else had seen anything like it since then.

"Strange how she's the only one who sees them," muttered someone behind me.

Koret ignored the remark. "Is that all?"

I nodded, and turned to leave. As I did, I saw the serf from the manor leaning wearily against the wall. "Let me take the boy out. He looks as if he's ready to collapse. I'll eat my boots if Melly won't take him. She can always use more help around here."

I didn't say Melly was a motherly soul who would take him under her wing, but everyone in the room except the boy knew it. Merewich gave me an approving smile, and I took that as permission.

When I extended my hand to help him to his feet, the boy eyed it warily and slid up against the wall until he stood on his own.

DESPITE IT ALL, I STEPPED OUT OF THE INN WITH A smile. Melly could be overwhelming to people who were not used to her, and occasionally to those of us who were. I cherished the look on the poor boy's face as she'd herded him to the bathing room with the determination of a sheepdog at shearing time.

The bright light of day assaulted my eyes after the dim interior of the inn, so I didn't see Poul until I bumped into him. Because of my momentary blindness, I couldn't tell if he stepped in front of me deliberately, or if it was an accident. But if he'd still been avoiding me, he wouldn't have been close enough to bump.

"Witch," he spat, stepping back from me as if my touch could contaminate him.

He had changed even more than I had over the past few months. New gray streaks ran through his beard, which had grown straggly. His hair was uncombed and his clothes ragged. They hung on him because of the weight he'd lost—but everyone had lost some weight.

"Yes," I agreed mildly, trying to step past him. I liked Poul. I didn't want this ugliness, especially not now, while I was so worried about Albrin.

There were several people gathering near the corner of the inn. It seemed to me that they were just curious—though I hadn't been keeping careful track of who belonged to the radical faction. I almost didn't care. I just wanted to find someplace quiet where I could deal with Albrin's death—for I knew that if Albrin wasn't dead, he soon would be.

"Why don't you just use your magic to destroy them instead of us, witch? Or are you helping them? There are evil spirits haunting the old cemetery now—but I don't suppose I need to tell you that." He looked unhealthy under his tan. "If you can see so much, why didn't you see the raiders' attack?"

I remembered the light in my sister Ani's eyes when she looked at her husband, and pushed aside my grief for a moment. Instead of the embittered, angry man in front of me, I saw the tenderness in his face when he held Ani after Kith brought home our brother's body. I saw . . .

. . . *my father's slow nod of thanks to Kith as he took Quilliar's limp corpse and helped lay it on the couch. Ani buried her face against Poul's shoulder and sobbed silently.*

"His neck is snapped. Must have been a bad fall," Father said, not looking at Kith.

"He's been dead for three days," said Kith, wearing the uniform of Moresh's own guard, as he had for two years. He shifted awkwardly away from the family, setting himself apart.

". . . *evil,"* spat Poul. I looked at him and saw only the mountain that rose behind him, the morning light highlighting the high ridges, the west-facing slope in shadows.

"The hob," I said numbly.

Poul looked taken aback. "The Hob? What does the mountain have to do with anything?"

I shook my head. The realization of what I could do began to make my heart pound. "No, not the mountain."

Briefly I saw again the face I'd seen only in visions. I pushed Poul aside and sprinted to the inn's stable, where I'd been keeping Duck when I wasn't using him for patrolling.

I grabbed his bridle, which I'd had mended, and slipped it on without bothering to take Duck out of his stall. He accepted the bit with his usual phlegmatic good humor, watching with interest as I scrambled to find a saddle big enough to fit him. The stable boy had been drafted to patrol, so the people who kept their horses here (Wandel and I) had to tend them themselves.

Not knowing how long it would take me to find the hob, I couldn't ride him bareback, as I usually did. Climbing mountains without a saddle would be miserable after a while. I cursed the time it took me to locate the one I'd used on the trip to Auberg. As I picked it up, the crossbow swung from its usual perch on my back, caught by a swaying stirrup. I was so used to wearing it now, I hardly noticed it, large as it was. But mindful of the task I'd chosen for myself, I set it in the saddle's place. Weapons wouldn't further my cause. If I ran into anything unfriendly, I had Duck and my knife.

By the time I mounted and set out of the barn, the elders' meeting had broken up and any number of people saw me leave. Duck caught my excitement and arched his neck, blowing like an eager stallion faced with a mare. I had to hold him back to a trot as I wove in and out among the people, ignoring their questions.

No one had said anything about raiders at the town bridge, so I assumed they would be concentrated at the eastern end of the valley for a while. I couldn't explain the urgency I felt, even to myself. It was a desperate conviction that I'd happened onto the only thing that could keep the tide of fate from turning against Fallbrook.

Duck's hooves clattered on the cobbles of the bridge as I settled him into a slow, easy trot he could maintain for a long time. Like everyone else, Duck had been honed by the necessity to survive this spring, but unlike many of our horses, he seemed to thrive on it.

The fields were barren of villager or raider, and even the songbirds seemed to have deserted the area. When I looked back from a higher place on the road, I could see a scavenger bird circling just beyond the manor house. Grimly, I turned Duck off the road and onto the narrow track Kith had taken me on this spring. The ground was rougher than the road had been, but Duck's steady trot didn't falter.

I watched his ears, trusting to his keener senses to let me know if any of the raiders were nearby. When he stiffened and brought both ears up to attention as we passed the sprite's castle Wandel had been so impressed with, I shifted my weight back to stop him. He didn't like stopping there, and let me know it by snapping his tail and dancing in place.

I took a deep breath because the raiders didn't bathe much. Since Kith had pointed it out to me, I'd smelled out several scouts whom I wouldn't have seen. Over the scent of hot, sweaty horse and hot, sweaty me, I could smell something sweet and aromatic.

Duck flattened his ears and bolted forward, making me glad I'd bothered with the saddle. He crow-hopped twice before settling into a thunderous gallop that took us well away from the clearing. I let him have his head. Whatever had startled Duck couldn't have missed the racket we'd made leaving; it would be best to put some distance behind us.

At last we came out from under the trees. As I rode beside the bits of cliff that had fallen here and there, I wondered exactly how I was going to attract the hob's attention.

HE KNEW THE MOMENT SHE RODE ONTO THE INITIAL slopes. It was the first clear communication from the mountain he'd heard since awakening, and it felt like coming home. He left off chasing the latest of the hill-grims who'd invaded his territory. They'd keep running anyway, never knowing he'd quit because they'd never seen him in the first place.

"Why did you summon her?" he asked out loud, just to hear the sound of his own voice.

The mountain couldn't form its thoughts the way the hobs did . . . had—not yet. Instead, it pushed until he understood what it wanted. The first part was easy. The woman had come for a hob's bargain, and the mountain wanted him to give her one. . . .

"No," he barked, feeling his ears flatten and his tail twitch like a cat's. Instantly he was drowned in the flood of a millennium of loneliness. Tears rose to his eyes.

"All right," he said, at last. "All right, just don't expect me—or them—to like it."

The mountain had an idea about that, too.

WHEN I FIRST REALIZED SOMEONE WAS PACING BESIDE Duck, it startled me. Duck and I were still climbing the foothills, and there was a hooded man walking beside us as if he'd been there forever.

He was average in height, a little taller than I was, but so wide he looked shorter. I thought at first he might be stout under his cloak. A brief observation of his movements proved he didn't sway like a fat person. He walked like . . . I tried for a comparison, but the only one I could come up with was Kith—but this man must have weighed half again what Kith did. The cloak he wore was an odd touch. This was high summer, far too warm for such a heavy garment.

He wore soft leather boots, rough-finished and undyed. His trousers, what I could see of them underneath the cloak, were dark brown, and there was some kind of embroidery on them. The cloak itself was of the same raw leather as his boots, but it was embroidered with all sorts of outlandish things. Minuscule red and black beads were sewn along the hem of the cloak as thickly as ants in their nest.

From his shoulders, strands of much larger red beads, some the size of walnuts, hung down in random lengths. Small, blue-black feathers were sewn into the hood, giving him the appearance of some sort of giant bird. In his left hand he held a wooden staff, dark and dull with age. The hand was charcoal gray and tipped with formidable claws.

I'd slowed Duck to a walk when we started the steep climb, and now I brought him to a halt. The hob, for I supposed it was he, stopped as well, turning to face me.

Under the hood of his cloak, his face was shrouded in shadows that seemed darker than the hood alone warranted. He did not speak, and now that I'd found what I had sought, I wondered if I could make him understand what I needed of him.

Finally, I cleared my throat and began, awkwardly, "My thanks, lord, for your rescue of me when the—"

"Hillgrim," he supplied, his voice as rough and earthy as the bark on an old elm tree, though his accent was as native as any born to Fallbrook. "Your folks called them hobgoblins as well. But as they're neither goblins nor hobs, I don't use that name. Mucky-smelling things, goblins—though not as annoying as the grims. I am no one's lord. You may call me . . . Caefawn."

He seemed friendly, though the hillgrim had fooled me in a similar fashion. I frowned at him a moment. Something about the way he spoke the last sentence called my attention to it. He'd sounded amused. "What does Caefawn mean?"

He drew back as if affronted, but there was amusement in his voice when he answered me. "It is who I am, Lady."

There was a story there, and if Caefawn was his real name, I'd eat my cinch. He sounded too satisfied with it. I narrowed my eyes at him, wondering for a moment if I was attributing human characteristics to someone—or something—arguably not human at all. I dismounted in order to give myself some time to think.

"If you are no lord, then I am no lady—call me Aren." I remembered something Gram said to me once, a reason the hob wouldn't give me his name. Names had power, she said, and the wildlings kept their names to themselves.

"Ah, but every lovely woman is a lady in her own right," he said.

I frowned at him. I couldn't afford to have him take me lightly—besides, I didn't like it. The village men talked down to all the women. I hadn't noticed it until they'd quit doing it to me. They treated me as they'd treat a man, even those who were wary or frightened of my talents. "Call me Aren if you want me to answer."

It occurred to me—too late, as usual—that arguing with the hob about names was a stupid thing to do when approaching him for help. I'd come here prepared to grovel, and I would, if he'd quit . . . flirting with me. No one knew where Kith was.

"Aren, then," he agreed blandly, but I had the impression he was laughing at me. "And Caefawn will do, Aren. It is not my name, but it is indeed what I am." He touched his staff to the ground gently. "You come for the hob's bargain."

"The what?"

"Ah," he said, and I could hear the smile in his voice. "Before the king's mages came, claiming this land for whatever kingdom they owed their allegiance, human and hob lived side by side. There were things the humans had that my people did not. For these our peoples would trade. One thing for another, by which bargain neither party was the worse."

"You"—he pushed back his hood—"need my help, no?"

I remembered those features clearly, but even so, face-to-face they were shocking. Reddish-brown eyes, cat-slitted and slanted, laughed out of a dark gray face. If he had been a carving, I would have said he was beautiful, but the color of his skin and eyes made it difficult to see past the strangeness. Black hair threaded with silver and white was pulled back into a thick braid that disappeared in the depths of his cloak.

His ears were pointed and large; the right one was

pierced several times with a chain that looked as if it were made of tiny wooden lengths woven in and out though the piercings. Three small, red feathers dangled from the end of the chain.

When he smiled at me, I saw his eyeteeth were long, like the fangs of a cat. His ears fanned gently; from the expression on his face, he did it to frighten me—like a child clapping his hands to tease a deer into running away.

The knowledge he was doing it on purpose didn't stop it from being unsettling, but it did make me mad. I felt my jaw jut out in an unladylike fashion that aggravated the soreness from the blow I'd taken in practice last night.

I'd rehearsed this speech all the way here, but I had intended to deliver it in supplicating tones, not bark at him like a territorial dog. "We need your help. There are raiders in the valley, and we can't stop them alone. I don't know what we can provide to you in return, but if you can help us, you are welcome to anything we have."

"Don't promise so easily," he chided, apparently not upset with my tone of voice. "I will talk to your elders before we seal the bargain." He tilted his head and looked out over the valley. "First, I will prove to them that my help is useful."

Duck pushed his nose into the hob's shoulder, bumping him with a strength that would have sent me stumbling forward. Caefawn swayed a little. He scratched the horse under his bridle, then pushed him away gently, murmuring something for Duck's ears alone.

Shaking his cloak back over his shoulders, the hob started back down the trail at a rapid pace.

When he pushed his cloak back, I saw he wasn't fat at all, not even muscularly fat like Koret. He was just broad. The other thing I noticed was that he had a tail. The very end was tufted with long, dark hair, silver-streaked like the hair on his head. The rest of his tail was covered in short silver hair, like a dog's, though it twitched with his irritation like a cat's.

For some reason the tail made him much more alien than the red cat-eyes and the fangs. He certainly didn't look like the hob in Wandel's song.

"Come, now," he said, without looking back. "If we do not use good speed, we won't be in time."

Though he didn't appear to hurry, the pace he set forced Duck into a slithering, sliding descent in order to keep up with him. I concentrated on staying on and bit my tongue against curiosity. It was enough he'd agreed to help us.

At the bottom of the steep section, the hob began to run. Duck snorted and broke into his lumbering canter, but the hob continued to outpace us until my horse sped into a gallop too fast for the rough ground. It was difficult to tell on such terrain, but I thought Duck's gait was choppier than usual. When Duck didn't respond to my weight or the reins, I called out to the hob.

He stopped immediately and waited for us to catch up, patting Duck's foaming shoulder remorsefully before I could speak. "Sorry about that. Been a long time since I ran with horses. This one looks a little lame, eh?"

I'd slipped off as soon as Duck stopped. "Right rear, I think."

The hob was there before me, looking at the swelling on the gelding's haunch, just over the stifle joint. "Faen," he commented, "best to avoid them if you can. Bite worse than a hornet, and they're twice as mean."

"Faen?" I asked.

Caefawn put his hand over the swelling. "Can't do anything for the poison; only time will disperse it. But I can make sure it won't hurt." The bump didn't look as if it changed any after he touched it.

"What is a faen?"

"Little people," he said, surprised. He held up his fingers with just enough space between his thumb and finger for a butterfly to fit into. "Don't remember that they minded humans, though the hob don't have much traffic with 'em. Can't trust them while your back is turned."

"Sprites?" I asked, remounting Duck.

"Hmm, I've heard them called that."

"There's a rock formation, it looks like a little castle—" I stopped speaking to settle more firmly in the saddle as the hob started off again and Duck followed. Whatever the hob had done to the swelling seemed to have worked, because Duck was no longer lame.

"Ah, yes." The hob's gait was slow enough for Duck to resume his distance-covering trot. "I had forgotten they had a place here. Does this trail go close enough to it that you can see them?"

"Yes." I ducked a low branch.

"No wonder they were upset. I'll have a word with them when we pass."

A little earthquake, like those which had plagued us this spring, caused the ground to shudder beneath us. Caefawn didn't appear to be upset by it. He cupped his hands around Duck's head and blew gently into the horse's nostrils. Duck mouthed his bit uncertainly, but his ears came up. Before the last of the vibrations died beneath his hooves, the tension was gone from his muscles.

Duck was far more upset when we approached the sprite's stone court than he had been during the earthquake. After seeing the welt on poor old Duck, I wasn't sure I wanted to get too close to the sprites either.

The hob stopped before we were in sight of the odd miniature building. He said a few foreign words in a courteous tone, waited a moment, then nodded.

"We'll wait here. That one was a guardian, didn't have the authority to let us pass. They're in the process of moving the trail away from their home, but it will take a week or two. In the meantime they're trying to shut down traffic through here. They would let you and me through—but they're not happy about the horse. Ah, here he is back."

The horse in question clamped his tail and shifted his weight, none too happy about the sprites. The hob talked a moment more, then started forward. Duck cringed as well as a big horse could until we were well past the court. I never did see a sprite.

When we came out of the shadows of the trees and into the open area of fields, I searched, but could see no sign of life.

"Be careful," I cautioned. "The raiders attacked on this side of the river last night. The battle was well on the other side of the manor house, maybe a league or so. But their victory there gave them this half of the valley."

"No," said the hob, unconcerned. "They're hunting a few archers and the berserker down by the other bridge."

"Kith?" I asked, forgetting that he could have no way of knowing who it was.

The hob looked at me without slackening his pace and nodded. "The one-armed man."

I shifted my weight forward, and Duck broke into a gallop. As we started to pass Caefawn, he reached out and grasped the gelding's nose, pulling him to a halt. "They'll still be there. No sense killing this lad to get there."

I closed my eyes briefly and nodded. When I looked up, I noticed a paving stone in the middle of the dirt path. Frowning at it, I sent Duck after the hob, who had resumed an easy jog. Scattered cobbles lay on the trail ahead, growing more numerous as we approached the King's Highway.

When we reached the rise before the bridge, I slowed Duck to a brisk walk to allow him to pick his way among the broken cobbles. It looked as if some giant had plowed the highway under. The earthquake hadn't felt that bad to me.

Caefawn slowed with me. "Good. The mountain wasn't

certain she could do this, but the bloodmagic seems to be weaker than she thought. Are you any good with the knife you wear?"

I couldn't pull my eyes from the damaged roadway. The mountain had done this? "My knife? No. Kith's been teaching me, but I doubt I'd stand up against anyone with experience."

"You'll do," he said. "When we get to the bridge, we'll let your horse return to his stable, and then you and I'll take care of the raiders."

That caught my attention. I looked incredulously at the top of his hood as I ran through his words again. I thought of several questions, but discarded them before they touched my tongue. "The two of us," I said finally.

He made a noise that could have been agreement, laughter, or both.

SIX

The hob made little noise threading his way through the trees. I tried to imitate him, but the thin yearling growths of willow snagged at my clothing and rustled as I moved past. Not that I couldn't move quietly in the woods, but *I* did it by avoiding dry leaves and dense growth like the stuff we were currently wading through.

I was so busy grumbling to myself that when Caefawn dropped to hands and knees, I almost tripped over him. I crouched and followed the motion of his chin to see a small group of raiders talking among themselves not much over a stone's throw away.

They were using the garbled language Wandel called the patois, so I couldn't tell what they were saying. If they'd been quieter, they would have heard me scuttling through the leaves.

The hob drew a hollow reed from a pocket of his cloak and slipped a dart made from a porcupine quill into the reed. Placing the tube against his lips, he blew, propelling the dart toward the raiders. I lost sight of it as it traveled through the air, but one of the men jumped and rubbed his thigh. Battle-roused, the others dropped low and looked for their unseen foe.

I held my breath and tried not to rustle.

The man who'd jumped first shook his head, laughing a little. "Just a bug," he said in the king's tongue.

The others relaxed—so did I. Then the man hit by the dart collapsed in the grass.

Eight of the men remaining held their weapons at the ready and crouched, each looking in a different direction. Both the hob and I held still. The ninth man dropped to his knees next to the hob's victim. From the relief on his face, I could tell the fallen man wasn't dead.

After we'd crouched there long enough for my feet to fall asleep, the raiders relaxed.

"Must have gone," said one, a big man with graying brown hair who seemed to be their leader.

"Or it really was a bug," commented another.

"What do you suppose it was?" asked the man who still crouched on the ground.

The leader shook his head. "How should I know? We've got people what disappear, leaving behind nothing but blood and weaponry. We've got horses lame from bug bites nastier'an anything I've ever seen—not even when we worked the swamps a couple of years back. Food goes foul too fast, and something's been robbing our supplies and scattering them. Now there's some freaking berserker lurking in the woods. Maybe the same bugs what got the horses got Henwit, too. I don't know."

Hmm, I thought, *if their leader is that spooked, the men mustn't be far behind.*

"What we going to do about him?" challenged the man on the ground. "I ain't leaving Henwit behind to get chewed up by whatever happens upon him."

The big man threw up his hands. "Take him back, then. You explain to the captain what happened."

The raider tried his best, but the unconscious man weighed more than he did. It was obvious he couldn't carry the limp body very far. Had Caefawn chosen the heaviest man on purpose?

Finally two of the raiders took the heavy man and staggered off with him. The rest of the party headed away from where Caefawn and I crouched. Almost a third of this bunch was out of the fight, without our killing a soul.

I twisted to look at the hob. He grinned back. It still looked rather alarming when done with fangs, but I was getting used to it. When he began backing quietly out of the brush, I followed.

I decided I needed to be armed with something better than a knife. Kith said by the time you could use a knife, you were too close. Even an idiot could kill you. Especially if you were fighting someone bigger, stronger, and better armed. Most of the people we'd be encountering would be all three. When we came to a tree with good stout branches, I stopped.

"You're too serious," Caefawn said, watching me hack at a solid branch of oak. "This should be fun."

I stopped hacking and turned to stare at him.

"Of course," he said, "it never hurts to be prepared."

He reached over and took the branch, breaking it off the tree as if it were a twig. Holding it in both hands, he fell to one knee and presented it to me, his tail curled around his feet.

"Your tree branch, my lady."

As he'd intended me to, I laughed as I took it from him—though for some reason his actions brought back that last morning with Daryn. I stripped the branch of its leaves and thought, *This one's for you, my heart's desire*.

The hob shook his head at me. "So sad." He reached over and touched my cheek with one black claw. "Come, let's find some more raiders to tease before you make me weep."

The second group we came upon had ten men in it as

well. This time the man Caefawn chose wasn't big enough to take two men to carry. When the rest of the group headed out, the direction they chose was right over the top of us.

Caefawn erupted from the underbrush before they knew we were there. The sight of him—ears, fangs, and tail—stopped them where they stood. I knocked one unconscious with a clout of my stick before any of them started fighting.

Satisfaction lent strength to my blows and speed to my reactions. I'd been waiting all spring and half the summer for this. While I swung my branch, I remembered Daryn defending my father's body with a walking stick.

These were lowlanders not much bigger than I was, but I wasn't as strong as a man my size would be. However, they were startled and off balance, whereas I . . . I jammed the end of the staff into the diaphragm of the man who'd tried to take me from behind. If Kith knew what rage I was feeding into my blows, he'd have my head. Anger might make me careless, but it felt really good.

The man I fought was not as good as Ice but better than Manta. If I'd been a man, I would have lost because he was better than I was, too. But he underestimated me. He brought his sword at my staff, thinking I'd be stupid and try to block it. Instead, I let it slide past and pushed his sword farther from his body, stepping into the opening I'd made. It worked just the way it had in practice.

Neither my staff nor his sword was usable in such close quarters. I dropped the branch and drew my knife. It was so easy, so smooth. I jammed the knife under his ribs and touched his heart.

His body took my knife as he fell, but I bent down and snatched up my staff. There were only two raiders left on their feet, and they were concentrating all their efforts on the hob, seeing him as the larger threat.

As I watched, Caefawn's tail caught the foot of the

man to his left while he bashed the head of the other with his staff. He spun around in a jingle of beads and feathers and tapped the head of the man still tangled in hob tail. He did it without effort. So much stronger and faster than the men he was fighting, he could choose to let them live. None of his moaning foes were dead. I was the only one who'd killed.

I waited for the flood of exultation, for release from the anger that had dogged my every step since that morning when I beat my hands bloody on the trapdoor of my cellar. I waited for triumph.

The hob turned to me, though I noticed he kept one ear cocked behind him to keep track of his victims. The man I'd hit in the diaphram continued to struggle for breath, making the other man, the one I'd stabbed, seem all the more quiet.

His face serious, the hob looked at me. I wondered if I'd violated some taboo by killing the raider, but after a moment he stepped to the dead man and took my dagger, cleaning it on the bottom of the man's shirt. Though he did a thorough job, the knife he handed to me was hard to take back.

I'd wanted to kill the raiders, all of them, ever since they'd destroyed my family. I dreamed of it at night, how it would feel to avenge their deaths. Instead, I felt sick and guilty.

"Come," said the hob, giving me another speculative look. "We need to leave before the rest of them recover."

I followed him into the woods. The next group we found were even easier than the first one. Not only was the man Caefawn brought down was the biggest of them. The rest of the party were lowlanders, three of them little more than boys. The leader sent all three of the youngsters off with their unconscious comrade. Swearing bitterly, the leader took four fewer men with him as he continued on.

The fourth group we came upon was very close to the

manor. The woods had begun to thin out, and the place we'd found to hide wouldn't conceal us from any kind of determined search. That didn't seem to bother the hob.

The leader of the raiders wore a horn around his neck, and a bit of gold cloth, battered and bedraggled, dangled from his belt. After the hob's quill had done its magic, the man knelt over his fallen comrade, drew his knife, and slit his throat. The rest of his men were silent.

The hob shook his head in disgust. "The fool. Let's teach him a bit of a lesson, shall we. Here, take this and follow me."

The underbrush where we crouched was dark, and I was distracted by what had happened. I took what he handed me and scuttled behind on my hands and knees as he approached the stone-faced mercenaries. Their leader said something short and curt, and one of the others nodded.

We edged closer . . . closer. The soft, velvet-covered rope I held in my hand twitched, and I realized what it was. I banged my head on a low tree limb. It's hard to pay attention to things like tree limbs when distracted by the . . . well, the *peculiarity* of holding on to someone's *tail*.

Caefawn kept going, though the cover was so thin now that if someone chanced to glance our way, they couldn't help but see us. Bright red feathers don't exactly blend into the landscape.

"Hush, now, and mind you don't lose your grip." The hob's voice was soft. The mercenaries, as jumpy as they were, didn't hear him.

Caefawn wove some magic and dropped from the sight of my eye sometime between one instant and the next. The only way I knew he was there was the reassuring pressure of his tail in my hand. I couldn't, quite, see myself either.

When the mercenaries started out, we did, too. I held my breath as we broke from cover. One of them looked right at me, but he called no warning. The dead man glared accusingly at me as we passed.

Their progress disguised any sounds we made. Caefawn tugged me forward until we were so close I could hear the last man muttering angry swearwords under his breath as he guarded their rear. And I'd thought Kith could curse.

When we reached the first of the manor gardens, the hob whistled softly. The swearing man turned to see who had made the noise, but the mercenary beside him cuffed him lightly to get his attention.

"Nawt but t'bird—*Look!*" The last word was drawn from the man in a shout, calling everyone's attention (including mine) to the edge of the garden.

Nearly half again as tall as a normal deer, the kindred deer, nearly twice the size of any other kind of deer, posed motionless, as if to say "Here I am, worship me." I'd seen a kindred deer a time or two, but they were rare here. I'd never heard of one that was white like this one was. His great golden antlers shimmered in the sunlight. Eyes blue as the sky settled first on the hob, then on me.

For a moment I thought they twinkled with the same mad humor the hob's did, but his gaze moved on. When it was through looking us over, the stag darted into graceful motion. The mercenaries, freed from the spell of surprise, dropped their weapons and ran to follow.

When we were alone, I released my grip on the hob's tail. I'd been holding it so hard that my hand was stiff.

"The white beast," I said in awe.

"If I find a safe place for you, will you stay there?" Caefawn asked abruptly. "The stag is a little too contemptuous of humans to watch out for his own safety."

"Fine," I agreed. I think that if he'd asked me to stake myself out as bait, I'd have agreed to that, too.

THE TREE LIMBS HAD LONG SINCE CEASED FEELING PRE-carious and had slipped into flimsy when the hob, climbing behind me, quit urging me farther up the ancient oak that dominated the grounds of the manor.

"There, now," he said, his voice a toneless whisper. "Without that thrice-damned road the oak listens to the mountain and will hide you from notice. The raiders are moving this way, so be careful." He placed my hands at apparently random places on the swaying branches. "Stay here until I come for you."

"Mmm," I said, which was as much of an agreement as I was prepared to make.

He apparently thought it agreement enough because he slipped down. I watched him leave, then put my forehead against the tree.

"Oh, Gram," I said out loud, "hobs, hillgrims, sprites, the white beast . . . and the day is not over yet."

I'd killed a man today, not because I had to but because I wanted to. I thought about it and decided I could live with it. But I also decided vengeance was for fools. If I'd killed him only because I'd had to, I wouldn't be feeling nearly this bad.

His death hadn't made Daryn less dead. Instead, I wondered if the raider'd had friends who'd mourn his passing.

A movement below caught my attention. One of the raiders crept stealthily forward, scanning the perimeter of the parkland. My perch, which had seemed so high moments before, now seemed pitifully vulnerable. I missed the reassuring weight of my crossbow. Next time I went hunting hobs, I'd be sure to bring it.

The man stopped just below me, crouching forward. He held a longbow and had a quiver strapped across his back. He was missing a finger from his right hand.

I was still staring at that missing finger when the thin shaft of an arrow slid through his throat at an angle, emerging gore-covered from the skin on the far side of his neck. His body convulsed, twisting with instinctive desire for life. I watched as he finally stilled, and I got a clear look at his face.

He was the man who'd shot Caulem as he went for help. Fighters, like farmers, often lose a finger or two, but I could not mistake the face.

The irony of it all made me laugh. Whoever killed him had saved me from testing my resolve to not look for vengeance.

As the raider's eyes glazed, the blood that had pumped from twin wounds slowed as the beating of his heart slowed. There had been too much death in the past few months for the gore to raise more than a hint of horror. Horror was watching Kith's face as he held down a man so Koret could cut off the farmer's infected hand, crushed in combat.

I looked around to see if I could find the archer. Hadn't the hob said the raiders were looking for a couple of archers as well as Kith? Even though I was watching, he was almost to the tree before I noticed him.

He wore a hooded, mottled green tunic and dark pants, and carried the bow that was Lord Moresh's pride and joy. Moresh had gotten it from a traveling merchant who'd brought it from far across the ocean. It was an exotic and powerful weapon—and to Moresh's chagrin, he'd never been able to draw it. He kept it on display in the manor.

The archer nocked his bow again, using the arrow he'd pulled from the dead man's throat. As he did so, he turned his head to the side and I saw his face clearly. Wandel's harp-calloused fingers pulled the bowstring with the same deft skill they had on the harp.

Almost gently he released the string. I tracked the arrow's flight to its target. A man crouching on one of the low walls separating the herb garden from the park fell to the ground. He'd been so still, I hadn't seen him until the arrow touched him.

I almost called out to Wandel, but decided it might

attract more than just his attention. Besides, the thought of the minstrel bending a bow that Moresh, a warrior born, could not, was oddly disturbing.

With all of the problems of this summer, the steward had let the grounds go. Usually the park was kept much shorter, but the waist-high grass served as cover for Wandel as he slid forward on his belly, snaking his way to a tree closer to the wall.

Something moved under my tree again. A raider armed with a crossbow scurried to the trunk, his gaze fixed on Wandel, who had chosen this moment to make a target of himself against the wall. The man under me spared no glance for his fallen comrade. He stepped on the stirrup at the end of his crossbow and cocked it with quiet speed.

Koret and Kith had both assured me that my knife was no good for throwing. Not that it would have mattered, because I didn't have any practice throwing knives. I'd have to try something else.

As quietly as I could, I began climbing down to a less lethal (for me) height from which to jump. I climbed down as far as I dared, finding a limb that left me an unobstructed path to the ground. Balancing there, I urged him silently to move forward. I thought for a moment that he was going to try to take his shot from the shelter of the oak, but he stepped away to get a better angle. Trying not to think about the dizzying distance between me and the ground, I dropped.

Even softened by his body, my landing was harder than I'd imagined. My knee caught him in the back of the neck and snapped the bone with an audible crack. After a moment, I rolled off him and dragged myself to my knees.

"Aren?" asked Wandel in a whisper.

I looked up blearily, realizing he must have heard the noise I'd made jumping on the raider and had come back to see what it was.

I must still have been a little stunned from the fall,

because I said, "I brought the hob from the mountain. I've got to get back up in the tree."

"Shh," said the harper, pulling me away from the bodies, his victim and mine. "Are you all right?"

I shook my head, pulling away from him enough to tuck my forehead down on my knees. When I spoke again, it was in a tone as quiet as his. "Sorry. Knocked the sense out of me."

"Anything hurt?"

Feeling better, I lifted my head to meet the harper's gaze. "No. I'll be black and blue by morning, and my left knee is not pleased with me. I'll get back in the tree."

"You said you brought the hob out of the mountain?" he asked cautiously. "Like the thing that attacked you?"

I grinned at him then. "That was a hillgrim. Last I saw the hob, he'd sent a group of raiders out after a white stag. He's wearing a brown cloak covered in feathers and beads. Don't shoot him."

Wandel grunted. "A feather cloak sounds pretty distinctive. Any fighting man worth his salt would remove it before his enemies began using it for target practice. If he's done that, how can I tell him from the others?"

"If he's taken off the cloak"—I scooted until my back was against the tree and slid up to get to my feet, a little rough on my back but it worked—"you'll know him when you see him."

BY THE TIME I REGAINED MY PERCH, MY KNEE HAD BE-gun to hurt. I found a more comfortable position and scanned the countryside. I couldn't see Wandel or the hob, but the number of raiders had dwindled significantly. I couldn't see any organized groups at all, just a few raiders wandering randomly here and there. I closed my eyes just for a moment to rest them.

"LASS, WAKE UP. WE'VE MORE WORK TO BE DONE."

I looked at the hob stupidly for a moment, then shifted

incautiously and almost tumbled out of the tree.

Caefawn steadied me, cinnamon eyes twinkling in his gray face. "Now, no sense falling out of the tree twice. This time there mayn't be a nice fat one to break your fall."

"Thanks," I said, taking a firmer grip on the branches, not questioning how he knew about my little adventure. Kith would have known as much just by glancing at the ground under the tree. If he could do it, there was no reason why the hob could not. "If you'll start down, I'll follow."

It was hard climbing down with my knee stiff and sore, but I managed it with the help of Caefawn's bracing hand. When we reached the ground, the hob bent and put his hand on my poor, sore knee and squeezed.

"Ouch," I said, jumping back. "That hurts."

"Let me look at it—there may be something I can do to help."

When he approached me again, I let him look. This time he was more careful when he put his hand on it. It still hurt.

"Well?" I asked.

He shook his head. "If I'd seen it when it first happened, I could have fixed it up tight. There's nothing wrong that a day's rest won't cure. I can do nothing about the swelling—you're not going to be able to walk far on that, at least not very quickly." He pursed his lips and whistled a little melody.

Since he was obviously waiting for something, I waited quietly, too—trying not to look at the dead men who lay nearby.

I didn't think it was obvious what I was doing, but after a moment the hob said, "They bother you?"

There was no ridicule in his voice, nor censure, so I nodded. "I can't help but think that the man I killed was someone's sweetheart, someone's son."

"He was," agreed the hob. "Best you remember it, or

you'll become more wicked than he ever was. The only thing worse than those who don't think about who they kill, are those who do, and enjoy it."

"Is that why you didn't kill anyone?" I asked.

He smiled, but there was no merriment in his eyes. "I killed a few today, but there aren't so many dead here as are sleeping or wandering. I'm thinking yon village is going to need every head it has to make it through the coming troubles. But it won't work as long as men like the one who chose to kill his own comrade still survive. I can't sort the good from the evil, but there are some helping me who can."

I really didn't want to know, but I had to ask just the same. "What's coming?"

"Ah." The hob pursed his lip. "Now that's something you shall see for yourself, *mah'folen*."

The sound of hooves on turf saved him from the back of my tongue. I didn't know what *mah'folen* meant, but it sounded loverlike, too familiar from a man—a hob— I'd just met. I turned to see a white pony jump the low park wall and canter toward us. For a moment the breath caught in my throat at the sight of him. Then it was merely a half-bred pony stallion.

He had straight, almost delicate, legs, but his neck was thick even for a stallion. His nose was convex, making his head appear too large for his body. Brambles were caught in his tail and in his mane, which fell haphazardly on either side of his neck, as if a comb had never touched him.

"Your ride, lady," said the hob with a bow, spoiling it by adding "I hope." He turned to the pony and said a few words in another language.

If the pony replied, I couldn't tell, but the hob motioned me forward. Mounting with my sore knee was even more interesting than climbing trees, but he wasn't tall, so I managed.

"Hold on," warned Caefawn, and sprang forward.

Without his warning I would have fallen as the pony surged forward to follow with a speed that lent validity to my first vision of the animal. This little wildling that looked like a hill pony made the fastest horse Albrin had bred seem a plodding workhorse in comparison. The hob didn't seem to have much trouble keeping ahead of it.

THE HOB WHO CALLED HIMSELF CAEFAWN GLANCED obliquely at the woman who rode Espe. The white beast snorted at him, telling him that he was too slow. The run had been good for Espe. Like Caefawn, the beast needed a good chase now and then to keep life interesting.

He wasn't so certain Aren was better for this day. Perhaps it hadn't been a good idea to bring her with him. Convincing the villagers wouldn't be all that hard. He'd been watching their struggles since he'd become aware of them this spring. They were losing, and losing people grasped at any straw, no matter how strange it appeared to them. Despite their distrust of magic, they would take his bargain and regret it later. He was trying for something better. Aren might be the key to that—or not.

Killing the raiders had done something to her. Remembering the rage she fought with, he hoped it had been the right something. Vengeance was a cold, hard thing.

He'd taken her not to use as a spokesperson in the village, but to see the enthusiasm she'd shown looking at the warning stone on his mountain this spring. Instead, she showed him that she could perform the dance of death with courage. A useful quality, but not much fun.

THE WAY WE TOOK WOUND THROUGH THE ORCHARD and berry brambles, over fence and hedge. My knee throbbed with every stride, but it was better when the hob and the pony slowed after only a few minutes of running. Never having wandered through the manor's pastureland from this direction, I wasn't certain where we were. Judging from the marshy ground and the thick brush, we might be close to the bridge. If the pony had been as big as Duck, we'd never have made it through.

Gradually I heard the murmur of quiet voices. Caefawn and the pony edged forward until I could hear plainly everything the raiders were saying. They used the king's tongue, not patois—gossip, not orders.

"Where's the capt'n?" The speaker was a boy with a thick southern accent.

"Off looking for some poor fool he can send into that copse to lure the berserker out of there." The second speaker was a man full grown, and his accent reminded me of Moresh and Wandel's. He must be noble-born, or raised among them.

"Why didn't he order us to do it?"

The older man laughed. "Too smart. He knows I'd refuse, and he's not good enough to force the issue—and he can't give the order to you while I'm here. Poor bugger."

"The capt'n or me?" There was a touch of humor in the boy's voice, and the man laughed.

"Neither. I meant the berserker. He's been trained—no way a one-armed man could fight that well without some training. He's got to know he has no chance. There aren't enough fighters in the whole village to push us out now—he'll have no rescue, but he'll take out as many as he can in the meantime."

"If he's no threat, can't we just let him go?" asked the boy softly.

"Not with Sharet as captain we can't." The older man sounded bitter, but after a moment he said, "No, that's unfair. I wouldn't leave him alive either. He's too good. He'd pick us off one by one while we slept. Bet you he's the one who got Edlen and those other fools. Edlen was nigh on as good as me with the sword, and from what I could tell, he didn't even manage to nick his attacker. No, the captain will lure him out in the open and I'll pick him off from a distance."

They were silent for a moment. Then the younger man said, "I wish, sometimes, that I'd never caught the capt'n's eye. That I was still back home herding goats."

The veteran sighed. "Be a fool if you didn't—or worse. But life's like that sometimes. Your village was overrun, Quilliar, and there's no one herding goats there anymore." I stiffened at the realization that the boy bore the same name as my brother. Not that it was an uncommon name, but hearing it was unsettling. "Much as I don't like killing civilians, the capt'n's right about this valley. There's no future in warfare, not the kind that's taking place now. There's only losers who fight never-ending battles. When we set up a permanent camp here, we'll make our own home and none will take it from us. You can herd goats here if you like."

The boy swallowed, then said in a hushed tone, "But couldn't we have found a valley not taken already, Rook?"

"Boy," said the man gently, "if a place isn't taken already, there's a reason for it. Life's not a game you can afford to lose."

"Life's what you make it," said the hob softly, stepping through the bushes.

Without prompting, the pony followed. Not that I would have wanted to remain hidden. Really.

The older man had stepped in front of the younger. He held his sword in his right hand, his left hand empty—though there was a crossbow lying on the ground nearby, as if he'd just tossed it there. His hair was gray and gold, longer than mine, and braided neatly, as was his beard. He was cleaner than most of the raiders I'd run into, nor was his clothing anything I'd have associated with a battlefield: green silk and brown velvet tunic over black leather trousers.

The boy behind him was beautiful, even prettier than Daryn. He, too, was blond. But where Daryn had been earth, this boy was air. He had a swordsman's body, not a farmer's, and his features might have been chiseled by an artist, they were so even and fine. A silver earring twinkled in one ear. He stepped to the side, not allowing the older man to protect him.

His eyes were older than Daryn's had ever been, and there was death on his blade—but I couldn't forget his name was Quilliar, and he was just a boy. I wondered what the hob had in store for them. I hoped these two would survive—actually, I'd like that for all four of us, five with the pony.

"What are you?" asked the older man softly, no fear in his voice. "One of the bloodmage's playthings?"

The hob laughed, and the boy flinched. Must have been the fangs. "No. I am a hob, but you may call me death if you wish. I hope that you do not. There are too many dead this day."

The warrior frowned at him. "Tell me how to call you by another name."

I noticed that while the older raider kept his attention on the hob, the boy's eyes never left me for long. Partners, I thought, each trusting the other to do his job. With a thread of mischief I owed the hob, I grinned at the boy, just to see what he would do. He stiffened slightly and tightened his fingers on his blade.

"Why do you fight what you can join?" asked the hob. "If you kill all the villagers, you will not survive the winter—there are things loosed in this place much more ill disposed to humankind than I am." The pony snorted, stamping his hoof.

"Words," observed the other man.

"Are you so lost in death you've given up hope?" I asked without meaning to. I was really getting tired of the *sight* controlling my tongue, but with the hob here, it should be safe. I quit fighting and let the vision take me where it would.

There was a time when laughter had been as natural as breath; when he had lain with fair maidens and fought raiders, driving them from his father's land with his brothers; when battle had brought satisfaction of work well done because he protected the people who made his family wealthy. Then there was bloodshed and betrayal, forcing him to flee and change his name.

Rook battled from bitterness and necessity. He'd taken only his horse and sword when he left so long ago he could not even picture his father in his mind's eye, though his voice haunted his nightmares. Mercenary or raider, it mattered not to him—they were his people to protect and to love.

"To protect and love," I said in a murmur, one hand on the raider's free arm as I looked into his dark eyes. I'm not sure how much of what I *saw* I told him. I was trying too hard not to show how scared I was to find myself clinging to him to think about it, or to stop my tongue from continuing. "Have you forgotten all that you were taught? Have you not seen that hatred and bitterness rots the soul?"

I sounded like a priest—I would never have been so maudlin, given a choice. Especially not with the boy's sword pressed into my side. I glanced at the boy's face, seeing from the readiness there that he was prepared to use it.

"Is killing what you want? Or do you want a home?" The hob's voice was calm, but then *he* didn't have a sword in *his* ribs.

"Home," spat the older man, looking from me to Cae-fawn. "What kind of a home would that be? Even if the villagers allowed us in as equals, we would not be accepted—not after the bodies that have fallen beneath our swords."

"You are right," I agreed, finding courage to speak from somewhere. "No more than I am accepted. But you will be needed. Do you have to be loved by all? Or isn't this one"—I nodded my head at the boy—"enough? Does your captain *accept* you?"

I heard the pleading in my voice. The hob seemed to think these two were important. I was willing to work toward his goal, especially if it meant the sword quit cutting into my skin.

That the raiders were listening at all was close to miraculous . . . or magical. I shot a glance at the pony calmly nibbling at the grass a few paces away. There were tales of the White Beast . . . but I'd seen the Beast today, and he was a deer. Besides, the White Beast wouldn't wander about with a branch of mountain ash tangled comically in his forelock.

"Uneasy allies become battle comrades after the fighting is over," said the hob. "Death has no friends, and there is much that might be death coming to these lands. The wildlings are free, and they've driven men out of these lands before."

"The captain will never agree."

"Ah," said the hob, "that is so. Perhaps, though, you might think on what we've said." He pulled a small feather from his cloak. "If you wish to speak again, burn this feather. If you are in the valley, I will find you."

"In a week there won't be a village to join," said the older mercenary softly, making no move to take the feather. "I am sorry." He sounded it.

"This rout hasn't been as one-sided as you think," replied the hob. "Most of the serfs are safely hiding in the fields. They'll come in when you're gone. There are five men dead at the bridge, but most of the village horses are running in the woods. I can see to it that they return to the villagers. See what results this day has produced before you make your decision." He took the mercenary's hand and set the feather in it. "Things are changing here faster than you know. A smart man learns to be ready to change with them."

The mercenary didn't look happy, but he put the feather in a bag at his hip. Jaw set, he nodded. "I'll keep it in mind. Quilliar, come. Skyboy should have been back a while ago. Let's see if we can locate him."

I waited until the mercenaries were gone, then said, "We've got to get to Kith."

The hob nodded, took a step toward the pony, and stopped. "You'd better go alone. He'll not trust you if I'm there. Do you know where he is?"

"I think so. There's a hiding place we used when we were children. It's not far from the Fell Bridge." I hesitated a moment, then said, "Wandel is here—the harper who was with us on the trip over the Hob. He knows more about what's wrong with Kith than I do. Do you think you could find him and tell him to meet me at the cairn by Fell Bridge? I think he knows where it is."

"Your wish is my command," he said softly, taking my hand in his and kissing it, as if I were a lady. "I'll have to keep the pony, though—he won't go with you unless I do. Tell your elders I'll meet them at yon manor house tomorrow late morning."

I thought I felt the bare touch of fangs on the back of my hand for a moment when he kissed it, but that could have been my imagination.

SINCE I DIDN'T KNOW THE LAY OF THE LAND HERE VERY well, I'd blundered about for some time before I caught sight of the old cairn. Buried under a thicket of thorn, the old stone mound held a good defensive position. Some long-ago lord had emptied the thing of its bones and treasures to use it to store grain for his pastured horses. The village boys often spent the night there to prove how brave they were.

As I started carefully down the steep slope, I found that as long as I didn't bend my knee, it didn't hurt much. It must not be badly hurt, which was a relief, but it made my progress pretty slow.

"Now, just where do you think you're going?" The raider who stepped out from the brambles was careful not to turn his back to the cairn. He held his sword easily as he smiled.

"Does it matter?" I tried to keep my voice even, though he'd startled me badly. I moved my right hand cautiously near my knife.

"No," he said softly, approaching me with all due caution. "It doesn't matter at all."

I didn't see anything, though I'd not taken my eyes off the raider. For an instant I wondered why he fell so abruptly. Then I realized the warmth on my face was blood. Finally my eyes registered Kith, shirtless, his knife in his hand. The blood from the raider's throat covered his knife, but his movement had been so swift I hadn't caught more than a suggestion of motion.

"Kith," I said, relieved. Then I looked into his eyes.

"Berserker" they had called him, both the hob and the raider, but I hadn't thought about what it meant. The man who stood before me had nothing human left in his eyes. I'd thought that a berserker's face would be twisted with rage, but Kith's expression was mild. I had no doubt, though, that he intended to kill me.

Remembering a trick Albrin had taught me when we were trying to catch a horse someone had brutalized, I collapsed to the ground, ignoring the pain from my knee. My position had made it clear to that mare that I was no threat; I didn't know what it would mean to a man—easy prey, perhaps. I dropped my eyes from his and sang some stupid children's song, just as I had to the mare.

I'd never been so frightened in my life, not even in the cellar the day the raiders came. It wasn't just my death I was afraid of, but of what it would do to Kith if he killed me. I finished one song and started another.

"Aren?" he asked, sounding bewildered.

Some instinct kept my eyes away from him. "Yes, Kith. It's all right now. Most of them are gone. It's time to go home."

"My father," he said. "He's in the cairn. I . . . bandaged him, but—"

"He's alive?" Forgetting my caution, I pushed myself to my feet, swearing as I twisted my knee again. "Plague it, Kith, help me get down there."

When he extended his arm, bloody knife and all, I grabbed it firmly for support and started down the slope. If an angry dog knows you're afraid, it will attack.

"We've got to get him out of here. Do you have a mount?" I asked in my best bossy Melly voice.

"Yes." His voice was slurred.

"Well, go get it," I snapped, letting go of his arm. The cairn was only a few steps away. Kith seemed a little dazed, and I hoped the task would give him time to return to himself.

When he was gone, I ducked inside the cairn. Albrin lay wrapped tightly in a cloak, though it was too dark to tell much more about his condition than that he was still breathing. He didn't feel feverish, but it was too early for that to be a sign one way or the other.

"Aren, girl?" he said, blinking a bit.

I rested my hand against his cheek for a moment. "Yes?"

"Sorry about . . . about—"

"It's all right. I know." I had to stop the terrible effort of his speech. "I understand. When I found out what had been done to Kith, I was angry, too."

"They . . . Kith . . ." The old man's voice faded. Funny, I'd never thought of him as old before—but he must be at least Merewich's age.

"Shh," I soothed him. "I know, sir. He's fine—I sent him off to get his horse. We've got to get you to the inn." I thought of the hob, and wished I'd brought him with me. He'd helped when Duck had been hurt.

"My horses," he said, "they wanted my horses."

"Shh. Rest, sir. The horses are safe." The hob said he'd see they returned. I touched Albrin's shoulder and left it there. It seemed to give him some peace, and comforted me as well. I fell into a light doze.

There was a spirit here, the thought came to me, a half-dream. It wasn't one to frighten small children—a guardian. It brushed against me, lifting my hair away from my brow, then settled in to wait with me. It knew about waiting.

I was too tired to do anything more than accept it, as I'd begun to accept the strange things that were happening to change the world into this new, bewildering place filled with hillgrims, sprites, and hobs. At last I heard the sounds of leather harness and hooves. I peered cautiously out of the entrance, and stepped out when I saw it was Kith.

"How is he?" he asked. This time it was *he* who wasn't meeting *my* eyes.

He was ashamed I had seen him as he had been earlier.

"He was conscious for a bit, he's resting now. I'm no healer, but he doesn't have the look of someone on the brink of death." This was difficult—I didn't want to hurt him. He was vulnerable now, and more tired than I was.

"Kith, you're not a monster." He looked up then, but I continued before he could speak. "Danci's breaking her heart over you—and you, you're in worse shape than she is. I've seen you sitting outside her house at night, hiding in the shadows. Don't you understand? Your choices are different now. There'll be no bloodmage, no Moresh to kill you as if you were a hawk with a broken wing."

He laughed, and there was such bitterness and mockery in it that it hurt me to hear it. "There are no choices, Aren. Who do you think Wandel is? The king's eyes and ears, sent to make certain that the nobles keep their bonds—and an assassin when need be. Why do you think Moresh was so generous with his hospitality? Did you think he was a music lover? There were other minstrels who came through here, and they didn't stay in the manor. That mare of his is worth a king's ransom—war-trained and royal-bred. Harpers don't make that kind of wealth, not the kind of harpers who travel from village to village. The king sent him here this year to make certain Moresh kept his word on certain matters. He came to me and talked to me about it after we returned from Auberg. We made a bargain, didn't we Wandel?" He didn't raise his voice or look away from me as he spoke the last.

"Yes." The harper stood halfway down the slope leading to the cairn.

I could see his face clearly in the afternoon sun. There was nothing left of the funny, sweet-talking harper that I knew. His eyes were as blank of emotion as his face. "We understand each other," he said.

"I am needed now," continued Kith. "When the danger is past, when the raiders are gone, then he will take care of the problem. Or"—he smiled, grinned, really—though there was no humor in his eyes—"maybe the problem will be taken care of for him."

If I said anything, it would be the wrong thing. I wanted to hit both of them, to scream at them—make them see reason. Stupid men who couldn't see the world had changed, was still changing while they remained caught up in what had been.

"Let's get Albrin to the inn, where someone who knows what they're doing can help him," I said finally. *Fight the most immediate battles first.*

Kith slipped back into the cairn, leaving me to glare balefully at Wandel. The unfamiliar coldness of his expression added to the surrealism of the day. Finally I turned away to rub Torch underneath the bridle's cheek strap where the sweat gathered. I laid my forehead wearily on his warm neck, keeping it there until I heard Kith step out of the cairn.

"Wandel, I need your help," he said. "I can't lift him properly with one hand, and I don't want him hurt any more than necessary."

As he turned back inside, Kith said, "Don't break your heart, Aren. I was dead when Moresh recruited me—don't hold the harper's vows against him."

"Vows I hold against no man," I said darkly. "Deeds are an entirely different matter."

SEVEN

By the time we got back to the village, it was almost dark. I slipped off my perch behind Wandel before we quite stopped. The Lass crow-hopped twice, making the harper soothe her so he could dismount. She hadn't liked carrying double.

"Melly!" I called from the yard.

She came to the door of the inn, wiping her hands on her apron. "What is it? Oh, lords and ladies, it's Albrin. And Kith as well." She dashed into the public room briefly and returned with a number of patrollers who were gathered at the inn before practice.

"No, no," she commanded as they started to take Albrin from Kith. "Wait. I sent Manta and Ice to get the door from the kitchen. He's been jostled enough."

The Beresforders had wasted no time; they showed up with the kitchen door on the heels of Melly's words. Carefully, Albrin was lowered to the door.

When I started in behind the boys carrying Albrin, Melly stepped in front of me. "Oh, no, you don't. You don't look much better than he does. I'll have too much help as it is, don't you frown so. I'll do better not having to clean you up off the floor, too. You go right on in there and pour yourself some of the mead I've heating by the fire, missy. When we've settled Albrin, I'll have a dinner brought to you. I've seen less tired faces on corpses, child. In with you."

As Albrin was carried up the stairs, I hovered in the doorway until Melly's flapping apron drove me into the tavern. I took a clean mug from behind the bar and poured it full of the sweet-smelling mead. Though the tavern itself was empty, I could hear noises from the public room beyond that indicated people were there.

Peering through the doorway, I saw a couple of the fishermen eating dinner at one of the tables. Engrossed in conversation, they didn't look up as I wandered in. The only other person in the room was Koret, slumped against the back wall with the remains of whatever he'd been drinking in the glass. From the look of the table, the helpers Melly had commandeered had been drinking with Koret. I don't know why he hadn't come himself.

He looked up and raised his eyebrows when he saw me. I brushed at my clothes somewhat ineffectually, but there really wasn't much I could do. I sat down opposite him, gingerly, stretching my leg out before drinking the warm mead.

"I heard you rode out after Kith," he said. His voice slurred slightly. "Not the smartest thing to do."

"No," I agreed, wondering if his surprise was at my survival rather than at seeing me here. Perhaps I ought to be offended.

"Kith's here. Wandel and Albrin, too," I told him, though he knew, already. "I'm not certain if Albrin's going to make it. They sent me here to get me out of the way." There was a spill on the tabletop and I touched it with my finger, pulling the moisture around in odd patterns.

Koret nodded, but he didn't look excited. "Live today . . . die tomorrow or next week like the rest of us. I'm not certain it matters."

I narrowed my gaze on him. "Actually, I didn't go out after Kith—at least not at first."

Koret knew how to listen even when he was depressed and half-drunk. He waited patiently, letting the silence linger between us like the caress of old lovers, expectant but not demanding.

"Do you remember what I told you about the thing that attacked me on the mountain this spring? That someone killed it and healed my arm before Kith and Wandel found me?" Deceptive Wandel, sweet-tongued killer. "That the harper and I found an inscription there on the side of the mountain?"

Koret nodded, straightening a little—though I think it was discomfort rather than interest sparking the move.

I looked down at the table. "With the raiders controlling Fell Bridge, with Albrin's people and the manor folk gone, I knew it was only a matter of time before the village died, too."

Koret gave me a small smile and sipped his ale. Doubtless, I thought, he'd seen it long before I had. He was experienced in warfare. My bench wobbled as Merewich seated himself beside me. I hadn't seen him when I'd come in. He topped my mug from Melly's pitcher.

"So I went for help." I looked at the table, wondering how I could get them to believe what had happened when I hardly believed it myself. "I found the hob—or at least a hob."

"So what is a hob?" asked Merewich.

"Well"—I considered the matter—"he's . . . not what I expected." I thought of how I trailed behind him, my hand wrapped around his tail, and grinned.

"How much of this has she had?" Merewich asked Koret.

"Rather less than he has," I said, though I could feel

my thoughts clouding pleasantly. Adding mead to no sleep and no food wasn't an aid to clearheadedness.

I sat forward and braced my elbows on the table, trying to put the hob into words. "He told me to call him Caefawn. I told him . . . I don't remember what I told him. He took me to the manor to show me what he could offer—in return for something the village has that he needs. The raiders were everywhere. He killed some. So did I. But most of them he put to sleep or had chasing a white stag hither and yon." I took a deep swallow of the mead, feeling the warmth of it seep to my bones. I decided I was more tired than drunk. "He wants to meet with the village elders tomorrow. He said something about a hob's bargain. I think he wants to help. I think he might be able to." Certainly I was more tired than drunk. More tired than anything now, with the mead taking the soreness from my knee.

"Tomorrow morning?" asked Merewich.

"What does the hob want?" asked Koret.

"Don't know." I yawned and folded my arms on the table, resting my forehead against my forearms. I closed my eyes.

I could feel the two men stare at me. The bench shifted as Merewich moved toward Koret.

"What do you think?"

Koret grunted, then said, "If I hadn't heard the stories of what the Beresforders faced getting here, I'd not believe it. But . . . I suppose we'll know in the morning, eh?"

"I want to believe it," confessed Merewich, almost in a whisper. "I want to believe it very much—but I don't trust in hope anymore."

WE MARCHED UP THROUGH THE EARTH AND INTO THE *enemy's home. Wooden boards and a heavy cloth covered the dirt beneath my feet, but I could still feel the earth's reassuring presence. . . .*

I awoke wide-eyed and breathing hard through my
nose. Without questioning why I was in a strange room,
I swung my legs from the bed and darted for the door. I
bolted down the inn stairs, ignoring Koret and Merewich,
who were running out of the public room. I sprinted to
the barn to collect my crossbow.

Too late, I thought, *too late*—but I hurried anyway.

The night air was still. The moon shone silver and gilt
as it touched the cobbles of the inn yard. The stones in
the yard cut into my feet, and I stubbed my toe on something in the dark barn before my scrabbling fingers
snagged my crossbow. Next to it I found the quiver with
the pouch that held the goatsfoot.

Too late, I thought feverishly, *too late*.

Only a short way down the street from the inn the
alarm bell was lit by the faint glow of the moon. The
alarm bell was closer than the baker's house.

The moon's illumination allowed me to take the flight
of stairs that led to the bell rope without slowing. Caefawn must have been right about my knee—I hardly noticed it. Rough hemp cut into my fingers when I set my
weight against the rope. I had to do it twice before the
clear tolling of the bell rang through the streets.

For a moment the stillness of the night continued, then
people spewed from their houses, children in the arms of
adults. The crowd grew with silent efficiency, gathering
around the bell to find out where the attack was coming
from. The response was better than the last drill Koret
had run.

"Belis!" I shouted to the quiet crowd, leaving off ringing the bell. "Has anyone seen the baker?"

They were beginning to murmur a bit and shuffle
around. I stepped up on the railing, holding one of the
bell posts for balance as I tried to look over the crowd
to see the fringes. Belis lived in one of the outskirt
houses, farthest from the river. It would take him longer
to reach us.

If he could.

I had seen just enough of the house in my vision to recognize the rug Gram had given Belis in return for a winter's supply of bread. I still wasn't certain what had invaded his house, but I had the impression that his house wasn't the only one they'd tunneled their way into. Merewich and Koret were working their way through the crowd—it occurred to me that if something didn't happen soon, I would have some explaining to do.

No one would listen to me without proof, not if matters had gotten far enough out of hand that the villagers killed Touched Banar. If Kith were in the crowd, it wouldn't have mattered. No one gainsaid Kith, and I could count on him to back me up. But Kith didn't come out of the inn.

Just as I was ready to give in to despair (too late, too late), I saw a group of people coming down a side street from the north side of town. Belis, tall and thin, stood out from the crowd, and I felt something inside me relax.

I set the nut and pulled out the goatsfoot, using it to draw the string to the nut and hook it. I pulled a bolt from the quiver and set it in place. The bow at the ready, I aimed for the darkness behind the small group of people who joined the rest of the village.

"Aren?" Koret's voice was a soft murmur as he mounted the stairs. Cautious.

It occurred to me that I must appear a bit touched, standing on the railing, wearing a man's nightshirt, and aiming a bow at the shadows no one. . . . But they ought to expect madness from someone who saw visions. Visions that had saved at least one man this morning.

There! I loosed the bolt and drew again, swearing at the time it took. After half a season's drilling, I no longer felt the strain in my forearms every time I cocked the bow, but it was not effortless and I wasn't as fast as I should be. The crossbow was not as quick as a longbow, and Kith, using one of the stirrup-drawn wooden bows,

could outdraw me even with only one arm. But I could
shoot almost as far as a good longbowman, and I hit what
I aimed at.

"Damn it, girl," bellowed Koret, reaching for my bow,
but a shout near the northeastern corner of the crowd
stopped him.

There was a shift in the people as they turned to face
the enemy gradually emerging from the side street Belis
had come from only a few moments earlier. Someone
called an order; children began to filter in from the edges
to gather under the bell podium. All at once the relative
hush of night gave way to the roar of battle.

Koret charged down the ladder, drawing his sword and
leaving me to shoot at will. I loosed a bolt at another
movement in the shadows.

Finally, from the darkness of the side street, a swarm
of . . . something boiled into the street. In the uncertain
light, I couldn't see them well. Better, I thought, if I
didn't.

As ferociously as the villagers fought, we could not
press back the tide of creatures. They were smaller than
a man—I could see that much—perhaps only half as tall,
though wider in the shoulders. Like a plague of locusts,
there seemed to be no end to them.

They weren't hillgrims. If they had been, there would
have been a lot more villagers lying in the mounting pile
of bodies. Instead of the graceful movements of the
grims, these new creatures moved with the stolid slow-
ness of a great bull. Their arms hung almost to the
ground, muscular and wickedly powerful—but merci-
fully slow. The villagers quickly learned to avoid the
blows, and after the first few minutes I didn't see anyone
fall. All the same, they pressed the villagers back by
sheer strength of numbers.

Before I ran out of quarrels, Manta dashed up the stairs
with two handfuls of bloody shafts.

"Here," he said shortly. "Koret sent these, says to stay

where you are. You're doing more damage here than you would in the thick of things."

He was gone before I could thank him. The arrows were warm and damp, and I wished for my gloves, which were, I supposed, somewhere in the inn with my clothes.

In the end it was the sun that saved us. As dawn began to show over Faran's Ridge, the creatures turned and sped away faster than they had come.

Spent, I slipped from my post on the railing. Laughter came unbidden—for once my *sight* had been in time. Just this once—but it helped make up for all the other times when I'd been too late. It was quiet laughter with a slightly hysterical touch, so I let it drift to silence beneath the soft moaning of the wounded lying in the streets.

I wiped my bloody hands on the tail of my borrowed nightshirt. It was unmannerly to stain someone else's clothing, but I couldn't bear the feel of the blood any longer. My hands ached from setting the goatsfoot. Training made me load the crossbow once more before I climbed down the stairs to see what it was I'd been killing.

Geol the cooper was surrounded by a group of people trying to stanch several wounds. Talon the smith sported a nasty gash on his forearm that he was awkwardly trying to bandage. Before I could offer my help, his wife bustled up to him. The bootmaker, Haronal, had a throwing ax embedded in his skull.

I didn't see any of the creatures bodies. At last I saw Koret kneeling beside a shuddering form near an alleyway, and went to him. The body was one of the things we'd been fighting.

It was vaguely human in feature, more so than the hillgrim. Standing, it (or rather he—the creature wore no clothes) might have been waist high. Curly, dark hair covered his head and the lower part of his jaw. His features were manlike, except he had no eyes. A horrible wound opened his belly, revealing internal organs.

"Is this what attacked you on the Hob?" asked Merewich, who'd joined us.

I shook my head, staring at the dying creature. If it had been human—a raider, maybe—I'd have been down on my knees holding the wound together and calling for someone to sew him up. It wasn't human, but it wasn't . . . Before I could decide if I wanted to try to save it, it died.

"Maybe the hob will know what he was," I said hollowly.

"Wait until you see this," said Koret intensely. "Wait."

The weak morning light touched the body, allowing me to see clearly what was happening to it. The tip of his nose and the ends of his fingers and hands changed, darkened, began to flake off.

Cracks split the skin of his face. The bloody gash in his abdomen quivered, filling suddenly with a dark, ashy matter that covered the details of the wound. The process sped up as it progressed. Each break in the creature's skin gave way to a multitude, until there was no body left.

Koret squatted on his heels and put his hand in the residual substance. My lips curled back in disgust as he rubbed it back and forth between his fingers, then held it up to his nose to smell.

"Mulm," he said, standing up and dusting his fingers lightly together. "Good planting soil."

"Pirates," commented Merewich sadly. "They have no sensibilities."

"Ah," replied Koret with a grin that told me at least part of his nonchalant manner was for our benefit. "I have noticed how delicate your sensibilities are, Merewich. That is why I didn't taste it." He wiped his hands on his pant leg. "So Aren," he said, "what made you come out here and ring the bell?"

"I dreamed," I said. "I dreamed I was burrowing up through the basement of Belis's house, prepared for battle. When I woke up, I realized it hadn't been a dream.

"How did you know that it wasn't a dream?" asked Merewich.

I shrugged uncomfortably. "I don't know." I looked for something else to talk about and said, "Where's Kith? I would have thought that he'd be out here in the fighting."

Merewich shook his head, "He collapsed after he got his father settled. Wandel said that it was to be expected after the day he'd been put through. I've never seen anyone fall into such a sound sleep so fast. I imagine he didn't even hear the alarm."

Koret had been looking over my shoulder as Merewich talked. He frowned suddenly. "Aren, I'd like you to go meet the . . . hob this morning. It's going to take a while to get everyone calmed down and decide who should meet with him. We'd like you to explain what happened, and see if you can't get him to be a little patient with us."

I nodded my head and started for the barn. I was saddling Duck before I connected Koret's frown, his sudden anxiety about the hob, and the way the villagers fell back, whispering and afraid, out of my path as I walked to the stables.

He was worried the attack would give added spark to the anger against magic—against me. It hurt. It didn't matter that I was the one who warned them. It only mattered that the creatures were wildlings, reminding everyone how evil magic was. I wondered what they'd think of the hob. Maybe they'd turn away from the only chance they had of saving themselves because the hob was a wildling.

Koret met me at the door of the barn and handed me a stone ax. "Take this with you. It belonged to one of our attackers. Maybe the hob will know something about them."

I took the weapon and mounted Duck before I replied.

I wanted to make certain he wouldn't hear how upset I was.

"I'll ask."

AS I APPROACHED THE MANOR, I PATTED DUCK'S SUN-warmed shoulder, more for my comfort than his. The silence of the abandoned building reminded me too much of Auberg. It was like some sort of spreading disease. By winter, Fallbrook might be shrouded in stillness, too.

The building was not fortified or designed for heavy defense. Generations ago there had been a great wooden fort, but the valley was too isolated to see much fighting. When Lord Moresh's many-times-great-grandfather had decided to modernize the old fort, he'd settled for a stone-walled manor. The walls were thick and the windows on the first floor were narrow, but that's as far as he'd gone for security's sake. It still would have taken more than the bandits' group to take the building if the lord's contingent were there.

I rode to the main entrance and dismounted, slipping the bit from Duck's mouth when it became apparent that no one else was there. Thus freed to eat, Duck nibbled on the long grass. The quiet munching sound was soothing, allowing me to ignore the hollowness of the building behind me.

The sun hit the grass and released its fragrance into the air. Like the smell of fresh-baked bread, the rich earthy scent was cheering. I couldn't change the villagers in a season, but perhaps time would help. When they weren't as frightened by the attack, maybe they'd remember I'd saved them from a surprise attack. Maybe Duck would sprout wings and fly.

I yawned, closing my eyes. When I opened them again, the hob was holding out an oatcake to me.

"Almost given you up," I commented, trying to sound nonchalant as I took the honeyed oatcake. As I took a bite, I realized I hadn't had anything to eat since I had gone to practice yesterday—no, the day before yesterday.

The hob sat cross-legged on the ground beside me, his cloak set to one side, munching on the twin of the treat he'd handed me.

"Sorry," he said. "I've been here a while. Waited a bit to see if others were coming, too."

He appeared to be enjoying his cake. I couldn't tell if he was concerned about the absence of the elders or not.

"They'll be along," I said, finishing the cake and accepting the waterskin he handed me. I drank (it *was* water, as far as I could tell) before explaining about the attack. "It could take the rest of the morning to get folks calmed down enough to listen, but they'll be here."

"Ah," he said, licking his fingers. I noticed he was careful to avoid touching his claws with his tongue. They must be as sharp as they looked.

I turned away so he wouldn't see me smile. It was odd seeing him doing something as human as licking his fingers, even if his tongue was black and his fingers had claws. It was odder still to find myself more comfortable in his company than I was with most of my fellow villagers. I'd known him a very short time, but that was enough for me to get used to his gray skin, fangs, and cat-eyes. Even his tail.

When I was sure I had control of my face, I turned back to see him watching me quizzically. When his left ear twitched at the sound of Duck's snort, the wooden chain bounced against his cheek.

"Didn't it hurt when they pierced your ear like that?" I asked.

The habitual hint of humor left his face. "I don't know."

Without the humor, his face was cold and frightening. Even though I'd seen what he'd done to the grim and to five . . . no, six raiders yesterday, I'd forgotten he was dangerous. The smile had only to leave his face and I could see the hob was a predator. I hoped he never considered me prey.

I decided it would be best to change the subject. "With those fangs," I said casually, "I'm surprised you eat oatcakes." Yeah, I thought sarcastically, that was a good subject change.

But it actually seemed to be one, because the hob grinned and said, "Oatcakes are good, but I do like a few hillgrims or a deer now and again. Trolls, though, are poor eating. No matter how well you clean them, they still taste like the north end of a southbound horse."

I laughed. This time, when his face sobered, it didn't scare me. I think it was because there was no coldness in his expression.

"I'm sorry," he said. "Ask me what you like, but I find that I don't remember a lot of personal things. It's . . . disconcerting. Some things are as clear as yesterday, but anything I cared about might as well not have happened. I suppose that's the mountain's doing. She has only me left."

He didn't seem to be finished, so I waited.

"We hobs tend to be a gregarious people," he said finally, after wiping his hands on the grass with rather more attention than such an action deserved. "I think she took my memories so I would live."

I thought about what I'd feel if someone took my memories from me. Took all the pain and guilt, leaving me free of it all—and marveled he still stayed near the mountain.

"Perhaps it's just the effect of the passage of time," I offered. "It has been a very long time."

He nodded his head politely.

"How is it that you survived, when no one else did?"

"There may be more hobs, elsewhere," he said. There was a wistful tone to his voice: as much as he wanted to, he didn't believe there were any more.

He ran his fingers up and down his staff. "I can re-

member a little. There was a battle with . . . something."
He looked at me out of the corner of his eye. "I think it
was an army of humans. Many of us were killed, and I
was hurt badly. My people took me to a cave we used
when our own magic wasn't enough, a place where the
mountain mends her children. I was there when the death-
mages did their work. I was the only one that the mountain could save." His nimble fingers fiddled with one of
the feathers on the chain in his ear, and he abruptly
changed the subject. "You said that you were attacked
this morning. By what?"

I launched into a description of the things that had
come boiling out of the baker's basement, though I was
thinking about his relationship with the mountain. Did it
serve him or did he serve it? When I handed him the
stone ax, he took it and tested it on a hair he plucked
from his head. Laid on the edge, the hair split neatly in
two.

"Turned to earth, eh?" he asked thoughtfully. "How
did the village celebration of the spring equinox go?"

"Equinox?" I stumbled over the word.

He raised an eyebrow. "The coming of spring."

I frowned. "We celebrate the harvest, but the spring is
planting season."

"Ah," he said. "Do you have a winter celebration? In
my day, folk—even humans—celebrated the changing
seasons: spring, summer, winter, and autumn."

"No," I said. "At least nothing devoted specifically to
the seasons. What does that have to do with anything?"

He grunted. "It might have nothing to do with it at
all—or not. Let me think on it."

A butterfly flew by and landed on a wildflower near
the wall of the manor. I watched it for a bit, rolling his
answer this way and that. He said I could ask anything.
"Why are you agreeing to help us? I mean, I know that
we need help—yours, someone's. You seem anxious that

we know how much you can help us. Why do you need us?"

An emotion crossed his face too fast for me to tell exactly what it was. He dug into the grass with his staff. "Because the mountain says I do. What is it that they do for you?"

Startled at his question, it took me a moment to reply. "What do you mean?"

He pursed his lips, looking at the place where his staff had dug through the grass into the dirt. "What do they do for you? The old man cares, perhaps, but it seems to me that he looks to you for aid in saving his village rather than having any true affection. The one-armed one, Kith, yes. But soon, I think, the singer will destroy him if he doesn't do it himself first. Maybe the big man with the beard cares. How long do you suppose the zealots, the ones who hate anything that hints of magic, will let you live?"

"Spying?" I asked angrily, raising my chin.

He said nothing.

It was my turn to look away. What he said hurt me, but I couldn't afford to forget that they needed him. And I needed them.

"They are *my* people." I said fiercely, after only a brief pause. "I will do my best for them whether they want me to or not." If I could make them people rather than "villagers," maybe it would help. "The baker's mother used to give me extra frosting on her sweet rolls when I was a child because once I found her lapdog. Kith's father taught me how to ride and how to track rabbits. Tevet, the woman who is the loudest to condemn me, taught me how to mend shirts so that no one would know they'd been torn. Her uncle was taken by the bloodmages."

"Ah," said Caefawn, "I see."

I stared at him, but he continued to look at the ground.

"No doubt you do," I said shortly. I don't know why I was angry with him—or if it *was* him I was angry with.

I pulled my knees up to my chest and buried my face against them, listening to the sounds of Duck ripping up grass and eating it. The hob was silent.

The wind picked up, rattling the branches of the trees. My anger left me, and a feeling close to self-pity replaced it. Bitterness and anger I could accept, but I'd had enough self-pity for a lifetime. Time to get up and do something. "Have you been inside the manor?"

"No."

I jumped to my feet. "Let me show you around, then. There's no one here to object any longer." Moresh's steward had been one of the men who died in the fighting. No one would care if we poked around. I pulled Duck's bridle off completely and tied it to the saddle. If he wandered off, he'd only go to the inn.

I took Caefawn to the kitchen door set in the side of the house, unobtrusively hidden behind a wall of hedge.

"The old cook, Fenwick, used to give bits of leftover food to the village children if the lord wasn't here. The old steward didn't mind, said it kept us from raiding the gardens. We'd all come in through here."

The kitchen was a mess. The bread oven was tipped on its side, its door flung several paces away. Broken bits of crockery were scattered here and there amid the litter of food on the floor. A bedraggled dog scuttled out as we came in. Flies buzzed about their business, unimpressed by visitors.

"Fenwick would be horrified," I commented, stepping over the mess as best I could. "She kept this place as if it were the king's kitchen."

It felt right leading him through the manor, introducing him to things I'd known all of my life: the small drawing room where the lord met with the villagers on business, the great hall where the harvest feast was served. I tried to let him see past the recent destruction, into the life of the valley before the mountain had fallen. That life had centered around the manor house. We villagers had our own lands, held in trust from the lord, and we served him and tithed to him to keep them. In return he protected us from raiders and, upon occasion, fed us in hard times.

The upper floors had fared better than those below. I had never been above the ground floor, so I fell as silent as the hob, letting my feet take me where they would.

The gaming room was full of tables with strange markings on them. I picked up a ball from a large table in the center of the room and sent it spinning off the edge and onto the floor. Caefawn ran his hands over the carving on the fireplace. His claws made light clicking sounds on the hard, polished surface.

I moved to the next room. It was shrouded—covered against the lord's return, I supposed. Even with the sheets, I could tell that it was a bedroom, though it was larger than my whole cottage. I wandered among the ghostly forms, trying to decide what each was. A table. A desk. Near the far wall was an object that defeated my guessing. It stood a full head taller than I was, narrow and rounded in shape. Finally admitting defeat, I pulled the sheet free.

A fully articulated human skeleton hung on a frame from an eye hook drilled into its skull, which stared emptily at me, jaw gaping wide. A strange thing to have in a bedroom. This must have been the bloodmage's domain.

I wasn't bothered so much by the skeleton as by the strange double vision I had that tried to tell me it was a young man instead. Chills ran down my spine as I looked at the skull hanging some inches above me. His eyes were honey-brown, framed by hair a shade darker than my own. A small scar trailed from the side of his right eye, like a tear that had been etched in. Laugh lines lightly touched the corners of his mouth. Something drew my attention back up the edge of the scar to his eyes; but this time they seemed . . . almost yellow.

I stepped forward, lifting my hand to touch bone or flesh and see which one was real. Before I could touch it, the skeleton glowed green and red briefly before dissolving into ashes at my feet. Dissolved by magic so strong I could smell its acrid scent in the air. Hob's magic.

"By the mountain, lady," growled the hob from behind me, " 'twas ill-done. That poor lad had enough to bear without being summoned back as a wraith."

"What?" I asked. Even to my ears my voice sounded foggy. His words were plain enough, but I didn't understand the meaning. Still captured by the memory of the skeleton's eyes, I found it hard to think. "A wraith?"

He glared at me a moment more, then frowned. His ears flared widely and he shook his head.

"Tell me, Lady, what magic do you possess?"

I rubbed my face briskly with my hands, but the vagueness didn't go away. He took my hands in his and spoke even more slowly. "What powers do you have, Aren?"

"I see visions." There, that was right.

"Of what?"

"Things that happen." That didn't seem a good enough explanation, so I made another effort. Finally the fog in my head dissipated. "I used to get just feelings mostly. You know, that something bad was going to happen. Now I *see* mostly events that have already taken place or are happening somewhere else. But I *saw* the things that attacked us this morning before they did." I shook the last of the fuzziness out of my head and smiled ruefully. "Sorry, that wasn't very coherent. I guess I'm a little dizzy. Too much excitement, too little sleep."

"Too much ignorance," he said in a disgusted voice.

I was about to ask him what he meant when the sounds of horses in the courtyard below announced the arrival of the people Merewich had chosen.

The hob said something in another language. From the

expression on his face, I didn't think it was a nice word.

I let him lead the way down while I tried to figure out what had happened in that room. I knew what a wraith was, or at least I'd heard stories of them. Nasty things that sucked the marrow from the bones of people and animals unfortunate enough to encounter them. Why would a touch transform a skeleton into a wraith? Was it something the bloodmage had done? Or was it—I looked down at my hands, which certainly didn't appear any different than they had before—was it *me*?

MEREWICH AND KORET WERE WAITING FOR US WITH THE priest, Cantier, and Ice. They looked grim-faced and a little pale. It might have been this morning's battle, but I suspected it was the first sight of the hob.

I stepped around him and bowed shallowly in an imitation of court manners. "My lord," I said to the hob, "may I introduce you to Headman Merewich, Martial Commander Koret, Elder Cantier, and Elder. . . ." I paused, because I couldn't for the life of me think of Ice's real name.

As I stared at him, he grinned suddenly. "Eannise, lord. Some folk call me Ice."

His good humor broke the tension a bit, enabling me to finish the introductions. "Goodmen, all, may I present to you Caefawn of the Hob?"

Merewich took over from there, as was proper. I took the horses and led them to where Duck grazed, hoping his good manners would keep them there—otherwise we'd all walk back to the village.

By the time I returned, the elders had found seats on the stairs that led to the manor's main entrance. Caefawn sat unconcernedly on the ground below them, legs crossed in a relaxed fashion. I stopped, unwilling to intrude.

"Can the lord's harvests feed the people you've got for

the winter?" Caefawn asked as I came close enough to hear.

"Aye, with a fair bit left over," replied Ice. "If we get the chance to harvest them."

"Right, then." The hob's voice became brisk. "What you need is help with the raiders, and with the creatures who are returning to this valley. Without help, it seems likely that you won't make it through the summer, let alone the winter. Am I right?"

Merewich wiggled his eyebrows. "I wouldn't have put it so bluntly myself, sir, but I suppose you've the right of it."

Caefawn nodded. "Well, then, I think I have a bargain for you." He flexed his hands on his thighs. "As I have demonstrated, I can help you with the bandits. I know a fair bit more than you about the returning wildlings." He smiled briefly, at some secret thought. "I can even help with the harvest. If I do these things, I require a gift in return."

"What is that?" asked Merewich.

The hob's face didn't change, but I heard a hint of bitterness in his tone. As if he liked what he was going to say even less than he expected them to. "The sacrifice of one of your women of childbearing years."

Dead silence fell.

Shock held me still. Clearly I remembered our conversation about the villagers—and about eating things. I wondered if he had been sounding me out for the position of sacrifice. Just how much did I owe these people? Gram would have said *everything*. I owed them because I was born as I was, with the power to see what could happen. I didn't need the *sight* to tell me this was the village's best chance for survival. Without the sacrifice the hob asked for, the village would die: I'd seen that last night in Koret's eyes.

"A sacrifice we cannot make," said Merewich finally. "Our village would never survive it. Our priest could never sanction it. The changes we've faced are already driving many of us to extremes, pulling the village apart. My own wife does nothing anymore except rock in her chair and stare at the wall. If I allowed this, the village would destroy itself before winter or raider could do so."

"Not if I'm the one you sacrifice," I said. *Stupid*, I thought, *to die for the people who want you dead. Stupid woman.* But if the villagers' dislike of me would aid their survival now, I was willing. "Few would regard my death as—"

"Death?" hissed the hob in surprise, ears flaring wide with a rattle of beads as he turned to look at me.

I looked from his dumbfounded face to Merewich's shocked countenance. I sat down where I was and began to laugh, though there was little enough humor in it. I don't know why I hadn't figured it out. He'd said he was the last one, the last of the mountain's children—and she, the mountain, was insisting he do something about it. He felt like a sacrifice to her cause, and so he asked us for another. "I take it you don't mean to burn me or cut out my heart as a tribute to the mountain?"

The hob bounced to his feet and sputtered.

Koret nodded his head gravely, though a dimple showed through his beard if you knew where to look for it. "I knew a man who traded from one island to the next. Spoke ten or twelve languages fluently. Managed to buy a pig when he thought he was bargaining for timber. Last I saw him, that pig was nigh on to a hundredweight and running his ship."

"Of childbearing years," said Cantier. "Looking for a wife."

"I could agree to a wife," said Merewich thoughtfully.

The hob sank back to his former seat and buried his face briefly in his hands. His shoulders shook. When he raised his head he said, eyes bright with merriment, "I see I have brought a moment of great import down to mere farce. I'm lucky I didn't end up with a hundred-pound pig. Well, enough. Time to make the bargain more clear."

He paused, and I sensed there was magic being wrought. "One year from today we will meet again. If you all agree I have helped the village survive, you will present me with a woman of childbearing years to wife. Think on it long and hard, gentlemen, before you agree. Death might seem worse, but mating with a creature outside of your race is no light thing."

"I agree," replied Merewich. "But something of this import requires the consent of us all. Koret?"

"Agreed."

Only Cantier, the wily old fisherman, shook his head. "Nay, can't see it, myself. Not without knowing who it is that will agree to wed him. My father always said never agree to a bargain that doesn't have the particulars worked out." He looked at me while he spoke.

I couldn't decline, not after having agreed to death. It would certainly be an insult if I did. The same reasons that made me an ideal candidate for death applied for marriage as well.

"I'll do it," I said. It *was* my doing that had brought us to this point, after all. I had found the hob and enlisted his aid. How I felt didn't matter.

"Willingly?" prodded Cantier.

I looked at Caefawn, who looked back at me. "Don't push it," I said. Caefawn grinned, his fangs gleaming in the bright sunlight.

"All right, then," said Cantier sourly. "I agree."

As he spoke, *something* happened. We all felt it.

"The bargain is struck." The hob sounded as enthusiastic as I felt: that is, of course, not at all.

EIGHT

Three days later, I woke up in the attic of the unoccupied house I'd been sleeping in since Kith told me to move camp until things in town quieted down. I think he believed I had moved farther away, but the deserted house on the east side of town suited me just fine. It had been deemed unfit to live in, but it worked for me.

I'd been dreaming of red-eyed demons chasing me through a forest. The reason the demons bore a striking resemblance to the hob was obvious, even to someone who was not a priest trained in dream interpretation. However, I could find no reason for the hob to be lying at my feet.

"Why are you lying at my feet?" I asked sharply—a result of sitting up too fast and hitting my head on a low beam. "How did you find me?"

"The little folk told me where you'd be. I've tried to catch you at night the last couple of days, but you were gone. So I decided to try before it got dark." The hob stretched, taking up even more space. His eyes glowed a little in the dark.

"I've been patrolling," I said in answer to his implied question. *Little folk? What little folk?* Fully awake, I was too intimidated by his presence, made even larger and darker in the confines of the attic, to ask him about little folk.

"I'm afraid I told the big man—Koret?—that I would be borrowing you from him for tonight. I promised to see what I could do about the earthens, and I need you to do it."

"Earthens?" I asked, slipping out of my blankets and rolling them into a tight bundle. Yesterday's clothes (which I had slept in) would just have to do. I wasn't changing with the hob looking on.

"The creatures that attacked your village were earthens. They're the earth spirit's minions, pretty harmless as such things go. Your folk were lucky the spirit is weak yet, or you'd have been facing something much nastier."

"Earth spirit?" I asked.

"I think," said Caefawn, "it might be better if I talk as we go. Koret explained it is important that no one find you here. If we continue to talk, the chances of someone discovering your sleeping place are greatly increased."

BY THE TIME WE WERE OUTSIDE THE VILLAGE PROPER, night had fallen. The moon was still in a brighter phase, but it was cloudy, so at intervals we were floundering (well, I was floundering) in darkness. I wondered why he'd picked me to go adventuring with instead of Kith or someone else more competent. Of course, there was the bargain between us.

"Where are we going?" I spoke softly because we weren't far from the village yet, having stopped just past the temple grounds.

"I was hoping that you would have a better idea than I," responded Caefawn.

I thought for a while, then said, carefully, "How would I know where we're going, when I don't even know why?"

"Form a picture in your mind of this half of the valley."

I frowned at him, but he didn't see because he'd closed his eyes. I could feel him gathering magic.

"Do it, Aren. Please."

I tried, but it was like trying to decide what the roof of a building looks like from the inside. I'd never considered the valley as a whole unit, just bits and pieces, one connected to the other.

"Mmm. Perhaps try one place at a time."

I started with the place I knew best, my parents' house. I thought of it as it had been when Quilliar had been there. Ma's roses in full bloom.

"Move on." The hob's voice was dark as a moonless night, slipping into my vision without intruding. His magic cloaked me as warmly as a blanket in winter, and as comforting. The tension I'd felt in his presence dissolved and my vision shifted until I saw the house as it was now: deserted and sad, the roses withering from lack of care.

"This isn't it. Try somewhere else," said the hob.

I tried my cottage next. The thatching was thick and snug; bits of brown poked out of bare dirt near one wall where I'd planted starts from Ma's flowers. There were *a couple of slats broken on the pasture fence near the barn. A rabbit moved cautiously through the doorway.*

"That's it," said the hob, and his hands came down on my shoulders.

A swooping feeling lifted me, like going over a high jump on a horse, but stronger. It was as if the whole valley were laid out before me. I could see the raiders as they went about their business, the patrollers who skulked in the shadows, an owl swooping upon an unsuspecting mouse.

"What am I looking for?" I asked again, but as I spoke, I found it.

An old snag marked the corner of Lyntle's fields near the easternmost fields. The earth beneath the snag glowed as if there were a hidden campfire sending red and yellow flames to light the night. The rye, planted earlier this spring, grew over the top of the place, but it was stunted and off-color.

"I found it," I said.

"I see it," answered the hob. His arms dropped away. As soon as he released me, so did the vision.

Dizzy from the abrupt change, I swayed; he steadied me.

I stepped away from him. "Now tell me about this earth spirit and what we need to do to stop it."

Caefawn grinned at my peremptory tone. "Patience is not one of your virtues, is it? Very well." He spread his hands wide in open imitation of Wandel beginning a story. He *had* been spying on the village. "Elemental spirits are the guardians of the world. They preserve the order. The mountain is an elemental, too—although less powerful than the earth spirit. The river has a spirit, too. I saw her myself a few weeks ago. When I lived here before, the valley belonged to an earth spirit more powerful than the mountain or river because of the villagers' celebrations and sacrifices. As far as I know, the bloodmage's meddling sent them all to sleep, and they are slowly awakening."

Was the hob one of the mountain spirit's minions, as the earthens belonged to the earth spirit? "So the earth spirit who guards this valley is awake and angry. Do you know why?"

The hob shrugged, leaning one shoulder against a tree trunk. Shadows covered his upper body. "Because your people farm the land and forget to ask permission and give thanks. The spirit, unlike the water guardian, who is fickle and mischievous, is a formal creature at heart."

"Why didn't you tell me about this before?" I asked.

"The mountain reminded me," he replied apologetically. "As I told you, my memories are foggy. It has been a long time, and I didn't deal with other guardians much."

"So I need to go talk to the earth spirit." It didn't sound like the smartest thing to do. Then again, if he killed me, I wouldn't have to worry about next summer. "Why me? Why not you? Aren't you the one who's supposed to save the village?"

The hob grinned. "It has to be a spirit speaker." He dug the base of his staff into the dirt, making a hillock of earth. "Your village is lucky to have one. Do you remember what happened with the skeleton in the manor?"

As if I could forget. When I wasn't having nightmares about marrying bloodsucking demons, I was dreaming of skeletons with glowing yellow eyes. I nodded shortly.

"It often goes with the visions, I think. Summoning the dead is something only a spirit speaker can do. If you were a bloodmage, you would be a necromancer. . . ." He stopped, considering his words. "I've heard the bloodmages took all the mageborn. How is it they didn't take you?"

"Women don't make good bloodmages."

The hob snorted. "Fools! Magic comes where it will. And women are capable of as much evil as men."

"My good luck they were fools," I said. "My brother wasn't so lucky."

"Your brother is a bloodmage?"

"No. My brother died so he wouldn't become one."

"Ah." The hob let Quilliar's death rest in the night.

A chill crept over my spine, and I twisted to look behind me. Thin white wisps clung to the branches and roots of the trees that bordered the temple graveyard. I froze, staring at them.

"Don't worry," said the hob softly. "The talk of death

draws them. They won't hurt us. The graveyard has been restless lately—too many newly dead." Poul had said something of the like the day I'd ridden to fetch the hob.

"Ghosts?" My throat felt dry, and I took a step closer to the hob, who had ceased to scare me. The memory of his magic was especially comforting.

Caefawn looked unperturbed. "Just a few of the restless ones, who have not yet gone on. Tell them to sleep."

A soft wisp touched my head and slowly took on a more solid form. As if my skin had allowed him to remember his form, Touched Banar sat on the ground and cuddled against my leg. He'd been small though wiry, but huddled next to me, he looked no older than a child. His thin hair was ruffled. Soot from the smithy fires smudged his face and clothes. The only thing different was the fear in his face.

Death should put an end to fear. But in Banar's eyes I saw the terror of his last moment. Pity drove away my jitters.

"Go to sleep," I said, using the words the hob had given me. "It's time to rest." I looked at the rest of the wisps, hoping Daryn and my family weren't among them. "Go to sleep. You're safe now."

They drifted back through the trees, some more slowly than others, but at last they were gone—except for Banar.

"Banar," I said, "they can't hurt you anymore. Go to sleep."

I touched his cheek, and gently stepped away. As soon as I pulled my hand away from his face, he was gone. No white fog drifting away, he was just gone.

"They won't rise again," said the hob after a moment.

"What?"

He smiled at me, and his tail wrapped about one of my ankles. Twice. "I told you, you're a spirit speaker. Something as weak as those ghosts can't defy you. When you told them to rest, they had to. You'd given the one more power by your recognition, and his fear gave him more. But names have power, too, even birth names. So he is at rest as well."

"Is that the right thing to do?" I asked, glancing uncomfortably at the hob's tail.

The hob shrugged. "Ghosts are spirit left when the soul has gone on. I'm not sure it matters whether they rest or not. They're not like ghouls or wraiths, twisted souls denied peace. Like as not, the ghosts here would have been gone in a year or two anyway."

I decided I didn't want to pursue it any further. "Right. All right. So much for ghosts. Tell me how we appease an angry earth spirit." I wiggled my leg lightly against his hold.

"First," he said, pulling his tail away, "you have to dress the part."

"No," I SAID FIRMLY. THE CREEK CARRIED RUNOFF FROM the snowpack high in the mountains. It was cold—really, really cold—and I wasn't going to get into it. Particularly not with the hob prepared to scrub me with a handful of moss.

"It's not that bad," he coaxed. "From the smell of your clothes, you could use a bath anyway."

I hope what I thought showed on my face. "I'm not going to strip off my clothes and freeze my rump off in the middle of the night with a stranger."

He widened his eyes in mock affront, but I could tell he was enjoying this. "How could I be a stranger?" I thought he was going to bring up our betrothal, but he was smarter than that. "We've fought side by side and shared magic."

I tapped my foot. "Sharing magic is not what I'm worried about."

He considered that a moment. "I'll close my eyes."

"I thought you had to scrub me or it wouldn't be a proper ceremonial bath."

"A-ren," he cajoled.

• • •

"FARAN-ROTTING COLD SPRING," I COMPLAINED, THEN squeaked. "You could be a little less thorough."

He ignored my complaints and took no more notice of my body than if I'd been a horse he was grooming. It was still curdling embarrassing—insulting, too, come to think of it.

He dried me with a soft cloth, then wrapped my shivering body in a single piece of silk that caught the moon's light and changed it into a thousand shades of green and gold. It wasn't very warm. I couldn't tell what made it stay where it was.

"Quit fussing with it or it'll be on the ground," the hob warned as he took a step back to look at me.

"I'm not fussing, I'm shivering."

He'd set aside his cloak when he started washing me. I snatched it from the ground and covered the sarong with it.

He grinned, and I had the childish urge to kick him in the shins. "Now we have to do something about your hair. Sit on this rock."

He took my hair from its braids and combed it out until it hung past my hips.

"There," he said at last, satisfaction in his voice. "Now to find the symbols of the earth's bounty. Wait here."

When he was gone, I found myself comparing these preparations with the ones I'd undergone for my marriage. Then it had been my mother and sister bathing me, preparing my hair. I drew Caefawn's cloak tighter against the memories, choosing instead to worry about meeting with the earth spirit.

The hob returned too soon for my peace of mind. With him he brought an armful of greenery. He sat at my feet and, whistling cheerfully, wove a tight circlet of rowan that he placed on my head before selecting wildflowers and tucking them around it.

"What is the earth spirit like?" I asked.

"I don't remember much about him," he replied, selecting some mountain aster from his booty. "Though I recall he'd associated with humans a long time. 'Twasn't much like the mountain; she's fair wild, she is—almost as informal as the water spirits, though they tend to be vulgar."

"The fisherfolk are like that, too." I asked him something that had been bothering me. "After I talk to the spirit, will I be bound to it—as you are to the mountain?"

He dropped the flowers on the ground in surprise. "Of course not. You're a human, not a hob. No elemental would ever take a human for a servant—too obstreperous."

I blinked at him, uncertain whether I felt more incredulous or insulted. "And *you're* the very paragon of tractability, I suppose?"

As quickly as that, his merry mood was gone. He tucked the last of the flowers in my hair and let out a slow breath. "The mountain commands and I obey."

My, but didn't he sound happy.

"If I felt like that about it, I wouldn't obey," I commented.

"That's why elementals avoid humans," said the hob.

I WALKED BAREFOOT IN THE HOB'S CLOAK AND A SA-rong of silk and moonlight with circlets of flowers around my head, my wrists, and my ankles. Caefawn walked in front of me, occasionally warning me of sticks and thorns—sometimes even before my feet found them first.

I wondered if what I was doing would offend the One God more than my being mageborn already had. My father said Tolleck, the new priest, was very young, but blessed with a gift enabling him to speak to the One God. Father'd smiled at me and said it gave him hope, seeing how a priest that close to the One God was a good man.

"Caefawn?"

"Hmm?"

"I won't be worshiping this spirit, will I?"

The moonlight allowed me to see his eyebrows raise. "No, indeed. Though I've heard of one or two elemental spirits who tried to require it. Not healthy for anyone concerned—even if the gods don't get involved. Just be respectful."

I stepped on another sharp rock, and swore.

MY FEET WERE SORE BY THE TIME WE REACHED THE OLD snag. In the night the ancient oak looked eerie, full of shadows and of silver where the light touched it.

"It's over here," I said, starting for the field.

"Wait here," he said, and stripped his cloak from my shoulders. "This is close enough. You don't want to force yourself on it."

"That's right," agreed a boyish voice. "It wouldn't do to force yourself where you aren't wanted."

The boy perched casually in the branches of the old snag. He wore rich-looking clothes of light-colored velvet; I couldn't tell whether they were pink or blue. One of his arms was twined in the branch above the one he sat on, the other rested negligently on one hip. Not what I'd expected of an earth spirit.

"I have to go a lot of places I couldn't, if I went only where I am wanted," I replied sharply—forgetting the one piece of advice the hob had given me. Be respectful, he'd said.

"I have to go a lot of places I couldn't, if I went only where I'm wanted," he said, repeating my words in a high singsong voice. It sounded even stupider the second time.

I swallowed my words and waited until I could speak calmly. Ridicule, I told myself sternly, was a childish game. Responding meant you lost.

"Spirit," I said calmly, even respectfully, "I have come to find out why you sent your servants to attack us."

He bounced off the tree to crouch at my feet. He was

so close I could smell the herbs on his breath.

"Killed and maimed the earthen, you did," he said in a sad voice. "Poor dead things." He said it in Caulem's voice.

In the tree, his face had been in shadows, so I had no warning until he was crouched in front of me and I looked into my husband's brother's face. But looking out through Caulem's clear eyes was someone else entirely.

"How dare you?" I grabbed the top of his shirt by the shoulders. "How dare you take the form of my kin?" I didn't yell, but rage thickened my voice. "It does not belong to you."

"Aren," warned the hob, his tail wrapping my ankle for the second time this night. It must have been a habitual gesture, but I found it distracting. My anger cooled enough for me to better consider my actions.

"Everything that goes to earth belongs to me!" the creature screamed. He was a wicked caricature of the boy I'd known. "You have not the right to deny me any form I choose, human."

"What is this?" A man's musical bass stroked my ears.

The being who wore my brother-by-marriage's form pulled from my grip and ran into the shadows whence the voice had issued. "It hurt me!" he cried piteously. "Oh, Master, save your poor shaper from the dreadful thing. Ow, ow, my shoulders. See where it bruised me?"

The moon came out in her full glory just before the new creature stepped out from the rye field. He was taller than either the hob or I by a good head, and his golden antlers were taller yet. Like me, he was clothed in a simple sarong, though his merely wrapped around his hips. I still couldn't tell how it stayed on. I reached up to make certain mine was still where it belonged.

The elemental's features were broad, with wide cheekbones and full, sensuous lips. His chin and lower jaw were coated with a dense beard that looked as much like moss as it did hair. Large, dark-colored eyes gazed upon me solemnly. His hair was shoulder length, wire-thick, and curly. His feet were cloven hooves.

"So you abuse my servant?" he said. There was no accusation in his tone, but I bristled anyway, ignoring the way the hob's tail tightened painfully around my ankle.

"Your servant wears the body of my kin, who died this spring." Anger at the shock and the sacrilege added an edge to my words.

The earth spirit made a chiding noise through his teeth, turning to the boy who crouched at his feet. "Is it so?" He didn't seem to need an answer, because he continued, "For shame, shaper. Go and change. Wear no more the forms of shades just to torment the living."

The boy cast me a malevolent look. "She hurt me, Master. Wilst punish her?"

"Go, now, child."

The boy hissed, but he left by the same path through the rye his master had taken earlier.

"Are you going to punish me?" I asked. I heard the hob draw in his breath at my challenging tone. Either that or he was laughing. In the darkness it was hard to tell.

"The fledgling was in the wrong," said the earth spirit. "I apologize for him." There was regal concession in his voice, but no real apology.

"You're not the one who owes me an apology," I replied.

The hob shook his head. This time I knew I heard a choked-off laugh. I ignored him.

The earth spirit spared Caefawn a glance, then turned to me. "Who are you, and why do you come to me here?"

Ah, here was the chance to use the speech I'd practiced all the way here. "I am Aren of Fallbrook. I've come to find out how we have angered you, that you sent your earthens to attack us." There it was, my speech, all of it.

The spirit shrugged his wide shoulders and dropped to the ground with sudden grace. I stood feeling awkward for a moment, but when the hob sat down as well, I did the same. The night enfolded us in its secrets while I waited for the spirit to speak.

"Where are the dances?" he asked after a while. The dark voice was heavy with sorrow. "Where the songs to gladden my heart? Where the thanks belonging to the earth? I am bereft." The pathos in his voice was so heartfelt that tears gathered in my eyes, though I didn't understand the reason for his sadness.

He continued to speak. "My ears have not heard the spring songs for so long that I do not even have the memory of them to hold. Yet the children of the village continued to rip my skin with their iron and forced me to bear them fruit whilst I could do nothing but sleep. But I am *awake* now. Should they not pay the price?" Wrath lit the bass reaches of his voice, and his eyes glowed green and brown with a light of their own. The strangeness of it reminded me how powerful this spirit could be. I'd seen the mountain cause an earthquake, and Caefawn said the earth spirit was stronger.

"What you say is true," I answered carefully, the germ of an idea beginning to sprout. "The songs were lost long ago, when the bloodmages bound the magic." His teeth peeled back from his lips at mention of the bloodmages (he had white teeth, large and flat). The glow in his eyes grew more green than brown. Good, it liked bloodmages as well as the hob—that was, not at all.

I continued slowly. "Like you, the world we know has slept. My people were kept in ignorance and fear by the bloodmages." *How nice to have a villain ready to hand.* Caefawn gave me a grin from behind the spirit's shoulder. I hoped the elemental wouldn't read me so easily. "That the earth and water have guardian spirits has been kept secret from us. Generations have been taught that the earth is dead."

The spirit had begun shaking his head as I finished the

last sentence, his action exaggerated by the stronger movement of his antlers.

"Life cannot come from a dead thing," he snapped.

"Does spring not come from winter? And winter is the season of the dead," murmured the hob.

"Be silent, servant of the mountain. Do not seek to twist my thoughts with your trickery." There was menace in the guardian's fierce glare.

"My lord," I said, aspiring to twist his thoughts with *my* trickery, "I tell you we were taught it was so—by those who should know better. This spring the bindings were torn from the land, and our world is reawakening into something that we no longer have means to comprehend. We have no memories to guide us, only the vague shadows of stories that have changed with the centuries. If we have offended you, hurt you, it is out of ignorance, not intention. We are willing to learn." I felt a strong urge to cross my fingers against the lie of the last sentence, as if I were a child speaking to her parents. It startled me when I realized that, other than the last sentence, I'd told the earth spirit nothing less than the truth. "We *must* learn—and we need you to teach us. We don't have the songs anymore." Still true.

"I care not what songs they sing," he replied harshly, but the fierce glow of his eyes faded. "Only that they are sung for the rebirth of spring, the promise of summer, the bounty of harvest, and the death that is winter."

Four ceremonies. Holy mares of the One God, how could I get four pagan ceremonies out of the village? Everyone knew how jealous the One God was of His worshipers. There wouldn't be many willing to risk angering Him in this time of need—especially when it was *me* telling them they had to. *Caefawn* would have a better chance. Let *him* try to explain to the villagers the difference between giving thanks and worshiping.

"Summer solstice is past," commented the hob.

"There will be no autumn harvest," said the spirit ominously. He waved his hand, and the plants around us began to wilt and die.

I fervently wished the hob would be quiet. He seemed only to irritate the spirit.

"Stay your hand," I said. Then, remembering I was here as a supplicant, I added, "Please. This will do you no more good that it does us. Where will your songs be if the land dies around you? You are the guardian of this land, not its destroyer." I hoped that was true. "Two weeks from tonight we will have a celebration here— beside this tree. A celebration of the reawakening of the land, of freedom from the yoke of the bloodmages, a welcoming feast."

How I was going to pull it off, I didn't know. Maybe the priest would be able to help—if he didn't burn me as a heretic first.

"A feast," said the spirit, obviously experiencing one of his mercurial mood changes. "A feast!" He bounded to his feet. "I will stay my hand for a fortnight. After the singing and dancing are over, I will reconsider."

He didn't walk away so much as blend in with the plants of the field. Caefawn stood up and offered me his arm. I took it and began the long walk home.

"SO," I SAID, SOME HOURS LATER, "YOU CAN SEE WE have a problem."

I sat in the private dining room at the inn. With me were Kith, his father—who was recovering from his wounds—and Tolleck the priest.

Tolleck groaned and held his head. "My dear, this is impossible! The village is already divided to the breaking point over the changes we've been forced to make. If I tell them we have to hold a feast to appease an earth elemental, they will likely burn me just before they do the same to you."

"Could you pronounce another reason for a feast?" asked Albrin. "I think the harper could be trusted to write songs that praise the earth without letting it slip that the earth is a real creature."

I shook my head. "I think he's going to be there. It's a little hard to hide a man with antlers and hooves. Someone is sure to notice him."

Tolleck laughed, but no one else did.

"The problem is belief," said Kith. "People will do amazing things to ensure their survival. But the villagers cannot conceive of a creature powerful enough to destroy all the crops."

"I don't really think a demonstration is in order," I said dryly. "It'd be like one of the serfs approaching Lord Moresh and saying, 'Excuse me, but I don't think any of the rest of the serfs believe you have the power to cut off my head.'"

"I'll seek answers from the temple," said Tolleck, rising to his feet. "Perhaps something will come to me. You were right to talk to me first. Give me a day or two to think about it before you do anything."

I rose when he did, and shook his hand. "Thank you." I hope he knew I was thanking him for his support as well as for coming here.

Tolleck started toward the door but stopped before he reached it. "You'd probably better let Merewich know about this. He's been running the village longer than I've been alive. If anyone might have an idea about how to get them to . . . *celebrate* the earth, it would be Merewich."

I FOUND MEREWICH EATING COLD OATMEAL IN THE kitchen of his home. He was alone except for his wife, who rocked in the chair before the small kitchen fire.

Creak back, *creak* forth, sigh. *Creak* back, *creak* forth, sigh. I was there for only a few minutes and it was enough to make me creak along with her.

"Two steps forward, one step back," sighed Merewich after he'd heard me out. He sighed at the same time his wife did. "You've already talked to Tolleck?"

"Hmm." I watched him eat the unappetizing gray stuff and noticed it was almost the same color as his skin. He needed a rest—perhaps Melly could send over one of the former serfs (whom she'd taken over like a hen with chicks). "I thought he might be the best one to decide if . . . well, if the ceremony might bring the wrath of the One God down upon our village."

"*Gods,*" exclaimed Merewich blasphemously. "I wouldn't have thought about that, but I suppose if I can believe in hobs and earth spirits, I'd better worry about the One God, too."

He quit eating and rubbed his face briefly with his hands. "Right. I'll speak with Tolleck. Perhaps you'd better go talk to Wandel. Tell him he needs to come up with some songs of praise, hmm?"

I FOUND WANDEL TRAINING IN THE SMALL ENCLOSURE behind the inn. I recognized some of the drills Koret was using for the patrol, but Wandel did them much faster than any of us. He saw me when I came through the stable door, but he finished his pattern before he acknowledged me. It was a long pattern, and it gave me a chance to study him.

What manner of man was he? Had he ever been the man I thought I knew—a musician with a talent for storytelling who could charm honey from the bees? Had he only been the king's assassin and spy?

His concentration was so intense I could almost touch it. I could *see* it. Like the ghosts in the woods, it looked like a foggy mist, but it clung to Wandel's body, moving as he did. The ghosts had glowed, but Wandel's spirit shimmered with fire and passion.

"People," the hob had told me last night on our way home, "have body, soul, and spirit. The soul is immortal, the body is not, but the spirit can be either."

Seeing Wandel's spirit didn't tell me anything about him I didn't already know.

"Aren," said the harper, wiping the sweat off his forehead with one arm.

"Merewich sent me to you." As soon as I tried to clear my sight, Wandel's spirit faded from view. Apparently I had better control over this new facet of magic than I had over my visions.

The harper listened to my story from beginning to end. A smile of awe grew on his face as I wound to a close.

"The Green Man," he said softly. "Who'd have thought—but I suppose we have legends popping up all over. Why not the Green Man? I know a number of songs already, but I can come up with a new one or two."

I *liked* Wandel. He was the only other person in the valley who found the wildlings fascinating rather than terrifying. *Or at least in addition to terrifying*, I thought, remembering yesterday's ghosts and the earth guardian.

"Merewich wonders if you can come up with any way to make the village more amiable to a celebration of the earth spirit. If you do, he'd like you to tell him, Koret, or Tolleck." I turned to leave.

"Aren, I'm sorry," he said suddenly.

I knew what he was talking about, and it wasn't the Green Man.

I turned back to him. "The king is dead. The world in which you made your vows to him is dead. Leave Kith be."

"Kith is dangerous. He knows it."

"And we need him!" I snapped. "Do you think the danger will be over when the raiders are gone? The hob doesn't. He's not nearly as worried about the raiders as he is about other things. Things like the hillgrim that attacked me. The wildlings are back, and most of them don't like humans very well—if they ever did."

"Look, Aren, most of the bloodmages' get commit suicide after a year or two. Kith's lasted longer than any other. The berserkers understand—Kith understands—that they are dead already, it's just a matter of time. If they're lucky, they die in battle."

I left without saying another word.

NINE

The hob was waiting for me when I woke up the next evening. This time he was holding a mug of something steaming that smelled sweet and milky.

"Here," he said. "It's a little chilly tonight. There's a storm blowing in. I thought you might like something warm to start the night with."

I wiggled around until I could take it from him, then sipped it cautiously. Some kind of tea with honey, but the blend was nothing I'd ever tasted before.

"Thanks," I said. He intimidated me a lot less than he had the night before, but I decided not to ask him why he was here tonight.

"I've come to teach you," he said. "Don't worry, I've cleared it with Koret. Tomorrow he'll need you, but tonight's mine."

I rolled my eyes at his mock leer, and he laughed. I didn't ask him what he was going to teach me. I should have—then I could have refused while I had a chance.

• • •

"BUT I DON'T WANT TO TALK TO GHOSTS."

The manor garden was unkempt, but still recognizable as deliberate planting. I was all too aware of the burial ground on the other side of the garden's stone wall.

"If you don't learn how to use your abilities, you'll be used by them," he said. *Hurrah, that sounded like fun.* "Aren, you've got to learn to protect yourself. You can summon spirits, but by the same token you can be summoned by them."

"Why you?" I asked nastily. It wasn't his fault, and I knew it, but he was there. "You aren't a speaker." Whatever that was.

"Because there's no one else," he explained, though I could see him fight a smile. He seemed to get some sadistic enjoyment out of my whining. "On this side of the river, I can deal with ghosts if I have to. But I'm hoping you'll be able to save yourself."

"How reassuring," I said witheringly.

This time he did grin. "Come on, lass. Likely you won't be summoning anyone you know. It won't hurt to talk a bit with the dead. If you can convince them to go on, as you did the ones who came to you last night, you'll be doing them a favor."

"Great," I said, shivering, though I wasn't cold.

Last night was a lot more frightening in memory than it seemed at the time. I was in no hurry to visit with more ghosts.

I thought of a possible way out of it. "Hold up a minute. Didn't you stop me from summoning the ghost of that poor skeleton?"

"There is a difference between summoning a soul back to its dead remains, and calling a ghost which is merely spirit."

"What's the difference between soul and spirit?" I asked.

"People like you and I are made of body, soul, and

spirit. The body is the physical and is tied very tightly to time. Humans are very rooted in the body—it's why there aren't more mages among you. Soul is what determines who you are—stubborn, impatient . . . the qualities that make you different from Kith or Koret. It is where emotions live. Hobs are tied most tightly to the soul. Spirit"—he hesitated—"spirit ties your body and soul together. It's where magic abides and it can take on aspects of both your soul and your body. That's why Touched Banar's ghost looked like his mortal body. It's why it was frightened as his soul was before it went on."

"So the soul and the spirit are immortal and the body is mortal." I said.

"Without the soul and body, the spirit usually dissipates after a while. If it doesn't you get ghosts."

"So I'm supposed to call a wandering spirit for a chat." *Hello, I'm Aren and you're dead.* Didn't sound like fun to me.

He nodded. "A ghost is a human or animal who has died, but has chosen not to go on to the spirit realms. Calling someone who has already gone on is an act of evil."

"And it creates wraiths," I speculated.

"One way to get them," he agreed. "Sit down."

I leaned my back against the garden wall and sank to my rump. The solid stone against my back was cold and damp. I crossed my legs.

He crouched in front of me, gripping his staff. "Now think about the dead. Just ghosts. Wisps of memory and being left here where they no longer belong."

"They must feel frightened," I said, thinking about it despite myself. Banar had been frightened.

"*Frightened*," it agreed, settling at my feet.

"Who are you?" I asked. The hob hadn't told me what to say to the ghosts when they came. I didn't really want to interrogate it.

"Mercenary," it said, the whispery voice a little stronger.

"Fighting the war. Our side was losing and the man who hired us dead. No money in it anymore. Captain said, 'Got to turn raider, boys. Lots of lords dead, estates left undefended. Find one of them.' " As it spoke, the wisps seemed to gather together and solidify.

One of the raiders. I didn't think it was one I'd killed.

"It's time to rest now," I told him. I didn't want to know what he'd do if he figured out I was one of the villagers.

"Rest?"

"You've done your duty, soldier," said the hob. "Sleep."

The ghosted started when the hob spoke, as if it hadn't noticed him there. Unlike the earth spirit, it didn't seem to troubled by the hob.

"Time to sleep," he agreed, though he didn't do anything but rest at my feet.

I whispered, "Sleep." I didn't know why I whispered, but it worked. The ghost faded away.

"That one was brighter than Banar was," I said softly when it was gone.

"The new ones glow almost as if they were still tied to a soul," said the hob, though he was looking uneasily around the garden. "The old ones can be shadows so dark even I can't see them unless they choose."

"Mistake, mistake, the mountain's slave made a mistake," crowed a voice from the wall over my head.

I knew *that* tone, though I didn't recognize the boy who bounced down on the ground in front of me. "Hob made a mistake. Hob made a mistake." The singsong was unmistakable. The earth spirit's servant wore the shape of a boy younger than Caulem. This one I didn't know.

"Quiet, shaper," said the hob, his attention still elsewhere. "Your place is on the other side of the river."

The shaper turned to me with a bright smile, "Hob forgets a lot. Forgets my master is *here*, too. Forgets some ghosts are not so weak. Forgets old places have their dangers."

"The shaper's right," said the hob, his voice lifeless with failure. "Being around humans makes me arrogant. I came here because I knew there were recent dead wandering—bound to be, after a battle. Should have thought there might be older spirits here."

Defeat was something I almost couldn't associate with the hob. Not even being left alone with only a mountain for company had given him such melancholy. Nor could I see any reason for it. I looked around suspiciously.

"There's a graveyard just over the wall," I offered, because what he'd said made me wonder if he knew. "Caefawn?"

The hob bowed his head and didn't answer.

"Show yourself," I commanded the air at large.

"Here I am," chortled the shaper.

"Be quiet or leave," I said sourly. "I have enough to work out. If you interfere, I swear it'll be the worse for you."

He subsided, except for a couple of smirks. I didn't know what he thought I could do to him, but I was glad he was threatened enough to desist.

"Show yourself, ghost." I said again. "Caefawn, don't you bring me out here, then leave me alone to deal with this thing."

It was there. Larger than the garden we were in, its substance covered the ground with a deep shadow.

"Caefawn," I said again. "Time enough for despair when there's nothing left to do."

"Hobs are emotional," observed the shaper. "Ghosts affect them more than they do you mortals."

The shadows continued to deepen in the garden, frightening the moon's light away. I reflected, not for the first time in the hob's company, that cat's sight would be extremely useful. Darkness crept over Caefawn, who was bent around his staff as if it comforted him.

The shadows stopped at my feet.

"Who are you?" it asked in a voice like fiddle music in the dawn. I thought that was supposed to be my question. "Why did you summon me?"

"I am Aren of Fallbrook," I answered it, as I had the earth spirit the day before. "I am here to be taught."

"Fallbrook," it said. "Taught what?"

"To speak to you," I replied.

Something touched me inside my head. It was the strangest feeling I'd ever had, as if something soft and ethereal drifted through my skin and bone. After an instant the touch turned to ice.

"Warm it," advised the shaper as he gripped both my hands and stared into my eyes. For once his face was serious. "Think of hot, rich food; the fire on a cold night; my master's eyes. Think of touch and life and light." Then, without loosing my eyes from his hold, he said in a different voice, "Hob, now would be a good time to help."

Would you like to join me?

I shuddered with the icy jolt that shot from my head to my spine. I thought of fires and soup, hot green-brown eyes that flared to red in an elemental's face.

I am so alone here.

Me, too, I thought before I caught myself. *I'm so alone.*

The shaper slapped my face. "Warmth and living, Aren."

Warmth. The touch of Daryn's hands on my flesh. Warmth slipped from his remembered touch to my cold skin. I concentrated on the one night we'd had, the passion and fire. When I ran out of memory, I built new ones. Dreaming about the dead didn't seem like the right thing to do under the circumstances, so for the new ones I substituted coal-gray skin for sun-browned, the nip of fangs gently wielded, a tail wrapped around my ankle. Thoughts curiosity had brought to me after the bargain was struck. I asked the question, *What would it be like to be wed to the hob?* The answers came whether I willed them or not.

The cold withdrew slowly, more slowly when desires replaced solid memory. So I tried another tack. I built the image of the gradual magic of rye and wheat pushing up through the earth, exchanging safe darkness for sunlight and warmth. Flowers opening for the first time to the dance of butterfly wings.

It was gone, and I was breathing as heavily as a drowning victim just rescued. I expect the analogy occurred to me because my clothes were wet with sweat. It started to rain. Lucky me.

"Good girl," said the shaper. "Did well enough for a mortal—better than the hob."

Behind the shaper crouched the ghost. I felt no fear of it now, for it was mine. It could do no more harm unless I set it free.

"But Caefawn's no speaker," I said with sudden knowledge of what that might mean. "The despair . . . that's a ghost's weapon, isn't it? It doesn't affect me."

Caefawn, his face drawn and remote, looked up from his staff. "That and fear. As a speaker you are immune to those and many other weapons of the spirit. The mountain could defend me from terror or gloom, not both. Not so far from her slopes."

Rather than tiring me out, holding the ghost under my control seemed to be giving me energy, as if I'd been drinking fizzies all night and was jittery with it.

All beings had spirits, not just ghosts. I thought that if I wanted to, I might be able to take the shaper as well, though not the hob. Not yet. It was as if I could see the will that each possessed, and measure my power against them.

See, said the ghost speaking secretly to me. *See what we could do?*

"Should be more cautious," advised the shaper. "Could

have killed her seeing if she could protect herself from ghosts. My master would have been unhappy. He sent me to watch you."

The ghost looked up at me with its eyeless face, as if we shared a secret. The double vision I'd had with the skeleton came back, and I could see the ghost as it had been in mortal form—a woman with hair of bright brass and laughter sweet as the south wind. A woman who had been afraid to be alone, to die.

Yes, her voice whispered in my mind, *I could give you power. Magic you could use to make the villagers like you again. Make them do as they ought, appease the earth guardian. You could save them from themselves.*

I knelt until I was level with its face.

"Go rest," I said slowly because it was difficult to speak. "Sleep now." It wasn't a suggestion, as I'd made to the raider, for this ghost I controlled absolutely. "Be at peace."

The ghost faded, as the other had. As it did, I felt that odd surge of power and awareness drift away.

I looked up into Caefawn's eyes.

"I didn't bring her here to see if she was strong enough to protect herself from the ghosts," he said.

"What, then?" demanded the shaper petulantly.

"He wanted to know if I'd give in to temptation," I said suddenly, not realizing it until the words were out of my mouth. " 'Death magic, blood magic slips easy down the throat'." I quoted an old lay softly. " 'Power calls with temptation's demand.' "

"I could have stopped you," Caefawn said. "Now, while you're just learning." *Could have killed me*, I thought.

"You didn't have to," I replied, getting to my feet like an old woman.

Stiff and sore, as though I'd been fighting rather than sitting in a garden, I tottered forward and kissed the hob's cheek. The surface was smoother than the skin my imagination had endowed him with. It was a relief to know I wouldn't have survived to do the things the ghost had offered to me.

The shaper hooted and blew raspberries, but the hob smiled as sweetly as if he read my thoughts.

WHEN I TOOK MY PATROL THE NEXT NIGHT, THE HOB came with me. Though "with" might be the wrong word. He'd run ahead and jump out from behind trees, laughing when I jumped and swore at him.

"No need to swear so quietly," he advised merrily. "The raiders are mostly in camp today. There's a small party by Wedding Pass, but they'll not cross our path."

I stopped short. "If there's no danger, why are we patrolling?"

He looked at me seriously for a moment. "Wouldn't do to get dependent on me. The bargain's for the survival of the village, remember. They need to be ready. Even when the raiders are taken care of, there are hillgrims, trolls, and a dozen other such nasties. I understand that in the past you've been protected here." He gestured widely to indicate the valley. "Not having to worry about much but the occasional bandit or wolf. It will never be that way again." He strolled through the field, passing an arm over my shoulder and letting his tail settle around my hips. "There was a reason the mages felt they had to bind the magic. Most of the wizards of the time felt the same way you do about bloodmages, blood magic. But they agreed to it all the same."

"Why not leave the lands to the wildlings?" I said. "There were other places to go."

He shook his head. "The wild was growing, pushing mankind back. I don't know how it was other places." He gave me a wry smile, acknowledging his tie to the mountain. "But here mankind was dying."

I walked with him, thinking about what he'd said. But I was also thinking about the arm slung so casually across my shoulders. Being courted by a hob wasn't as different as it could have been. But it was different enough for me. I grinned to myself as I bent to unhook his tail.

SO I DIDN'T TELL KORET THE HOB KNEW WHERE THE raiders were most of the time. When I patrolled, Caefawn joined me as often as not. Sometimes the earth spirit's shaper came, too, never in the same shape twice but never again in the body of anyone I knew. When I wasn't patrolling, the hob continued my lessons. Sometimes I wasn't certain whether he was teaching me, teasing me, or courting me—often as not, it was all three.

"Come on, then, the raiders aren't going anywhere today," he said, pulling me proprietorially in the direction opposite from the one I should be going.

"And how do you know that?" I asked, though I fell in beside him willingly enough.

He grinned and twitched his tail with mischief. "A few of my acquaintances are having fun tonight. They'll do no harm—except to the raiders' pride, and you'll have more time to learn."

"Did you talk to your 'acquaintances' about the thefts in the village?"

"None of them admit to it, though that's no surety. If you could talk the people into leaving something out for the little folk, it might go better for them."

"Better for whom, the little folk, or the villagers?" I asked. "The widow Shona left a handful of cookies out last night, and this morning something had unwoven the better part of the blanket she was working and tracked blue dye all over the walls and ceiling."

The hob chuckled. "I'll look at it. Happen I'll recognize the footprints."

We crossed Fell Bridge. There was no guard there. The hob had advised against it, saying the raiders were unlikely to harm the crops before harvest, or to take any of Albrin's livestock out of the valley. What went missing could be retaken closer to a time it would be of use. Put up a few herdsmen with the animals to guard against predators and give them orders to run at the first sight of the raiders. Koret had agreed. The raiders seemed to have the same philosophy, for no one had seen them on the manor side of the river since the last attack.

"Where are we going?" I asked, climbing over a stone wall that divided one pasture from another.

"To the bogs," he said. "I'm hoping to find a few noe-glins or maybe a will-o'-wisps. You'd like the will-o'-wisps: when they sing, the flowers bloom even at night."

We found a large rock to sit on by the edge of the Fell bogs. The air was damp and chilly despite its being summer. The bog smelled of rotting vegetation and sweet bogflower.

"It'd be easier to do this inside the marsh," Caefawn informed me. "But then we'd get wet and smell like a bog for days. We'll try for noeglins first. They're about as strong as ghosts, and guaranteed to fight you with anything in their power. They'll be good experience for you."

We sat for a while. His tail snuck around my waist. I pried it off and set it politely between us with a pat. I hadn't realized just how strong his tail was. If he hadn't let me, I'd never have gotten it off.

"Is the rock uncomfortable?"

I quit twitching my hips. "Quite. So how do I call a hooglin?"

"Noeglin," he corrected. "Hmm, this might be a problem. I'll try to describe it, and we'll see what happens. Think of a creature formed from the stench of the swamp. They aren't too intelligent, nor yet too—" He broke off abruptly and pointed.

In the dark, only its movement allowed me to see the creature scuffling about the edges of the swamp. It had a dark, furry pelt and looked almost bearlike, but was much smaller. It might have been the size of a herd dog.

"Pikka," said the hob when it was gone. "They're a true animal, but I'd be careful just the same. They've a nasty temper—I'd rather face a bear than a pikka. Most times a bear will leave you alone."

"They use magic?" I asked. Otherwise, why would they come back after the bonds were lifted? I'd certainly never heard of a pikka before.

The hob nodded. "For stealth, mostly. A pikka can slip into a herd of sheep and eat a lamb lying beside its mother without disturbing any of the sheep."

"Caefawn," I asked, "where are they all coming from— the fairies and such? Spirits are immortal, and I know how you survived—but what about the pikka and earthens?"

"The guardian spirits like the earth spirit, mostly, I suspect." His tail slipped off the rock, almost as if it were accidental. I gave it a suspicious look. His eyes crinkled, but he kept his mouth seriously straight as he continued. "I suppose a few of them were here anyway, just hiding. The only time you'll ever find a dwarf is when he wants you to. The earthens are a manifestation of the earth spirit—not really creatures in their own right. Most of the things the village has been seeing lately are under the earth spirit's guardianship. Except, of course, the winkies that tangled the nets and made Cantier so angry. They belong to the river guardian."

"The mountain had only you?"

"Of my kind," he replied.

There was something in his voice. *Pain*, I thought, *or at least sorrow*, so I changed the subject. "Hooglins are formed from the stink of the swamp. . . ."

The hob settled more comfortably on the rock. "Noeglins are mischievous. One of their favorite tricks is to creep up behind some poor unsuspecting traveler and scare the bejeebers out of him."

"Like a hob-of-the-bog?" I suggested.

He cleared his throat, so straight-faced I worried he

was offended until he spoke. "Well, hobs don't generally eat their victims . . . unless they're hillgrims. Hillgrims taste really good raw, but they're best when cooked for a day in a pot with onions and butter." His tail now rested on the rock again, this time on my right (the hob sat on my left).

"How can they eat if they don't have a body?" I looked at his tail suspiciously, but it lay virtuously still.

"Very few creatures are pure spirit," he said seriously. "Ghosts are, and poltergeists. But all things are tied more strongly to either body, soul, or spirit. The ones you can call are tied strongest to the spirit. Sometimes, like the noeglins or the earth guardian, they can put off and on the physical body as easily as I shed my cloak."

"So you call them spirits, even though they have a body?"

"And a soul, most of them." He nodded. "There are three types of living creatures: mortals like humans and dwarves, soulfuls like hobs and cats, and spirits like the guardians and noeglins."

"Cats?" I said.

A flurry of sticks flew at us out of a growth of bog-weed. They hurt when they hit—and most of them hit. Caefawn snarled, startling me, for he sounded like a wolf and I'd been thinking of him as though he were human, despite his talk of eating hillgrims. Overlaying the smell of the bog was a acrid smell. After a moment I couldn't smell anything else.

"Right," the hob said after the deluge was finished. "There's a noeglin. You need to keep him from hurting you and get him out into the open."

"Come here, you nasty noeglin," I coaxed. A speaker's voice seemed to have some power with the earth spirit and the ghosts. Maybe it would work with a noeglin.

"Here I be," said a soft, sibilant, hate-filled hiss. Then, like the ghost, it attacked my mind.

It was easier to fight than the ghost had been, though

the noeglin didn't attack in precisely the same way. I tried to block his advance into my head. It seemed to work best when I envisioned something solid.

So I held a mental door before the noeglin, a stout barn door that stopped it where it was. Before it could try something else, I put doors all around it, trapping it there, though I could see it hanging over the swamp like a misty clump of rotting weeds.

I don't know what part of it I held trapped, no more than I could have said what part of the ghost I'd caught. These were creatures of spirit, not body—so I thought I'd ask the self-appointed expert.

"How can I hold it in my mind and yet it is still there?" I asked, pointing at the noeglin.

"Bloodmages take a bit of an enemy's hair or skin and attach it to a vole or mouse by magic," said the hob soberly. "When they kill the mouse, they can kill their enemy, too. Sympathetic magic. You can hold a small bit of it in your mind and affect the whole of it."

The noeglin wriggled suddenly, spouting a series of sounds that boomed and hurt my ears. "Me go," it said.

"It wants you to let it go," translated the hob unnecessarily.

I opened one of the doors, releasing the noeglin from my control. The spirit sank tiredly into the dark mud of the swamp, taking the noxious odor with it.

"How is it that it—and you—speak the same language I do?" I asked, when the noeglin was gone.

" 'Tis a gift of the hobs to speak whatever tongue they hear, a gift the guardian spirits share when they will," he said. "As for the other—another human wouldn't have understood the noeglin. But you are a speaker, and what good would your gift be if you couldn't understand the spirits you call? Now about the will-o'-wisps—"

SPEAKING TO THE SPIRITS, ONCE I KNEW I COULD DO IT, was easier than the visions. Calling them was simply a

matter of knowing what they were. Caefawn had started
with ghosts because they were relatively powerless, and
I already knew what they were. He seemed to think it
was his duty to stuff my head full of every kind of spirit
I was likely to meet. He made me memorize the names
and characteristics of any number of them. Most of the
creatures, he said, he'd never seen.

Spirits had no body in their natural state—which is
what made them spirits, I suppose. Ghosts, ghasts, noeglins, and poltergeists were lesser spirits who were often
hostile. He hadn't found any ghasts here, but I met most
of the rest of the very weak and horrid. Poltergeists, he
said, were both powerless and mindless—not worth the
effort of approaching them.

The weaker benevolent spirits like dryads and naiads
he'd shown me as well. The dryad had been soft-spoken
and solid-seeming; he reminded me of the ancient oak he
called home. The naiad had been shy, leaving as quickly
as she'd responded. Caefawn hadn't seen her, though
he'd been sitting beside me the whole time.

Some of the spirits we'd looked for, like the will-o'-
wisps, we couldn't find. I could tell it made Caefawn sad,
though he didn't say anything.

One or two of the creatures had attacked me. Sometimes their attacks were physical, like the noeglin throwing sticks. More often they were mental. As I learned to
defend myself, the hob would find a new, stronger, more
contentious thing to call.

Caefawn said that most of the stronger spirits, like the
earth guardian, would know when I was about and come
on their own if they chose. I could summon the lesser
spirits whether they willed it or not. Some of them I
could dominate if I chose—but it made me increasingly
uncomfortable to do so. It felt wrong, even evil, to do
more than defend myself. Gram always said that if something felt wrong, it probably was.

●   ●   ●

"SO WHAT'S IT TONIGHT?" I ASKED CHEERFULLY. I WAS starting to feel brave in the night. Facing off with noeglins and ghosts had made me less afraid of the darkness. *Silly me.*

Still, it was easier than facing the villagers. Someone had decided it was best to tell the village about the necessity of appeasing the earth spirit. Predictably, it was seen as my fault. As of yesterday, none of the patrollers except for Ice would talk to me.

"There's a fetch abroad here," Caefawn said. "They weren't very common Before, and you might not get another chance to meet one."

There were stories about fetches. I decided missing my only chance to meet one might be a good idea. "Isn't it dangerous to meet a fetch?"

"Yes," he said, stopping beside one of Soul's Creek's little waterfalls. "But so are ghosts and noeglins."

We were half a league or so above my old croft. I leaned against a tree, panting a little. The hob was hard to keep up with, even when he was obviously slowing down for me.

"Are we here?" I asked hopefully.

"As close as we need to be," he answered. He waited, gathering his thoughts. "I wouldn't willingly take you to meet the fetch. They have too much power over humans, and I'm not certain how much your talents will help you against it. And it's too far from the mountain for me to help much."

I'd learned a lot about the hob. Away from the mountain his magic—which mainly concerned things of the hunt, like hiding or tracking—faded, though his great strength and speed seemed to stay with him.

I frowned at him. "You're scaring me."

He nodded solemnly. "Good. You'll be more wary that way. I don't think it would be a good idea to try to control it—I'm not certain you're good enough. However, you don't want to let it wander around the valley for long—it'll start to take victims."

I shook my head. "So what am I supposed to do with it?"

"You'll have to decide that yourself." Caefawn sat down on the ground, wrapping his tail around one of *his* ankles for a change.

We waited in silence for a while, a peaceful silence. I could hear Soul's Creek running behind me. A nightjar cried out.

"Tell me about names," I said.

"Names?" he asked.

"My gram always said the wildlings guarded their names, and I know Caefawn isn't your name. You enjoyed it too much when you gave it to me."

He snickered. "I'll tell you what it means sometime. Right. Names, then. Names have power."

"What power? Should I worry that everyone and their dog knows my name?"

He shook his head. "You don't have a name, not really. Birth names are weak things, tied to the body, not the soul. There aren't many in your village who have real names. The priest does, and he knows enough to keep his real name secret. Real names are given in a ceremony with earth, air, fire, water, and magic. If someone knows your real name, it gives them power over you—an advantage. Focusing a spell on someone with their real name makes it harder to fight or unspell. If you knew the real name of the earth spirit, you could call him and he would have to come."

"If real names are so dangerous, why would anyone want one?" I asked.

He laughed. "Real names add power to your magic as well. When you know enough about your magic to know what you are choosing, you can decide if you want a real name and I will help gift you with one."

"Hmm." I considered what he said, shifting against my

tree because my shoulder was going numb. "What did you say I should do with the fetch if she comes?"

"Anything you want to," replied a low feminine voice in sultry tones.

I turned, but it was too dark under the trees to see anything more than a shadow. The voice sounded familiar. Knowing what little I did about fetches, I would have bet that its voice sounded just like mine—though I don't think I'd ever sounded quite so sultry. There was an old saying, "If you ever meet your fetch, if you don't die today, you'll die the next."

I felt outward with the *sight*. At some point in our excursions, I'd discovered that the *sight* and this spirit-speaking were very close. It was the *sight* that allowed me to see the spirits when even the hob couldn't. Calling and seeing were just two sides of the same thing, like talking and listening. Not that I was good at controlling either one, but I was getting there.

A woman dressed in boy's clothing walked out from the shadows of the trees where I'd been watching. Her face was strong, though not pretty. Her dark hair was drawn untidily back into a thick braid. I'd thought it might be like looking into a mirror, but it wasn't. I'd thought it might be like looking at Caulem animated by the shaper, but it wasn't like that either. She was a stranger; if I hadn't known she was a fetch, I wouldn't have noticed she looked like me.

"What do you see?" I asked Caefawn.

He shrugged with his ever-present grin, though his eyes were wary. "Nothing, but I heard it speak."

"Leave this valley," I said, turning back to the woman.

"He brings you here to me," she purred. I never purr, at least not in public. I began to feel a little indignant, but she continued. "So kind of him. He never told you what happens to a human who meets their fetch, did he?"

A few days ago, I would have believed her. Believed the mere sight of her would kill me. But I trusted Caefawn. He wouldn't have brought me here if death was the only thing to win.

"I've heard the stories," I agreed mildly. "But you cannot harm me, a speaker." The look on her face told me that what I said was true, and that she wasn't happy I said it. Me, I was happy. I'd hoped that, as with the ghosts, my magic would serve to protect me.

"Not if I don't believe you can hurt me," I continued, watching her face closely to see if I was right. I was.

"We don't believe in you anymore," I said cheerfully. This one was as easy as the noeglins had been. "If someone meets you and talks with you, when he is home, he'll dismiss it as his imagination. It's been too long since your kind has been here. You'll have to find other prey."

She laughed. Not good. She approached me, gripped my hand with hers. I could see the pale scar the hillgrim had left me winding down her forearm. The hair on the back of my neck lifted, and I met her eyes. She smiled and looked at her arm as I'd just done, drawing my gaze with hers. The skin on her arms began to dry. It cracked and pulled back, curling away from the flesh. I stared at it, unable to break her spell.

The skin broke along the lines of the hillgrim's scar, and for a moment, just an instant, I thought the arm I stared at was mine. I cried out with the sharp pain of it and with revulsion at the ugly wound. The pain made it more real, so when I shifted my gaze away from her arm to mine, I wasn't surprised to see that my scar had split, too. Yellow pus oozed out like a tear and dropped to the ground. The distinctive odor of rotting flesh filled the air. I felt the hob's hands on my shoulders, but I couldn't pull away.

"Break it," he said hoarsely. Good, he was scared, too, how comforting. "Break her hold."

Very helpful, I thought, but he was right. I thought of how I had broken the ghost's hold in the garden and tried thinking of Daryn again. The fetch giggled and ran her tongue into the same ear Daryn had. Her saliva burned, and I couldn't hear out of the ear.

Passion didn't work. I'd try something else, then. Caefawn had enveloped me in his arms from behind. I could feel his heart beat against my back like a drum, like hoofbeats.

A vision came, and I grabbed it with both hands, unsure whether it would help me or her.

Duck's hooves drummed against the ground shaded with golden light from the sunset's fading glow. I sat him without saddle, reins resting loosely on his neck.

I remembered the day clearly, several weeks after we'd come back from Auberg. Memories shifted to accommodate the vision, subtly strengthening both sight and memory.

I laughed as the wind caught my hair and spilled it out of its loose braid. Free, I was free. Free of hiding what I was. Free of being less than I could be. I gloried in my strength, my freedom. The price had been too high, but it was paid. Now there was no one to hold me in subtle chains of wifehood, womanhood. No one to belittle my warnings because I was a woman, and women are given to such fits and starts. No need to hide what I was behind the image of what I should be.

I let out a war cry and shook my hair in the wind. Letting the cool fingers of air wash my other self behind me. The weak woman who cowered in her cellar was gone forever. The woman I was now had grown beyond her.

I stretched out my arms until they felt like wings as Duck ran down the mountain.

I came to myself slowly. I looked at the fetch and said, softly. "Go away."

Her eyes faded from brown to sea-green; her face shifted subtly, leaving behind cheeks more rounded, lips softer, jaw narrower than they had been. She snarled at me, and her face looked less than human. Then she was gone.

"About time," growled Caefawn.

I sank to my rump on the cold grass, which was damp from the spray of the small waterfall. My arm hurt as if it had been savagely ripped open, but there was nothing wrong with it. The hillgrim's scar was as it had been, and my wrist was unbruised. I covered my face with my hands and took deep, slow breaths until I felt like myself again.

THE HOB WATCHED AREN PUT HERSELF TOGETHER again, one layer at a time. First she put aside the fear, then the rush of danger. She did it so thoroughly he could barely smell the remnant emotions on her. She had such control. He wondered if she'd learned it, or if she'd always been that way.

"Why is it that strong feelings broke her hold on me, just as it broke the ghost's hold in the garden?" Her voice was soft and calm.

"How do you control the spirits?" He asked not because he couldn't have told her the answer, but because she'd learn it better if she found it herself.

It was hard for her to articulate what she'd done. *A limitation of the language*, he thought. He wondered if the bloodmages had their own language for what they did.

"I take a little bit of their spirit inside of me," she said. "If I separate it from the rest of the creature, they cannot attack me. I learned that from the noeglins."

He nodded. "It's like knowing their real names. You have a part of them, and they cannot struggle against you effectively."

"So why can I break their hold by thinking about"— she hesitated. He could see in the darkness as easily as the light, so he watched the blush highlight her cheeks.

"By thinking about strong emotions? It worked with the ghost, and now with the fetch."

"Not just any emotions," he said, speculating about what strong emotions she'd been using. He could make a good guess, and it delighted him. "Only things that make your spirit want to stay with your body." Experimentally, he ran his tail in a swift caress over her heated cheek. She was still nervous about his hands—perhaps it was his claws. But his tail she found amusing and peculiarly safe, and he used it to his advantage.

She appeared to be lost in thought, and pretended not to notice when his tail slid over her shoulder and wrapped around her wrist. It was the slight dimpling of her cheek that gave her pretense away.

Controlled she was, but there was also humor in her, if not mischief. He could almost remember having a mate with mischief—but he would make do with humor. She was so much better than being Alone. He tightened his tail a bit, though not enough to betray his desperation. He could make do with Aren.

TEN

I wiggled onto my stomach to get away from the raiders' camp. The earth guardian's shaper, who wore the body of an old, old man with none of the infirmities such a body should have, wiggled with me. I wasn't sure if the earth guardian sent him to watch over us, or to keep the shaper out of trouble.

The hob moved much more quietly than either of us, his gray coloring and brown clothes blending into the early morning light so well, that he almost disappeared in the grasses without magic.

The raiders had chosen to hide their camp in the trees, reasoning that if we couldn't find it, we wouldn't be sneaking up on them from the forest. Even so, they would keep a heavy guard on that side of the camp because the trees afforded an attacking enemy good cover.

We'd sneaked up on them from the field side because they wouldn't be looking for trouble from there, and because we had the hob's ability to hide in plain sight. I'd decided to count sleepers for Koret, so we'd have a better idea of the number of raiders. There were fewer than I'd expected.

We were almost safe when it started to rain again, making the mud . . .

. . . *soft under my fingers. Hunger was hard in my belly. I looked across the field of sleeping men and smiled in anticipation of the blood that would flow. I heard a snigger beside me and turned to hush that one. If they didn't hear us until we were upon them, there would be better eating. On the other hand, fighting was good, too. I remembered the feeling of bone breaking beneath my fingers and the feeling was good.*

Caefawn's hand was hard over my mouth and his body covered mine, holding it still. I struggled underneath him, but he was amazingly strong. None of the bits of training Koret and Kith had given me had any effect at all.

Behind the hold of his hand I screamed in frustration, and a little in the age-old fear of a fish caught in a net. If he didn't let me up to warn them, the raiders whose camp we'd been spying on were going to end up dinner (or breakfast) for the hillgrims.

I resorted to an old trick I'd learned when Quilliar used to cover my mouth. Caefawn's hand was locked under my chin, but I managed to stick out my tongue anyway. His hand tasted of mud and rotting leaves, but my resolve was rewarded when he pulled it away in instinctive revulsion. The mud removed the last lingering taste of remembered blood, but I wasn't sure it was really an improvement.

I spit out a piece of grass and grunted, "Get off me."

He rolled off. I gathered my legs under me, and sprinted back to the camp we'd just left. We'd almost made it back to the trees, and the first stretch of field I ran over had been turned by Daryn's plow, but hadn't been harrowed to smoothness. Plow horses didn't have much trouble with the ground, but people did. I fell twice, but used the momentum to roll again to my feet.

"Ware, to arms, to arms," I bellowed. If I was grinning, it was because I was imagining the expression on Caefawn's face. He must think I'd lost my mind. Only shock could have stopped him from catching me. "Attack coming from the hills! Hillgrims!" Not that anyone in the camp would know what a hillgrim was, but the name sounded nasty enough to carry its own warning.

As I pelted across the smooth part of the field, heading toward the rise where their camp was, it occurred to me that running into a camp of nervous raiders who thought I was the enemy wasn't a bright idea. I was armed only with a knife; the crossbow was hanging under a tree on the other side of the field. It would be hard enough to crawl through the muck, and I hadn't wanted to do it with my crossbow because the harness that held it to my back wasn't tight enough to hold it steady while I crawled. I'd have to fix that, but for tonight I'd left it on a tree.

I had time, running across the field, to wonder why I was so worried about hillgrims munching on a few raiders.

"Beware, hillgrims," bellowed a deeper voice just behind me.

It wasn't the hob, so it must have been the shaper. I glanced to my right and was treated to the sight of a hundred-year-old man running like a deer. He grinned at me happily. I didn't see Caefawn.

The men were on their feet and armed as I topped the rise. Most of them were looking at me—the moon was still old enough so they could see me in its light—so I pointed frantically behind them.

"The west, the west!" I screamed.

But from the swearing beginning on the hill side of their camp, I suspected that my cries wouldn't be necessary much longer. There was a howling battle cry, and most of the men turned from me and ran to face the real threat.

Unfortunately, two of them remained. One of them was staring at the old man, who grabbed a stout stick from the woodpile and jumped over an empty cooking pot half as high as he was, all the while howling madly, "Hillgrims! Hillgrims! Fun to kill hillgrims!"

The other took a step closer to me, sword at the ready. "You?"

It was Quilliar. The other Quilliar.

I nodded. When he didn't strike immediately, I headed for the woodpile, too.

Quilliar was still waiting when I turned, his sword blocking the other man, who apparently had recovered enough from the sight of the shaper to decide I was a threat.

"Why did you warn us?" Quilliar asked.

Why indeed? Because I trusted Caefawn's judgment, I'd come to accept that the village might need them to survive. Acceptance was a long way from risking my life to save them. They'd killed my family. When I thought of it, I knew I would kill the raiders I'd killed again if I were given the chance. Why fight for them, then? The answer, when it came, bothered me. I shoved it to the side and gave them a simple answer they could accept.

"Have you ever seen a hillgrim?" I asked, an arm-long stick in each hand. "If you had, you wouldn't ask me. Besides, I suspect our village and your company are going to need each other once the wild fully recovers. The hob tells me that goblins and trolls are hard to fight."

He weighed my answer, then turned to the other man. "She's with us. At least for now."

He was right. I would welcome the chance to die for the village because I didn't believe they'd ever let me live with them. A sort of variation upon the adolescent theme of "I'll die, and then they'll be sorry." I would always be alone.

I heard the shaper's howl again and, involuntarily, I

grinned. I wasn't alone. I had the earth spirit's guard and the hob.

I started toward the sounds of battle, more because I was distracted by my thoughts than because I was eager to fight. Because something had occurred to me.

I had never really been alone. Why had I thought that Quill and I were the only ones hiding what we were?

Fallbrook and Beresford both were thick with magic. There wasn't a family in either village who didn't have a near relative taken by the bloodmages in the last three generations. I could even make a fair stab at guessing who the village mageborn were: the ones who hated me the most. I'd felt so alone after Quilliar died. It hadn't occurred to me that I wasn't.

I darted around a tent and found a raider struggling with a hillgrim on his back. He'd dropped his sword and was trying to pry it off, but the 'grim had locked its jaws in the thick leather of a gaudy protective collar the raider wore around his throat.

My weapons were too stout to do what I intended, so I grabbed a pair of wooden tent spikes set nearby. Stepping behind them both, I slid my chosen weapons between them. I braced the free end of each stick against the raider's leather-armored back and used the leverage to force the hillgrim to break its hold or let my sticks crush its throat.

It released the raider, reached behind, and grabbed me across the shoulder, wedging its claws in the soft flesh under my arm.

A crossbow bolt took the 'grim through the skull, about two fingerspans from my nose, with a dull sound. With such a close-up view, I could tell it was from my bow.

"Thanks, Caefawn," I murmured, shaking free of the dead hillgrim.

Trust the hob to do the most useful thing and grab my crossbow. No doubt he was perched high in one of the trees, killing hillgrims much more efficiently than any of us on the ground.

"Thanks, brother," said the man, whose back was bleeding from the scratches the hillgrim had made.

He picked up his sword. He turned to me, and his jaw dropped. I tapped him on the head with a spike. Gently.

"Close your mouth and watch your front," I said, nodding at the hillgrim darting under someone's legs to attack him. Then, remembering the odd stillness that had held me when the hillgrim had attacked me on the Hob, I added, "Don't meet their eyes."

As I left the raider to aid another man with a similar problem, I called a belated "You're welcome."

This time I didn't try subtlety, I just jabbed one end of my right spike into the hillgrim's ear with the weight of my body behind it. The end of the spike was sharp and slid easily for a few inches. I pulled my knife and used the handle to hammer the spike in deeply enough to kill the hillgrim. I had to pry the creature's jaw open to free the raider, who'd fallen to his face, crying for help from the One God. A true believer, I thought. There were no more unoccupied hillgrims in the immediate area, so I took a good look at the raider's wound.

"The One God was with you today," I announced briskly. "The 'grim got a mouthful of your leather armor, but not even a bit of flesh."

He turned over, a lad even younger than Quilliar. The bridge of his nose was freckled. He looked at me for a moment, then took my hand when I offered it, and got to his feet.

Without a word we both turned back to the fight.

It didn't take me long to realize that I was able to help the other fighters because anytime a wildling started for me, it was felled with a crossbow bolt. Caefawn was good; no, better than good, because I was good and he was better.

I caught occasional views of the shaper in his old

man's body as he put his club to good use. More often I heard him, cackling like a demented fiend and singing nonsense songs in a high, carrying voice. Even to me, who knew what he was, it was uncanny. It didn't seem to bother the hillgrims, but it was fair spooking the raiders.

"We need to get out now," said Caefawn quietly in my ear. "Move slowly, and don't look anyone in the eye. The hillgrims are retreating and the raiders will notice you before long, so it's time to go. As long as no one thinks to look for you, he won't see you."

His hand on my shoulder, he guided me around the battlefield. I wished he'd move his fingers so they weren't pressed to the wound the first 'grim had given me, but I didn't want to say anything to break his spell.

The hob's grip kept me to a slow walk until we reached the cover of the trees. Then he pulled us to a run. Exhaustion from the fighting caught up with me too soon, but the raiders wouldn't be searching through these woods for a while. At least not until they'd counted their dead and wounded.

I sat down on a rock that looked smooth enough to be more comfortable than the wet, pine needle-covered ground.

"What's wrong with your arm?" asked Caefawn after studying me a while.

He didn't give me a chance to answer, just pulled aside my shirt. Ignoring my yelps, the hob took a look at the cuts under my arm.

"Sore," he determined, "but not serious."

He took a little flask from one of the bags he wore around his waist. I could smell the alcohol before it hit my skin, and I whined as softly as I could when it hit.

"This is like a cat scratch," he said. "It'll feel better once it's cleaned off."

I muttered something uncomplimentary, and he laughed.

"Mischief," he said obscurely, then chided me. "Next time you want to alert a camp of armed men, do me a favor and think of a safer way. I suppose we also need to do something about those visions. If I hadn't been there, you'd have had the whole of them upon you before you could defend yourself."

The euphoria of the run came back to me as the pain of my cuts faded. I grinned at him. "Good thing you were there." I gave him a speculative look. "I thought you couldn't do that invisible trick from this side of the river."

"You mean when I got you out of it? We weren't invisible, just camouflaged. In the heat of a battle, there's more than enough confusion to make it as effective as invisibility. If someone had been looking for you, they'd have seen us."

Having caught my wind, I stood up and started back toward the village. It was going on to full daylight, and I needed to get some sleep. "I wonder what the raiders will make of my warning them."

He sniggered. "I hadn't figured on you. If Rook is smart, your village won't have any more serious problems from the raiders."

I raised my eyebrows at him. "Who?"

"Remember the two raiders who listened to you *speak* that first day?"

He gave speak the same emphasis that I gave the *sight*. Perhaps it hadn't been the White Beast's presence that encouraged the raiders to listen.

"Yes."

"The older one is Rook, second in command. I've been talking to him quite a bit. The raiders have been having some problems. Something's been getting into their stores. Horses are going lame for no reason. Their leader's getting a reputation for bad luck."

I laughed. "Rook will be better?"

"He's come to see the error of their ways," replied the hob. "It should work."

He sounded a little tentative, but I'd come to believe in his infallibility. The hob had changed the villagers' luck. Smiling, I looked down upon my cottage from the slopes above it. We'd come up with a way to appease the earth spirit; the raiders would join us and help; Fall-brook would grow and thrive. With the luck of the hob on our side, what else could happen?

"WHY ARE WE GOING ALL THE WAY UP HERE?" I ASKED from Duck's back as we trotted up the path to the Hob. It was light out, but the rain made it less pleasant than it might have been. I yawned; I hadn't gotten much sleep after coming back from fighting the raiders. Caefawn had awakened me before the sun had risen well past the top of the mountains.

The hob looked at me as if I were an idiot. "Didn't you ask me to teach you how to keep the visions from overwhelming you?"

I considered it. "I think that was your idea."

"Do *I* know anything about how visions work?" he asked, then continued without giving me a chance to say anything. "Of course not. No self-respecting hob would ever dream of having visions."

I pulled off my wet hat and hit him with it lightly. "No hob would ever dream of being self-respecting," I returned roundly as I set the hat back on my head. "If he found he was in danger of it, he'd have to do something drastic."

He laughed. "True, lady. All too true. Well, then, I ask you, how am I to help you control your visions?"

"I thought that was what I should ask you," I said, yawning again. "Seeing as you're so determined to teach me."

"True, but you didn't know to ask it, did you?" He

gave me a flirtatious glance before turning his attention back to where he was running.

If he was going to play with words, I could, too. "Then why are you asking me to answer it?" I ducked under a low-hanging branch.

"Because I am not a respectable hob."

I laughed. "Enough, already. Why are we going to the Hob?"

"Because I think I know how to help you—but I need the mountain to show you."

We took a different path up the mountain than I had ever taken. But then, I'd been on the Hob only a handful of times. The rain stopped falling, leaving behind the fresh scent of a newly washed world. The sun began warming the wetness from my rough wool cloak.

Duck enjoyed the sun, snorting and curveting as no responsible farm horse ever would. The hob was certainly having an effect on my horse—on me, too, for that matter. By all rights I should have been fretting and stewing about how we were going to appease the earth spirit and keep the villagers from assassinating me on sight, or I should have been examining my possibly upcoming nuptials and chewing my nails. Instead, I was chasing after the hob and enjoying it. His boundless energy and enthusiasm, coupled with the warm sun, made worry impossible.

The path we took wasn't well suited for a horse. Duck and I jumped over several piles of trees, and slipped and slid around a boulder too big to jump. The faint trail we followed didn't climb up the mountain, but meandered here and there around her sides.

We topped a rise into a small meadow flanked by steep mountainsides. On the far side of the meadow was a tight growth of brush and trees. I sat back, and Duck halted with a snort and toss of his head, mouthing the bit and making it jingle musically.

"Faker," I accused him. "I didn't even pull the reins."

Duck snorted and took advantage of the loose reins to drop his head and snitch a mouthful of grass.

"Well trained horses don't eat with a bit in their mouths," I informed him. He ignored me, so I turned my attention to Caefawn. "This is as far as Duck can go. There's no way for him to get through that mess of trees, and the sides of the mountain are too steep for him to climb."

The hob nodded. "If you wait for me here, I'll get what we came for. It'll take me but a minute." He strode across the meadow, then stopped. "We'll be here a while after that, so you might as well unsaddle Duck." He continued toward the greenery, keeping to a brisk walk for a few strides then breaking into a run—as if unable to contain himself another moment.

I slid off Duck's back and, following Caefawn's advice, unsaddled him. After a moment's thought, I took off his bridle. We'd become close comrades over the past few months. I didn't think that he'd run off; the grass here was long and full of clover. I'd probably have a hard time getting him to leave it.

I lay across a large, flat boulder. If I bent just right, I could avoid most of the sharp places. The grass was too wet to be comfortable. I closed my eyes, just for a while. I dozed, dreaming of a motherly woman who patted my hand and told me, oddly enough, that I was most pleasing. I couldn't quite work up the energy to ask pleasing to whom or for what.

"Sleeping again?" asked the hob.

He was sitting beside me and, like Duck, he had a strand of grass sticking out of his mouth.

"I usually do, if I'm up all night fighting hillgrims." I rolled to my feet. "What is that?"

He held a body length of cedar in his hands, twisted and knotted as cedar tends to be, though the end effect was a straight line. Long, stringy bits of bark dangled from it, and there were twigs of greenery here and there.

"Cedar," he said, as if I didn't know.

"And what's it for?" I persisted with obvious patience.

"For an anchor, my sweet. Cedar's hold is as strong as its scent."

He broke off the remaining leaves, then drew one of his claws down the side of the limb to break the surface of the bark. He peeled the bark off in long strips, wet with the yellow tissue that protected the inner wood. When he was finished, he held a gaudy staff of wood striped pale and red, with knots and twists aplenty.

"Take this," he said, handing the staff to me.

It was heavier than I expected. If it had all been stretched straight, it would have been half again as long, which explained the extra weight.

"Now what?" I asked.

"Well," he said, "when you were telling me about your visions, I thought of a kite in the wind—tugged here and there, willy-nilly. It occurred to me that you needed a string to tie you to yourself, so when the wind blows, it cannot pull you too far without your consent."

"It looks more like a staff than a string to me," I said, tongue in cheek.

He snorted. "Feckless lass. It's a serious business. I've seen you when the visions take you—you've no defenses. If that ghost had come when you were looking at some ancient ancestor of mine as he carved a silly warning in the rock, you'd be haunting my mountain even now."

"*You're* calling *me* feckless?" I said with mock incredulity.

He showed his fangs. "I'm not the one who ran into a camp of armed enemy, my sweet. The cedar might not help at all, I don't know. But you can try."

So I sat on the ground with the staff across my legs, holding it with both hands. Caefawn folded his legs nimbly, one across the other, and faced me, tail twitching like an anxious cat's.

"Call the vision," he said.

While he was tutoring me in spirit-speaking, I'd realized summoning a vision wasn't all that different from calling spirits. Some of the most powerful approached me, and the others might come to my beckoning. I hadn't applied it to my visions yet, but this was as good a time as any to try.

What I really wanted to know was what was happening with the raiders—but whatever it was that kept me from seeing them was still in effect. So I received something different.

Music drifted from his strings, called by skillful fingers. Wandel hummed a bit with the music, absorbed in the chords he summoned. He stopped abruptly and shook his head. He played four or five notes over several times, varying the last note until he was satisfied.

"Come back now, Aren."

When I had visions, it seemed like my body became less real than the sights or sounds that passed through my mind. This time was no exception, but the cedar staff held substance my body did not. Even as I thought about it, I broke free of the vision.

"It worked," I said, smiling. Both Caefawn's prop and my new technique. It wouldn't save me from falling off Duck when a vision struck (which I'd done once), but at least I could avoid lying around waiting for marauding hillgrims (or whatever new creepy-crawly appeared next) to find me.

He matched my smile with one of his own. "Good. Cedar's pull is not all that strong. Once you understand how it works, you can do without it. No sense getting dependent on props. Try it again."

I tried the raiders' camp again, but instead of focusing on the raiders, I tried to picture Rook's face. I hadn't tried an individual before, and this time the *sight* started to come to my call. The sensation of pressure against my temples was almost too strong to bear. It wasn't exactly painful, but extremely uncomfortable. I kept my eyes open, mostly to see if I could.

Caefawn's face faded to blackness, but nothing replaced it but the strong smell of meat cooking over an open fire.

"So what are we going to do now?" The voice belonged to Rook's Quilliar.

"I don't know." Rook's voice was unhurried. *"I suppose—it's time to come back now."*

His voice slid into Caefawn's deeper tones.

This time it was easier to pull back to myself. Maybe because the vision wasn't as strong, but I felt as if I were controlling it rather than the other way around.

"Good," said Caefawn, as my eyes refocused on his face.

I grinned in triumph. Not only was I learning to control my vision, but I'd gotten past whatever it was that guarded the raiders. Before I could tell him, though, the *sight* caught me up in an implacable grip. The strength of its hold made my attempts to avoid it seem like the fluttering of a chick just hatched. The smell of cedar faded to nothing.

When the hob was trying to get me to find the earth spirit, I'd had the sensation of soaring over the ground. Now I felt a sensation very similar. I could *see* . . .

. . . the two of us staring at one another, the hob's tail wrapped around my wrist and his hands at my shoulders before I was pulled away. The Hob—the mountain version—lay beneath me and I floated over her ridges and past them to Silvertooth's broken body, which was covered with new growth of grass and thorn. Something grabbed me, and my speed increased until the ridges below me became a blur. Then it stopped. I couldn't be certain where I was, for the trails and ridges were no longer familiar. But the man . . . I knew the man.

He rode a dark horse and wore a bloodred cloak. Behind him trotted three men dressed in black, Kith's old uniform, on horses tired and wet. Rain poured down as the sky wept. Lightning flashed and the wind turned branches into whips that beat and slashed at those who dared ride through the weather.

For an instant, then again as lightning scrawled across the sky, I could see the rocky outcrop topping the crest of the mountain they rode around. One of the horses stumbled over nothing. His rider called something—I could hear his voice but not his words. The front rider stopped his horse and listened. Lightning flashed, and his white face stood out in bas-relief. Mad eyes in a face that might have come from any family in Fallbrook—though his features were oddly misshapen, melting from the fire beneath. Gray threaded through his mahogany hair, the contrast more vivid because of the additional darkness the rain lent to the rest of his hair.

The bloodmage shook his head and goaded his horse on with sharpened spurs.

"Come on back, love," said the hob.

It was his voice this time, not the staff, that anchored me and drew me back. The smell of green cedar sharp in my nose, I turned to Caefawn.

Fear and rage fought for ascendency. The fear was for Kith, for I knew of nothing else that would have brought the bloodmage here. He had come to kill his creation. Buried underneath was another fear. Too many people who didn't like me knew what I was. The bloodmage would find out and demand my death, as was his king- and god-given right—the price of that long-ago binding of the wildlings.

Fear shortened my breath and caused my limbs to tremble, but it was the rage that won.

My lips drew away from my teeth, hating the raiders had been too difficult. Their Quilliar was no more evil than my Quilliar had been, though it had taken the hob, death, and the duplication of my brother's name to show me that. Their Quilliar had been a sheepherder; Rook (so my vision of him had told me), a lord far more able and kind than Moresh. In a different world they would have been men just like my father and husband, perhaps better men. My parents' death, my husband's death were the fault of some cosmic madness that haunted men of war— deaths I might have been able to stop.

My brother's death, though, belonged to the blood-mage. As the disaster that had descended upon Fallbrook belonged to the bloodmages, all of them. Without them there would have been no unraveling of the binding. No war. No mercenaries-turned-bandits. So I gave Moresh's mage the guilt for all of the deaths of this spring and summer, for every evil thing that had befallen me and mine.

There was some inconsistency in my logic—I knew it even then—but anger clouded my thoughts, and it felt good. I gathered my righteous rage around me like a warm blanket. There was someone to blame for this. I'd thought the bloodmage dead, safe from my wrath. I felt the fury pounding in my blood as if Quilliar's death were just yesterday.

"Aren!" Caefawn peered worriedly into my face. "Aren, what did you see?"

I tamped the rage down gently for later use and said, "Moresh's bloodmage is coming back. I saw him on the old road that runs around the back of Faran's Ridge, near Mole Rock." Caefawn frowned, coming to his feet and pulling me to mine. "He's come for Kith—to kill him."

"When?"

"Moresh gave him three months. Until last spring planting. When the mountain fell, when Moresh died, I thought that would be an end to it."

Caefawn shook his head. "Not yesterday; there was no lightning storm on the ridge yesterday. Not today either, or at least not this morning, although it might rain on the ridge between now and nightfall." He took a deep breath and closed his eyes. After a moment he opened them and shook his head. "The mountain says there won't be such a storm today. Maybe tomorrow."

"Which puts him at the village tomorrow, or possibly the day after." I hugged myself tightly, though I wasn't cold.

Time was giving me perspective, and I felt the rage seeping away. Moresh's bloodmage was no more responsible for my situation than the raiders were. He'd once been a victim, too: I'd never heard of anyone apprenticing to the bloodmages happily. Remembering the relief I'd felt giving him all the guilt and fear that were mine, it was easier to understand the villagers who hated me.

Rage or not, the bloodmage had to be stopped. Though it would have been nice to have more time to prepare, it really didn't matter. I knew what Kith would do—nothing. He'd believed all along that he was living on borrowed time, and he didn't seem very willing to fight for more. Albrin would fight—but he was not yet in shape to be any help. Koret was a trained fighter, but he knew nothing of magic. In any case, the village needed Koret in order to survive; I couldn't risk getting him killed. No more than I would risk Caefawn in a battle that was not his.

There was no one to fight the mage except me.

"So how do I fight a bloodmage?" I asked him.

I noticed for the first time that the hob's ears were pinned back against his skull, though his smile was easy enough. "That's a very good question, but you're asking the wrong person. You forget what the bloodmages did to my people. I was there—and didn't fight very well." His hand flexed on his staff. He continued softly, "I don't remember it, but I dream of it every night."

"You couldn't have done anything," I said, his pain drawing me out of my preoccupation with the bloodmage. "You were wounded so badly your people gave you to the mountain because they could not help you.

What could you have done that your people did not? From the stories I've heard about the binding, the magic was worked far from here, far from the Hob. There were no battles to be fought. It's said they sacrificed a dragon to power the spell. If the mountain couldn't fight it, there was nothing you could do."

"Whatever happened, it is long since over," he agreed bitterly. Bitterness was not something I would have credited the hob with, though he had cause for it.

I didn't want to hurt him further and risk bringing back memories that the mountain had seen fit to take. However, still less did I want to face the bloodmage without any idea of how to oppose him. So I rephrased my question.

"Have you battled anything with magic?"

"Yes," he said curtly. "Though when it was and what it was I don't know. Detailed advice wouldn't help you anyway. Your powers are not my own, but they are not the bloodmage's either. Use that against him."

"Use what?" I asked, losing my own battle with bitterness. "Visions? Shall I ask him to meet me in the night so I can call up ghosts? Ghosts he can doubtless use better than I can—death dealer that he is."

He spread his hands apart in a gesture of surrender. "I have nothing more to offer you. I'm not certain there is a way to vanquish such a one, but I'll help as I can."

"No," I said. I didn't want to risk the hob, not just because he was the key to the village's survival, but because I didn't want to risk losing him as I'd lost so many people I loved. I stared at him, and admitted to myself that I loved him.

Caefawn rose to his feet, shaking out his cloak. He said mildly, "I swore to help the village survive. If I think that its chances are better with Kith alive and willing to fight, it's no one's business but my own. Come, I'll escort you far enough so that you can find your own way back. Then I need to look into a few things."

• • •

I WASN'T SLEEPY AT ALL ON THE RIDE BACK. IF THE mage wasn't enough, there were the berserkers who followed him. One-armed, Kith'd been able to stand off the raiders for the better part of a day. What could he have done had he been whole?

To fight the berserkers, the village only had two well-trained fighters. Two. And one of them wouldn't fight. I knew Kith—better now than before he'd left for war. He'd already accepted his death, distancing himself from people whenever possible. Not only because he'd been altered by magic into some kind of superior soldier, as I'd thought when he'd first returned, but because he knew he had only a short time to live. He wouldn't fight it, because deep inside he felt that he deserved nothing better. He'd been tainted with death magic, and the One God taught that such men were already dead.

Koret was good, but he had nowhere near Kith's proficiency. I'd seen them spar a time or two, and even I could tell the difference. He would stand little chance against the bloodmage's men.

There was Wandel. From what he and Kith had said, they both considered him able to fulfill the king's command to kill Kith if Moresh failed to do so. I thought about the harper, who was even now writing songs of thanks to the earth, and wondered how he'd stand up against a berserker.

Duck tripped over a small, downed tree hidden beneath a clump of grass. I noticed then that we were alone; Caefawn must have decided I could find my way down from here.

He would help, he'd said so—there was no reason to feel abandoned. A sudden thought caught me like a fist in my stomach. I remembered his ears pulled back against his head like a stallion whose territory was threatened. I sat back, and Duck stopped.

He wouldn't, I thought, *not so far from the mountain,*

where his powers would be little better than nothing. But even as I thought it, I worried. The woods were his element, and even so far from the mountain he might feel confident. Three berserkers and a mage against a hob— would those odds worry the hob, who ate (if he could be believed) hillgrims for breakfast? Who'd greeted my suicidal run this morning with laughter and a "be smarter next time" speech?

I tried to convince myself I was wrong. But all I could see was the look in his eyes when he told me that he, of all people, would be of no use against a bloodmage. It wasn't just sorrow there, or anger. It was guilt.

Who better than I to understand that? By virtue of my *sight*, I'd been given guilt enough to fell an ox. Guilt for Daryn and my family. Guilt for surviving when they had not. How much more would the hob feel it? He was the last of his kind, the only one the mountain had saved.

I threw myself forward, and Duck, catching my sudden urgency, took off like a shot. He was traveling far too fast for the track, but I didn't care. I had the sick feeling I'd traded one person I loved for another. I didn't want to be responsible for anyone else's death, least of all Caefawn's. If I could get to town soon enough, perhaps I could arm the village—or at least the patrollers. If I could get enough people and run them up to Faran's Ridge, maybe Caefawn would stand a chance.

The track we followed turned onto a trail both Duck and I recognized, and he stretched out even more. Running downhill always felt like falling to me, with the horse frantically trying to get his feet down faster than his body.

The mountain shuddered under Duck's hooves, and we fell. Luckily the slope was shallow, and Duck scrambled to his feet almost before I quite knew we'd gone down. I could feel the mountain's rage, and knew my suppositions about the hob were correct. He'd told her where he was going, and she knew who'd told him about the bloodmage. She wasn't happy with me.

Fear sped Duck faster than any goad, and we jumped and dodged and wove like a shepherd's dog as Duck fled down the side of the mountain. Tree branches caught at the cedar staff, but I held it fast.

"I know," I shouted, though I wasn't certain the mountain would hear me. "I'm getting help."

Duck fell to his knees again as the solid footing shifted under him a second time. I steadied him as he scrambled to his feet, and he redoubled his speed. Great muscles trembled with his effort and his breath escaped in noisy gulps. If we did get off the mountain, there was a good chance he'd never run again.

The brief break from the rain was over, and the ground grew wet and slippery. The mountain sent rocks tumbling after us, some of them as big as Duck. One crashed into a nearby tree, knocking the old giant to the ground in front of us.

Given no choice in the matter, Duck bunched his hind legs underneath him and jumped with the power bred to drag an iron plow deep into the earth. I'd just enough warning to bury both hands in his mane and hang on.

It wasn't a graceful jump; he landed with both hind feet tangled in branches and went down for a third time. But those same branches cushioned our fall. I threw myself as far away from him as I could get, to give him room as he somehow scrambled up.

Duck stood there a moment, head hanging in exhaustion. His chest was foam-covered, and a good portion of the water dripping off his back was not rain. His knees were cut and scratched from his earlier falls, but only the skin was damaged, as far as I could tell.

The earth shook slightly one more time, but there were no more boulders or rocks. The sudden silence made me realize just how loud the earth had been. Now there was only the sound of the rain. A flash of lightning hit in the direction of Faran's Ridge.

"I thought you said there wouldn't be a thunderstorm tonight," I accused, but the mountain didn't answer.

The lightning meant there would be no time to get help. I didn't doubt the hob could make it to Faran's Ridge to confront the bloodmage, but it would take us mere humans a full day to get there.

Duck and I continued toward the village at a slow walk.

I didn't doubt that the bloodmage would reach Fall-brook. I *knew* it. If I let go of the staff I held, I would see it, too. The vision hovered just behind my eyes. I gripped the staff tighter and tried not to think.

I WALKED BESIDE DUCK ALL THE WAY TO THE INN. There were a few people out in the rain. The smith's wife gathered her children together and hustled them into the smithy. I guess I must have looked pretty battered.

Duck picked up his pace for a few steps when he saw the inn, but he soon slowed again. He waited patiently as I stripped him of his tack and wiped him off with a knobby towel. I put him in his stall and measured him a bit of grain. His chest was wet with sweat and rain, but cool from the long walk. I wouldn't have to worry about giving him too much water.

"What's wrong?" Kith's voice didn't surprise me, even though I hadn't heard him come in.

I hooked the stall door and turned around. In the silence between us I played out what would happen if I told him.

He would tell the villagers that it was between him and the bloodmage. They would let him surrender himself. His father was too ill to protest; Merewich could not risk losing what control he had of the village; Koret would see it as Kith's choice.

If the village gave Kith to the bloodmage, the mage

wouldn't harm the village. He would stay here; there was no other place for him to go. Me, he would kill, but he might be persuaded not to kill Kith because all of the reasons to kill him were gone. Though from what I knew and what Kith had said about him, that was not likely. Then what?

If the earth spirit had not believed me when I told him we were not allied with the bloodmages, he would have destroyed Fallbrook's food supply. What would he do when he discovered a bloodmage living here?

I had the means to defeat the mage. I had known it all along—I'm sure the hob did, too. But I wouldn't have done it for revenge or to save Kith's life. But for the village, I would do what I wouldn't for the man who was as close to me as my brother. In order to accomplish it, I'd need to confront the bloodmage alone. I looked into Kith's eyes and knew he wouldn't let me do that. So I lied.

"Nothing." No, that wouldn't do. It had to be obvious from Duck's condition that something had happened. So I added, "Pox-eaten hob. Went off to get himself killed." The tears in my voice were real.

Kith's body tightened with . . . eagerness, I thought. "Where?"

I widened my eyes at him. "What, and get you killed, too? Besides, he's right; it's his business." His chance to drive away the demons that rode him at night. I wish I thought he'd banish them. I knew something of what the hob could do, and what he could not. Three berserkers and a bloodmage, off the mountain, were too much even for him.

"I see," said Kith, relaxing a little.

If I closed my eyes, I knew I would *see*, too. So I reached over and grabbed the cedar staff I'd laid against the stable wall. Time enough for visions when I was alone.

Focusing on Kith had helped. I wiped the tears from

my eyes, so I could see him. Before I brought my arm down, Kith caught me in an awkward hug that was over almost before it had begun.

It must have embarrassed him as much as it startled me, for he turned and took a few brisk steps toward the entrance. He stopped, then turned on his heel to face me. "Aren, I could love you no more dearly had you been my own sister."

"I love you, too, Kith," I replied, wondering why he'd chosen this moment for his revelation.

He nodded his head as if we'd been discussing the weather, and continued out the door.

As soon as he was gone, I sat outside Duck's stall and relaxed my mental hold on the cedar, though I left my hand on it. It hadn't helped the last time, when the *sight* was strong, but it couldn't hurt. The vision swept in like an unwelcome guest left knocking at the door too long.

The bloodmage rode into Fallbrook alone. The streets were deserted. The only sound was the breeze whispering past the chimes that hung from several doorways.

There was a tear in the mage's cloak that widened and narrowed with the rhythm of his horse's gait. The horse walked slowly. It looked as if it were held up only by the reins that the mage held in his left hand. His right hand held a handful of small wooden beads strung on a minuscule black chain.

It ended there, by no effort of my own. I was glad it had. I knew enough. He would ride into town in the late morning from the east. He must be coming over Fell Bridge. I didn't know why the streets were empty, but I knew why there was a howl of grief locked in my chest. The chain he'd held was the same one Caefawn wore in his ear. It was black with dried blood, hob's blood.

There in the shadows of the stable, I snarled with rage. I held that rage to my heart with all my will, for behind the anger were sorrow and fear. If I wasn't successful, the village would die.

I had the evening and night to gather my forces. I used the cedar staff and levered myself to my feet. Time enough for grief when it was over. For now I harnessed my rage. At the very least the bloodmage would know that he had been opposed. I owed that to Kith. To Caefawn.

ELEVEN

I led Torch from his stall. Duck had given all he had, and Torch was the only other horse I trusted not to run when the spirits came. He'd been trained as a warhorse for Kith, so he'd stand for things any sane horse would run from. It also meant he'd be testy with anyone but Kith on him. I was hoping he'd remember me from when I'd helped train him.

I talked to him while I put Kith's saddle on his back and tightened the cinch. "It's partly for him, you know. If someone doesn't step in, he'll die. So you're going to have to bear with me, just for tonight. Quiet, now, I don't want him back here. I don't want him to know what I'm up to, or he'll fight for the wrong side."

I adjusted the stirrups, untying the laces, pulling the leather shorter, then retying the laces with the speed of long practice. There was an old waterproof cloak hanging at the back door of the stables. The deerhide it was made from was still soft and pliable despite its obvious age.

Leading Torch, I walked out to the small run behind

the barn. The field wasn't much, just enough to let a horse stretch his legs a bit. It was surrounded on four sides by buildings, but there was a narrow alleyway between it and the fourth building. While I'd been in the stable, the rain had turned into a downpour.

Wandel's mare was turned out. She raised her head briefly, but when she saw it was only us, she dropped her muzzle to nibble at the overgrazed stubble covering the ground.

Torch stiffened and blew air when I mounted.

"Come on, Torchy. You know me. I'm not stealing you, just borrowing you for a bit." I kept my body loose and my voice soft. If I got nervous now, he'd fight. I was counting on some very old memories to get us through this.

His dark-tipped ears flattened and released, signaling his uncertainty. He stomped a front foot impatiently, then lifted both off the ground briefly. On Faran's Ridge lightning struck again; I tried not to pay attention.

I asked Torch to move forward. He hesitated before crossing the field in a stiff-backed walk. I set him through his paces: slow walk; speed it up; shift his front quarters to one side or the other; then turn attention to his hind legs. We sidepassed left, then right. By the time we'd worked into a canter, he'd decided I belonged on his back. I collected him and stopped him at the corner where the stable met the inn. By taking the diagonal across the field, I could work up enough speed for him to jump the fence.

I set him at it. We'd take the fence at the opposite corner. It would make the obstacle he had to jump wider, but it would give him half a stride more landing room. It was no wider nor higher than jumps I'd taken on him before. But I hadn't taken him out in a thunderstorm.

Torch danced with eagerness, knowing, as horses will, what it was I intended to ask of him. He took the fence handily, resenting it when I asked him to slow to a walk.

I intended to take him through the village by the alley-
ways; if we trotted, someone was sure to hear us. It
would be best if no one saw me, especially riding Kith's
horse.

The alleys in Fallbrook twisted around more than the
roads—which weren't exactly the King's Highway.
Some of the alleys were cobbled, and the heavy rain
made them slick.

I rode around the edge of someone's storage shed, then
down a gully into someone else's backyard. That's when
I heard voices ahead. There were a number of people
talking quietly. Torch stopped almost before I asked him.
I couldn't see into the next yard because of a bramble
rose hedge and a sharp rise to the ground.

I was still trying to remember who lived in the next
house when someone screamed.

I leaned forward, and Torch climbed the steep, mud-
slick surface of the alley at a flat-out run. The hedge
continued around the alley end of the yard, but it was
lower, and Torch popped over it without slowing his
headlong flight.

There were six or seven people in the yard. One of
them was down, rolling from side to side with something
dark and furry on his back. In the two strides it took
Torch to reach the man's side, I saw that the animal was
one of the odd creatures I'd seen in the Fell bog.

Pikka, that's what Caefawn had called it. I jumped off
Torch's back while he was still running and used the
momentum to lend strength to the blow I struck with my
cedar staff. It hit the creature in the ribs with a satisfying
crunch.

The pikka shrieked and, unlike the hillgrim, it let go
and turned to face me. Pig-sized, intelligent eyes assessed
me as I appraised it in return. Growling low in its throat,
the pikka paced back and forth, looking for a path to me
that would elude the bite of my staff. I backed away,
little by little, trying to lure it from the fallen man.

Pikka used magic to go undetected.

If I'd been riding Duck, the second pikka would have killed me. As it was, I heard Torch squeal and felt the ground shake beneath his hooves. I turned my head just in time to see him strike another pikka behind me. My lapse in attention gave the wounded one time to slip past the cedar staff and attack.

I turned farther away from it, and the pikka grabbed for the nape of my neck. It got a mouthful of hair and cloak instead. I dropped over backward, on top of the pikka, jerking loose the frayed strings that held the cloak to me. I rolled over without shifting my weight off the animal. Its sharp claws and sharper teeth were, for the moment, tangled in the tough old cloak. I tried to reach for my knife, but when I loosened my hold on the cloak, the pikka's struggles increased and I had to take a better grip. I could see my knife, touch the haft with my elbow, but it was tantalizingly out of reach.

And then it wasn't.

The knife slid out of its sheath and onto the cloak. Despite the thrashing of the pikka, the knife traveled smoothly up the cloak until I could shift and snatch it up.

Knife in hand, I looked across the wet grass to the pikka's victim. It was Poul. He'd rolled over onto his stomach and his eyes were on mine. He gave a short, painful nod, then his eyes closed as he grimaced in pain.

My left hand held the pikka's head against the ground while my knees on its shifting shoulders kept it relatively still. I drove the blade of my knife into its throat through the cloak. I stayed where I was until the creature was still.

I looked up and saw the people who'd been gathered in the neat garden. I had to laugh at the irony. The pikka had interrupted a meeting of magic-haters. Poul's mother was there, and the smith's wife. I wondered if the smith knew his wife was involved with the people who'd killed his brother. No, I'd forgotten, he'd been told it was the raiders. Perhaps it had been—or the fetch, or any one of a number of deadly creatures. The pikka weren't the only things invading the valley.

I couldn't help but wonder if the smith's wife had found Touched Banar a burden she could do without— a grown man who couldn't tie his own bootlaces without help. Had she encouraged these people to kill him?

Since everyone was too scared to come closer—scared of me or the pikka, I didn't want to guess—I left the pikka's cloaked body and hurried to Poul. Poul, who'd saved me by using magic to give me the knife.

Poul lay limp, but I could see his chest rise and fall. His shoulder was a mess. Someone should have been trying to stop the bleeding while I was fighting the pikka. He'd lost a lot of blood.

I could almost hear Gram's dry voice saying, "The bleeding will ensure the wound is clean—if it doesn't kill him."

I stripped out of Caulem's green tunic, wadded it up, and pressed it into the wound. Poul's mother knelt on Poul's other side and pulled off her apron. She ripped it into strips and began wrapping the cloth around his shoulder over the tunic, to hold it in place.

"It's bled freely enough to take care of most chances of infection," I said, my voice sounding shaky to my ears. "My gram would tell you to leave the bandaging alone for a bit to let the bleeding stop."

"I've been tending my menfolk long before you were born," she said in the same sour tones she'd always used to hide her soft heart.

I backed away from Poul, glad he wouldn't die—at least not today. My cloak lay in the mud where I'd thrown it. Like me, it was covered in blood. Clad only in Caulem's thin linen undershirt, I shivered in the cold.

I couldn't look at any of the people in the yard. They were the core of the hatred that threatened the village every bit as much as the bloodmage and the earth spirit. I couldn't bear it. So I walked to the pikka Torch had killed. Kith's horse had done a fair job at pounding it flat. I took a close look at the wounds and noticed blistering where Torch's iron-shod hooves had touched flesh.

I pulled the cloak off the one I'd killed. This one had taken far less damage. Long, black fangs showed through lips pulled back by death. It looked more like a small bear than a dog or cat, but its face was narrower. The pikka's side was caved in where my staff had hit it. It would have died soon even if I hadn't managed to slit its throat.

Someone threw a dry cloak around my shoulders. I looked up to meet Poul's mother's eyes.

"I've got to go," I said abruptly. "I have business to attend to. Someone might get the priest—he and Koret have been studying the new creatures that've been plaguing us. Tell him that I think it's a creature the hob called a pikka."

"We'll take care of it," she said.

I looked away and nodded. "Thanks. If more show up, you might try fighting them with steel. The hob says that some of the wildlings are sensitive to it."

Torch was waiting patiently, his rump turned so he wasn't facing into the rain. I looked him over for wounds as best I could in the dimming light. His legs and underside were covered with mud. He didn't limp when I walked him out. I swung to the saddle and settled the cloak so it didn't interfere with riding.

"Aren," she said.

I looked up.

"When people are hurt and scared, they do stupid things. Cruel things."

I thought about Touched Banar and glanced around the yard at the people clustered about Poul, people who almost certainly had something to do with Banar's death. The smith's wife looked up and met my eyes briefly.

I rubbed my face wearily, heartsick, and said, "I hope that thought comforts you, madam." I was going to do something evil myself—who was I to judge these people? "I hope it comforts me, too."

I think she would have said something more, but I leaned forward and Torch lifted into an easy canter, then popped back over the hedge.

I CALLED THE SPIRITS OF THE BOG FIRST, THINKING IT was only just to follow the order Caefawn had laid out. Ghosts, with their ties to bloodmagic, I would leave alone.

The ground gave off sucking sounds as I stepped closer to the bog. My call was strong, driven by my anger and by my hatred of the kind of person I was soon to become. My call echoed in my head like a shepherd's horn.

The noeglins came, not just one this time but all of them. As my call strengthened, I could feel them inside my head, a great, dark wave of maliciousness.

I'd learned a few things about magic from the hob—rituals to twist for my use. I held up a branch of mountain ash, what Caefawn called rowan, stolen from a tree in someone's backyard. My knife in one hand, the branch in the other, I said, "By rowan and iron I bind you to me. By iron, rowan, and the bit of you I hold, you will obey my words."

The slight breeze wafting across the bog stilled for a moment as I spoke.

"You will await me at the eastern entrance to the town tomorrow at dawn. There's a two-story cottage"—where I'd been sleeping—"with moss growing on the roof and a maple tree set to the north of the main doorway. You will stay there, in the attic, until I call for you."

I waited until all the protesting was done before sending them off. I kept something of them inside me, imprisoned in that cold part of my mind. Evil, I thought, not cold. To fight evil, I had to become evil myself.

I tested the power I held. It wasn't a tithe on what the ghost had offered. But the ghost was old, older than the manor, maybe older than the hob's long sleep—and she was gone anyway. I couldn't use ghosts. The bloodmage used death magic, and he was more experienced than I— a valid excuse, but not the real truth. I just couldn't forget Touched Banar's ghost cuddling against me as if I could protect him. They had been human once; the newer ones could be people I knew. I couldn't expose them to the evil I was doing.

Torch shoved his head against my shoulder, and I turned to find him wet with sweat and white-eyed. I patted him consolingly, trying to ignore the noeglins' presence in my mind.

"Come on, Torch," I said. "It'll get worse before it gets better."

So I called the widdles from the gardens and houses, the afanc and fuath from the river, and the frittenings and groggies from the woodlands. Locking them in their own cells in my mind until I thought I might go mad with the screaming, the piteous weeping, the insidious seep of evil.

The sun finished its run in the west, and the weariness of its setting bore down upon my shoulders. But Fallbrook couldn't afford to have me give in to fatigue.

The last of the groggies left my sight. Dizzy with the taste of power, unable to concentrate from the noise in my head, I turned toward Torch and stumbled forward. I didn't see the woman holding his reins until I was near to touching her.

She stood in the open, letting the pale light from the moon touch her face so I could see it better. Her face was ashen, the stubborn mouth tight with fear and sorrow. Her eyes held a wildness, like a trapped wolf. There was something strange about those eyes, and I stared at her until I picked it out. Her pupils were pinpoints, though the night should have opened them until her dark brown eyes were black as night.

I recognized her, of course. "Fetch," I said, though for some reason it was hard to twist my lips around the word.

She smiled, putting Torch's reins into my hand. As soon as the reins left her hands, Torch's ears flattened and his eyes rolled so that I could see the whites. He pranced until I stood between her and him, but he was too well-trained to pull against the bit, though he shook with fear.

"I waited for this," she said, sliding the hand that had held the reins to my cheek. She stepped nearer and pressed her body against mine, her mouth to my mouth, kissing me wetly. "Waited to find you tired and alone." She whispered it in a lover's voice against my lips.

I stood stiffly in her embrace. "Oh, sister," I said, fear tightening my spine. Belief and fear were her weapons: fear of death and pain. "You mischose your time." And I took her with the knowledge I had gained this night. I stole her essence and locked it with the gates of my mind. It was easy because I feared myself far more than I did her.

I was becoming a bloodmage. I'd come to understand it wasn't just the deaths that made bloodmagic so foul, but taking without repayment or consent.

I gave her the same direction that I'd given the other spirits this night, and she replied, "I am with you." Then she faded into nothing.

I mounted Torch and he caught my fear, dancing and snorting until I thought I'd never get him headed home. I could hold nothing more. The meeting with the fetch left me shaking in spasms close to sobs. I was so powerful that I didn't even need to fear a creature such as she.

What I held imprisoned in my mind tainted me until I wanted to wash in the waters of the river, though I knew I would never be clean again—because I wanted the power I held, wanted to roll in it and throw it into the faces of those who'd killed Touched Banar. *Here*, I wanted to say, *here is what you should fear, not the poor god-stricken man whose worst deed was less than a dust mote to my mountain.*

The trapped spirits moaned, but the fetch laughed with my laughter while tears slid down my face.

TORCH WAS SWAYING WITH WEARINESS WHEN I BROUGHT him back to the stables in the dark. I wasn't any better. The spirits under my control wailed and shrieked pleadingly until I wanted to scream at them to be quiet.

Instead, I curried and rubbed Torch until he was clean and dry. I led him to his stall and grained him. I sat down on a bench and leaned against Duck's stall. Daryn's red gelding blew gently in my hair before wandering back to the shadows of his straw-filled box.

Though I fought against sleep, fearing the trapped creatures would escape, my eyes closed . . .

. . . *running through the trees in the dark, faster than humanly possible, the pounding of feet, pulse, and the mad joy of the chase. Ah! This was more gloriously fun than anything he could remember in a long time. Ducking roll to dodge an arrow from nowhere that sent him halfway to the bottom of the mountainside he'd been climbing—all the better to avoid capture.*

Careful not to go too fast and get ahead; they might give up. . . .

Intense red-hot agony as an arrow took Caefawn in the knee. His fall twisted the arrow inside the wound, which popped and cracked heartrendingly.

DARYN SAT ON DUCK'S BACK, SHAKING HIS HEAD.

"You should have told me your nature before I married you. I would have known then that you would be the death of me, for that is the nature of all your breed."

I tried to talk, to explain that it was not my fault, but

somehow the mounted figure turned into Poul cradling a wrapped infant in his arms.

"My son," he said proudly, dismounting and walking closer so that I could see what he held.

When I reached out to open the blankets, there was nothing but the tiny skeleton I'd last seen in Auberg.

Ani came from behind me, pushing me away. "Let me tend the child now, you'll make him cry."

I tried to explain that there was only a skeleton inside the blankets. But before I could finish, she turned back to me. The flesh peeled away from her face.

Poul cried out in horror and ran from her, leaving me alone with his dead wife. My sister.

"It's fine, dear," she said calmly, patting the blanketed baby that rattled every time she touched it. "I'm dead, too. Eaten by the pikka."

Rain began to pour down, slicking my hair to my head.

"Here," said Caefawn, his left leg scarlet with blood from knee to boot. "He won't cry if I hold him."

The arrow was still there in his knee, and it wiggled when he walked.

"Let me get that out for you," I said, kneeling in front of him.

"No!"

But I had already taken hold of the arrow and pulled it out. Lifeblood pooled on the floor and wouldn't stop, no matter how frantically I tried to seal the wound with Caulem's green tunic.

Caefawn reached down and touched my face. "Be at peace. Never you mind, sweetheart. Just remember my name is Neklevar; it means "light in the darkness." Someone should remember the name of the last hob.

"What does Caefawn mean?" I asked, hands wet with his blood. I took one red finger and traced it down my cheek, drawing one of the runes Wandel and I had found carved into a rock on Hob's Mountain.

He touched the rune gently, then his hand fell strength-

*less to his side. "A caefawn is a trader who tricks people
out of their money. He sells a pot for a copper, but when
you take it home, it turns into a feather and flies away."*

*Caefawn turned into a falcon and took flight, spraying
me with blood. I followed him, running as fast as I could.
But there was no sight of him when I came out of the
trees and into a clearing. The earth spirit's snag sat there
with the spirit upon it.*

*He leaned down toward me and said, "What are you
doing here?"*

*I knelt before him, covered in the hob's blood, and
lifted my hands. Blood pooled in my cupped palms and
dripped to the ground.*

*"I see you've been busy, speaker," said the earth
spirit, leaning nearer. "Look at what you've become."*

*I cried, for he said what I already knew. The tears
turned to rain and thunder, and I became a pikka, feeding
on the bodies of my dead.*

I AWOKE IN THE EARLY DAWN WITH THE TASTE OF FRESH
blood in my mouth, and threw up on the ground. Shaking, I opened Duck's stall and took a mouthful of water
from the bucket suspended on a hook near his manger.
The wailing in my mind continued unabated.

Luckily I hadn't fouled my clothes. Ignoring the noise
in my head, I used a forkload of hay to clean up the mess
I'd left. I was just finishing when Kith walked through
the door.

"If you'd asked, I'd have loaned you Torch," he said.

My mind was too busy to allow for clever replies, so
I just nodded and leaned against the wall. I must have
looked really bad, because he walked up to me and put
his hand on my face.

"Not sick," I said, "just tired." My face felt stiff, and
my mouth felt cold and slow. I wanted to bathe the stink
from my soul.

"Rescuing Poul from a . . . what was that word? Pikka?"

I nodded, regretting it almost immediately. The movement brought a rush of pain to join the shouting.

"Merewich swears it's a wolverine, though he's never seen one with curly, black fur."

I grunted this time; it was safer than moving my head.

"Where were you going in such a hurry that it couldn't wait for the rain to let up?" He stepped close to me, touching my collarbone with his hand, staring into my eyes. I wondered if my pupils were pinpoints like the fetch's. "Aren, what's wrong?"

I don't know what I would have told him, but just then the alarm bell rang. Kith hesitated, then turned on his heel and ran.

I could just manage to walk, if I did it slowly. I set the pitchfork aside and picked up the cedar staff from where it had fallen on the ground while I slept. One end was black with dried blood.

By the time I left the stable, there was a fair crowd around the bell. I edged toward the front. Merewich, looking old and frail, stood several paces before the villagers. Behind him, Koret waited silently.

Facing them . . . us, was Rook mounted on a big, nervy gray. On each side of him were two men, also well mounted. Rook had a nasty cut on his lower lip and a bruise on the side of his face.

". . . bought our services in the war," he explained. "But the lord was killed, and the side we fought for was losing. The other side had no need to hire, and ours had no money. We knew—the captain knew—if we continued, we'd be dead in a month at the outside. So he took us raiding."

Rook took a deep breath and continued. "It was something he'd done before, though not recently. There were enough former bandits in our midst that those of us who wished to protest were outnumbered. There weren't many." His horse shifted restlessly.

"Bastards!" spat Talon. The smith broke free from the crowd and took several running steps forward. "Killed my brother, who wouldn't hurt a fly."

Kith slipped out of the crowd behind Talon and touched the big man on the shoulder, whispering something to him. I couldn't tell what it was, but Talon relaxed a little. Perhaps Kith had blamed Banar's death on the wildlings.

Rook's gray tossed his head, dancing a bit. When Rook saw Talon had finished, he continued in the same calm voice. "When he saw this valley, the captain decided we'd stay here. It was small with few defenses. He fancied himself lord of the manor, I think. Before anyone could change his mind, the earthquake hit, and we were trapped here."

"If we agree to accept your offer, what guarantee of behavior do we have?" asked Merewich in the long silence following Rook's narrative. "Many of us have lost family to you."

"The hob suggested we camp outside the town for now," replied Rook. "We'll send no more than two men at a time into the village unless there's an alert."

"At which time you fight for us," Merewich stated, the doubt in his voice obvious. "Let me ask those whose families suffered the most from your predations. Jarol? You lost your brothers in the fighting at the manor."

"Aye," replied Jarol's laconic voice from somewhere behind me. I was dizzy, so I didn't turn to look at him. "But I've another brother, a wife, and two children. Happen I would be happy if the fighting stopped."

Jarol was a mild-mannered farmer, slow to anger. A clever man, too. I wasn't surprised by his reply. Nor would Merewich have been. That Merewich called upon him told me the headman wanted this truce, and was too smart to jump enthusiastically at it until the village was behind him.

"Aren?" asked Merewich without looking at me.

He took me by surprise, for I'd no idea he'd noticed me—besides, who would listen to me? "About what, exactly? I just got here." The spirits I held, sensing my preoccupation, chose to fight for their freedom again. I could have drawn on the strength of one and held them all. I felt the power gathered for the asking, but I chose not to ask. Instead, I drew on the remnants of stubbornness that were all mine to use.

"Aren?" Merewich frowned, turning his head.

Kith shouldered his way to my side and gripped my arm, but I shook him off irritably. "They've come to ask for truce," he said. "Their captain is dead, deposed by this man." He nodded toward Rook.

"She's the one who warned us when the creatures attacked us from the hills," said Rook after a moment. "It's because of her actions I thought we stood a chance of sharing this valley."

I nodded my head. That was right. *Silly me, they'd killed my family and* . . . I bit my lip to clear my head. The impulse to cry "Kill them all" came from the blood lust of those I held and not from any need I had for revenge. Revenge I would save for the bloodmage. At that thought the spirits grew silent, but there was an eagerness now in their waiting stillness.

For now, I had to think. I was a speaker; that should mean something here, too. If only I could think clearly. I had a talk with Kith once. He'd said something about the men he'd fought with. . . .

"Fighting men learn to follow the man who leads them—not just orders, but obedience." My voice was slurring a bit, and I had to overpronounce everything so my audience could understand me. "They have to know what he wants and do it before he asks—otherwise they will die." That much was true. "They cannot afford to ask themselves if what he wants is right or wrong, not if they want to survive. If they cannot fight together, they will die. Just like Fallbrook."

Poul's mother was there, and I met her gaze. "The deeds of the mercenaries must fall upon their captain's back." *Each person is responsible for his actions*, I thought. But there was too much guilt here. If we didn't give some of it to the dead, we would all drown in it.

I took a deep breath through my nose. "Their captain was a ravening beast—I saw him slay one of his wounded out of hand. The mercenaries had to follow his lead. Would you blame a herd dog for following the directions of the shepherd?" I looked at Rook. Who would have named a blond man for a raven? Perhaps it was all the sparkly things on his clothes. *Steady, Aren*, I thought, *keep your mind on the business at hand.*

"This man is a decent man. I have *seen* that." I paused, looking at the smith's wife, Poul's mother, and the others who'd been in the yard when I'd killed the pikka. "You all understand what it is to do a wrong thing because you feel you must." Suddenly I was so tired I could barely form the words. "Let us have peace."

There had been magic in my words, but I couldn't tell if it had done any good. I was too tired to worry about it.

Merewich called another's name, but I didn't hear who it was. Merewich would make peace if the villagers let him. I worked my way through the crowd toward the stable.

The morning sun was rising, and I had a place to be.

TWELVE

I saddled Duck, fumbling with the knot of the cinch. My fingers were clumsy, so finally I took the saddle off altogether. Holding the spirits seemed to be affecting my coordination; moving was like wading through deep water.

Slowly, I climbed the side of the stall to mount. Duck gave me an odd look, but stood patiently while I steadied myself on his back. If I had thought I could walk to the far end of town without falling, I would have. Riding was better than walking, but only a little.

Death, murmured the things that I held. *Death.*

Now, when they pushed and tugged at the barriers I'd drawn around them, it was with eagerness for the kill rather than anger at being captured.

I bent and picked up the cedar staff that leaned against the stall. Duck sidestepped abruptly so I didn't fall off. I wondered how much of the weakness I felt in my knees was due to what I planned and how much to lack of food. I didn't remember eating since yesterday morning, but every time I thought of food, I could taste the blood of my dreams.

Outside the stable, the loud sound of men's voices tried to draw my attention. But that part of the village's survival was Merewich's; I had other work to do. The sun had continued on its journey; I must have been in the stable longer than I had thought. There wasn't much time now.

Once away from the bell where the raiders and villagers worked out their differences, the streets were deserted, just as in my vision of the bloodmage. Without the raiders, without the bloodmage, Fallbrook had a chance to survive. They would have to appease the earth spirit, but no doubt Merewich could manage it somehow. Perhaps the death of the bloodmage would be appeasement enough.

I stopped at the place where I'd seen the mage in my vision. On my right was the house where I'd forced the creatures to wait for me. The noeglins' stench was spooking Duck, or maybe he could smell the wiggins' corpse-rot odor. The latter was more subtle, but I found it harder to bear.

Slowly, I slid off. When I was steady on my feet, I took the bridle off Duck's head and shook it. He planted his feet and snorted at me, until I yelled at him. My yell became a shriek I couldn't control as the power from my captives threatened to shake me apart. I plugged my ears and dropped to the ground. The sharp pain in my knees from the little bits of rock I'd fallen on cleared my head a bit, and I was able to stop shrieking.

Duck was gone, but the fetch knelt on the stones beside me, a smile on her face. I closed my eyes, unwilling to let her distract me. Gradually the creatures subsided, satisfied they would be free only when I chose.

The battle over for the moment, I rolled to my feet and opened my eyes. The fetch's clothes were wrinkled and stiff with dirt and sweat. Dark hair had escaped its braid almost entirely, and she was paler than before. She smiled, and I saw that her lip was puffy and bleeding slightly—I didn't remember doing that.

"I thought that you could only come out at night." I tasted the blood on my lip when I spoke.

The smile turned to a velvety, smokey laugh, and for the first time I saw that her eyes were still in that odd, almost pupilless state. No wonder Kith had stared at me. "With your call I can go where you demand. Without you, do you think the noeglins could escape their bog?"

"When I release you, you will go back where you came from," I stated with more confidence than I felt. What if I'd released these things to terrorize the village? Without me or the hob to protect them, the people would be help-less.

She laughed harder. It was difficult to believe, looking at her, that she wasn't exactly what she appeared to be. As soon as the thought crossed my mind, she stopped laughing and dropped her head to meet my eyes. She stepped toward me with snakelike smoothness.

"Yes," she said, "believe in me."

I took a deep breath. "Go now and wait in the house for what will come."

She raised her chin, but I was too tired for theatrics. "Go."

I put all the force I could muster into my voice. It must have been enough, for she left.

I'd called the spirits to this place because I wasn't cer-tain I could draw upon their power if they weren't near. I hadn't paid enough attention when the ghost had shown me how it was done. Maybe if I failed, the creatures would strike the bloodmage down before they left for their usual haunts. I took a firmer grip on my cedar staff as if it would save me.

The wait seemed to last forever. Bored and terrified, I stood until I swayed, then sat on the ground and drew pictures in the dust of the road. Big loopy flowers were easy, even with the awkward length of the staff. I erased them and drew a square. A few more lines and it was the widow's house. While I rubbed the house out with my hand, I glanced up and saw the bloodmage.

The sun was at his back, and I squinted against the glare. He started his horse toward me, so he must have stopped when he saw me. I stood up and dusted my hands, one at a time, on my skirt.

He stopped again, just a few paces away, playing with the hob's chain, rolling the little beads through his fingers, which were stained, like the earring, with the hob's blood. He rode alone, as the *sight* had foretold. Caefawn must have found a way to lure the berserkers away, perhaps even killed them before he died. The blood on the beads was dry and it flaked off, drifting to the bloodmage's hand.

The sight stilled my doubts. The spirits I held were quiet as I gathered their power to use against the mage. It took longer than I'd expected. Each spirit had to be dealt with separately; each extracted something of me for its gift. We were interbound until I felt there was little left that was only me.

"Well, now," said the mage, who'd watched me patiently. His voice was a polite, mellow tenor.

"Sir," I said politely, more from habit than anything else. A polite greeting of strangers.

Moresh's bloodmage had given me nightmares as a child, nightmares that had worsened after Quilliar's death. Even then, the red clothing made more of an impression than anything else about the man. He was only my height, with ordinary features, dark coloring, and Beresforder blue eyes. There was little in his face that hinted at what he was—only the subtle softening of what had once been a sharp-featured face. His eyes were quite mad.

For the first time since I took the initial noeglins, I felt that I was thinking clearly again. Facing the bloodmage at last, a deep calmness had taken root in my soul. Within me I held the power to destroy him. It was a heady feeling. My whole life I had feared this man, and now I did not. The power I held vibrated my bones like a building storm—of evil.

How, then, was I different from the bloodmage?

He was talking, but I didn't hear him. My own question consumed me.

Death! roared the spirit of evil in my head, a spirit made of the bits of my servants. *Kill it, and all will be gained! We shall not fear the Green Man. What can he do to us? We can save the village from him as we save Kith from the bloodmage.*

"How could I have missed you?" murmured the bloodmage in my ear. He must have dismounted while I was distracted, because he stood just behind me now, embracing me like a lover.

Yes, shrieked my spirit, *take him now. Bind him and make him ours. Hurry! Do it quickly. Take his power.*

A surge of magic shook me.

"Never seen anyone with this kind of power," continued the bloodmage. He gripped my shoulders and turned me toward him. His expression was filled with the same greed for power that had seized me far more tightly than the mage's hands.

When the spirits whispered to me, the bits of them that were becoming part of me answered. I knew then that if I managed to kill the bloodmage this way, I'd be an even greater danger to the village than he was. Merewich, Koret, and Tolleck trusted me. There were other mageborn in the village; I knew that, and so did the vile things who'd sifted it from my mind. Mageborn without the benefit of the hob's training, and thus easy victims. Part of me writhed in horror, part of me thought, *Prey.*

No wonder Caefawn had watched me when I called the ghosts. He had been willing to kill me, rather than let me access the ghost's power—now, too late, I knew why.

I twisted out of the bloodmage's hold and shouted, "Go!" Using the voice of command I'd learned had a strong effect on the spirits, a matter of emphasis rather than volume. And I released the spirits, all of them. I returned the power they'd given and took the little bits of myself, of my spirit back. I could feel their disappointment as they scattered.

The widow's house rattled and creaked.

"What was that?" said the mage, turning to look at the house where the spirits had waited.

His distraction gave me time to realize I had nothing to fight the bloodmage with. For a while I'd forgotten to fear him. I remembered now, remembered just why I'd been so desperate to destroy him. But it was too late. I'd used what little power I'd had to hold the spirits. Sweat dripped down my forehead as if I'd run a league rather than waited here for the bloodmage.

"My dear," he crooned after he'd determined there was no danger in the widow's house. "You are a treasure." He stepped to me and locked his hands on my face.

He took my mind.

Oh, not all of it. Some cool part of me observed what he was doing. It was not so different from what I had done to the spirits I'd taken. Perhaps, in a different time, he would have had the *sight* and been a spirit speaker.

He broke something within me, part of a deep tie between spirit and . . . soul, I suppose. I almost heard it give, like a bone crushed by a hillgrim. It broke, and I was his.

He stepped back, pulled his mind away, and left me an observer in my own body. He patted my cheek, but I felt it only remotely. "We'll wait here for Kith. I've called him, so it shouldn't be long now. I have three other berserkers I managed to save. They were out hunting, but I've called them back to me. I'll need a few more men from here, too. With a guard attachment I should be able to reach a more civilized place again and sell my skills."

My eyes, drifting without direction, caught on the hob's ear piece, still laced through the bloodmage's fingers like a talisman.

"You may call me ... Caefawn," said the hob.

The knowledge that Caefawn was dead brought tears to my eyes.

"What are you crying about, child?" asked the bloodmage with little interest.

I would have answered him if I could have, but the broken part of me seemed to have lost the ability to turn thoughts to words. I stared at him silently, and he shrugged. He started to *do* something more to me, but the sound of hoofbeats stopped him. He left whatever it was he was trying half-done.

It was one of his berserkers. He and his horse were covered with mud. His coloring was lowlander, but he was bigger than even Koret, and very young. But his eyes held the same old knowledge Kith's did. It made me sad even through my terror.

"Fennigyr, I felt your call." His voice was emotionless, and he moved with the same bone-weariness his horse did.

"Well? Where are the others?"

"Gone. Renwyr took off after a white horse, and I lost Stemm in a mudslide. I've been looking for them, but then you called."

"They're not dead," the bloodmage said after a moment. "One of them is hurt, though. We'll have to find them later."

Frantically I tried to figure out what the bloodmage had done to me, how he'd separated my soul from my spirit. Caefawn had told me that people (and his definition of "people" was considerably broader than mine) were composed of three parts: body, spirit, and soul. The mage had separated my soul from my spirit and body.

It was my spirit now that controlled my body, like a different sort of ghost. Not precisely without intelligence, but it was an intelligence obedient to the mage's will, just as the ghosts had obeyed me.

Horse hooves clattered on the road. My head turned, and I could see Torch approach at an easy canter. Kith sat so still that he appeared less real than the fetch had. He'd crossed the stirrup leathers (sized for me) in front of him. His face, I saw as he neared us, was as frozen as stone.

"Fennigyr, I heard your call," he said. "What do you wish?"

"Dismount," said Fennigyr, pursing his lips in thought.

She (I couldn't think of her as me, though I suppose she was) picked up the staff of cedar from the road and began drawing flowers in the dust, turning her attention away from the men.

I could hear them talking, but I was forced to stare at the dust flowers. The restriction reminded me of a vision. *A vision,* I thought, looking at the cedar she held in her hand. Oh, she was looking at it, too, but not the way I was. I focused on the cedar and pulled at it with my mind. Caefawn told me to use it as an anchor. I hoped it would help me to bridge the division the bloodmage had drawn. I could feel a weakness in his spell, perhaps where he'd begun to alter it when the berserker distracted him.

"Ah, Kith," Fennigyr said, "you were my best, my favorite. Did you know? I always liked the men with a little less bulk and more speed. I had to talk Moresh into using you at all—he liked them with more bulge and height. I asked him, Who'd you have an easier time hearing in the woods, a moose or a ferret?"

The force of Kith's stare drew her attention away from the cedar staff.

"In this light you almost glow, Firehair," continued the mage. "I always like my works of art to be pretty as well as functional, and I've always been partial to red."

Kith's eyes were still holding mine. If I hadn't known him so well, I wouldn't have seen his mouth tense when the mage called him Firehair. I wouldn't have *seen* the power that name had over him. It bound him to the mage. I could see the tie, spirit to spirit.

I remembered what Caefawn had told me about names. Kith had a name, given him by earth, air, fire, water, and magic. Given to him by the bloodmage—who was evidently a man of little imagination. *Firehair? My poor Kith.*

I could feel the part of me constrained by the mage's spell. It itched like an infected tooth, and I pushed against it.

"I'm not Moresh," the mage said. "He didn't know how much of myself I put in each of you."

He spoke like an artisan—didn't the saddlemaker say that very thing so often it had become a running joke in the village? I paused in my thoughts—hadn't I given part of myself to the creatures I'd commanded? Perhaps Fennigyr meant it literally.

I focused on Kith, trying to see him as I'd seen Wandel while he'd practiced, as I'd seen Kith's ties to the bloodmage a moment ago.

Kith broke into the bloodmage's speech. "What did you do to the girl?"

"She's not your concern," purred the mage. "One of the things I liked best about you was that you were never quite tamed. Moresh thought it was a weakness. He feared you, did you know? What he couldn't see was that the difference made you better than the others. You're older than any of my other men." The mage stared sadly at the sky. "Such hard work to make, and so easily destroyed. He didn't see you were more than just a man without a shield arm. I could kill you. . . ."

She looked at the sky, too, but all we saw was clouds. I needed to see Kith. Or my staff. If I could have spoken,

I'd have sworn. I swore to myself anyway, though I continued to struggle with the spell and my fear.

A harsh grunt returned her flittering attention to Kith. He was on his knees, and I could see the veins in his forehead. I could *see* how the mage used his bonds to cause pain.

". . . how easy it would be?" asked the mage. He hurt Kith some more.

Kith's fair skin had turned dark red.

I fought; the itch turned to an ache—how strange without a body, and at that moment it turned to outright pain as something tore. I would have screamed if I could. I'd done more damage, but I'd also damaged Fennigyr's control.

I'd freed my magic, too, what little there was of it.

Firehair, I thought. Holding Kith's real name to me, I *looked* at him. With his name, my spiritsight was much clearer than it had been with the harper. Like Wandel's, Kith's spirit was full of light. If ghosts were a candle, then living spirits were a glass, magnifying the light of the soul. I could see the little bits of foreign spirit tied into his own, and I plucked at them. But when I pulled one away, I had to replace it, because I *saw* I'd damaged Kith. Without those little bits, Kith's spirit would be wounded beyond healing. So I attacked the spirit bond that tied him to Fennigyr instead. It fell apart like a poorly knitted sock, leaving Kith's spirit damaged, but free.

"What?" exclaimed the bloodmage, staring at Kith.

Kith gasped a deep breath of air, unaware that it was not the mage who had released him. The mage was not so handicapped. Kith didn't have time to look up before the mage's swiftly drawn sword slid into his back and out his belly.

She turned her face away from Kith's death as wild grief sliced through me. Her gaze passed by the other berserker, and I could see the pain on his face. The low-lander had loved Kith, too.

Failure and agony almost distracted me enough that I didn't see what lurked behind the berserker, but no one could miss the solid thwack as Caefawn's staff hit the berserker in the head.

Caefawn's cloak was gone, and his remaining clothes were in rags. His charcoal gray coloring was somehow more foreign, exposed so openly. The neat silver-black braid of hair was loosed, spilling in a wild curtain about him. His right knee was bandaged heavily, and his ears, pinned tightly against his head, were free of ornamentation.

"Bloodmage," growled Caefawn, sounding something more than human.

Hope flared inside me for a moment, but I'd lost my belief in the hob's omnipotence sometime since the day I'd ridden up to fetch him from his mountain. The hob did not have the power to take on the bloodmage, not on this side of the river. I could feel the bindings that held him to the mountain and drained his strength. For the first time I understood that not only did the mountain augment his power, but he also fed her.

I would get to watch him die while I wondered if I could have fought the bloodmage better if I hadn't weakened myself by taking the spirits for their power.

"So you're the thing that's got my berserkers chasing their tails," observed the mage, sounding fascinated. I could hear nothing in his voice that suggested killing Kith had bothered him, though he'd sounded like a love-struck boy just moments before. "What are you?"

The hob snarled like a cornered lynx, beautiful and inhuman. His red eyes glowed even in the full light of day. "I am Death," he hissed.

"No," breathed the bloodmage. "I am."

Something dark left his hand, something vile that made my spirit flinch and step back. It hit Caefawn and spread down his chest. But as if it couldn't adhere to his skin, it dripped off him to puddle on the ground. The dirt beneath the hob's feet melted and steamed beneath the force of Fennigyr's magic.

Caefawn sprang onto the mage but hit some invisible barrier a foot away from Fennigyr's body. It propelled the hob backward a bodylength, and when the hob came to his feet he was clearly favoring his bandaged knee.

"I am your death." There was mock sorrow in the mage's voice.

Frenzied by the hob's danger, I *pushed* the edges of the broken place inside my head where the mage's spell was slowly unraveling.

Fennigyr waved his hand gently and the hob staggered back. The mage laughed and displayed the earring he held. "Yours, I believe?" He closed his hand on it. "It is enough to make you mine. I have just been forced to kill one of my children—was it you who set him free? But you will make an admirable replacement. Whatever you are, you have magic to feed me with."

The hob was frozen where he stood. I could see the sweat gathering on his forehead as he fought the mage's hold. But it was no use. If he could have forced the battle into a physical contest, Caefawn would have won, but magic for magic, the mage was an easy victor. I didn't think the bloodmage could tamper with the ties binding the hob to the mountain because they were part of the hob, not an addition like the berserkers' ties to Fennigyr. But I never doubted the bloodmage could kill Caefawn.

I was so tired, and my head hurt and itched in places I couldn't scratch. I rubbed my temples, trying to get some relief.

I rubbed my temples.

I'd broken through the spell at last, at least part of it. I had a moment to savor it, then the spell unwound. The shock of it left me lying on the cobbles, but my body was my own again.

A groan from Caefawn caught my attention. Neither he nor Fennigyr appeared to have noticed my momentary fit. Caefawn's face was drawn back in a grimace of pain and effort.

Neklavar, I thought, giving Caefawn the name he'd told me while I dreamed. True dreams they'd been, for my vision cleared and I could see far deeper into Caefawn's spirit than I had before—as it had when I'd used Kith's real name.

Thick cords of green and gold reached from his soul through his spirit into the ground, his ties to the mountain. With spiritsight, I could see the bindings that the bloodmage was trying to put on him. They looped the hob loosely, but slid off without attaching.

The bloodmage didn't have the hob's real name.

Fennigyr, my father had called him when the mage came to collect my brother's body and raged over its uselessness. The lowland berserker had called him Fennigyr as well. But this spring, on the top of Hob's Mountain, Kith had called him Nahag.

It might have been a nickname.

I focused on the bloodmage, whose face was smooth and blank, though his body shook with the effort of the magic he was using. I tried to say his name, but my throat wouldn't work right—I just couldn't form the word. So I thought it instead.

Nahag.

It wasn't just a nickname.

I could *see* the reason bloodmages all went insane. Rather than looking like a brighter version of a ghost, Nahag's spirit was like a beggar's cloak, rags and tatters covered here and there by different colored fabrics, pieces of other people's spirit. I thought of the little bits I'd taken from the noeglins and the bits of myself I'd had to give in return, and was sickened.

When I'd looked at Kith or Caefawn with his real name held tightly to me, I'd seen his soul, a rich, warm form enveloped in body and spirit. But the bloodmage's soul was small and dark, turned upon itself as if it could not bear to touch his corrupted spirit.

One of the foreign bits belonged to Kith. I ripped it away: fury spurred my path without giving me a chance to wonder if I could do such a thing or how I could do it. As soon as it lost contact with Nahag, it disappeared from my *sight*.

The other ragged bits fluttered and whined, disturbed by something. It was probably my imagination, but I thought they were trying to attract my attention to their unnatural plight.

With no better plan, I decided to see what would happen if I took them away from Nahag, hoping the power he'd gained from the people he'd stolen from would abandon him.

Like plucking geese, it was a job that soon grew wearying. I stopped now and then to look, but the mage was concentrating on the hob. I couldn't tell if I was doing any good or not.

My head ached with effort, and something else was wrong, too. I'd damaged myself breaking Nahag's spell, but I didn't have time to worry about it. As my father said, *"You have to finish what you start, Aren. Or all your work's for naught."*

I curled my hands around the cedar and fought off the vision so I could continue to work.

I had to rest, and took the moment to see how Caefawn was faring. His skin had lightened to a pale gray and sweat matted his hair, but otherwise he appeared unhurt.

I looked beyond him and saw a circle of villagers ringing the three of us. They'd come, drawn here by Duck's riderless state, or perhaps by Kith's abrupt leave-taking. But they stayed well away from the silent, motionless battle in the center of the street. There was grim fear on most of their faces. I wondered if they feared the hob or the bloodmage, and decided it was probably both. However, one person had joined the fight.

Rook approached the bloodmage cautiously. With a well-worn knife, he probed the magic that had kept the hob from hitting Nahag. Nahag made a brushing gesture and Rook was tossed to the cobbles. He lay there for a few counts, rolled to his feet, and tried again.

"Enough," whispered Nahag to the determined raider.

"I won't let you kill him," said Rook. There was a fierce determination in his pose. I wondered if Caefawn had teased the bleakness from Rook's soul as well as he'd done it for me.

"You can stop nothing." Nahag's voice was tight with impatience. He spoke a few words and gestured—I recognized it as the same spell he'd thrown at me, and waited for Rook to react. Nothing happened; there was too little magic behind the spell.

Rook looked almost as surprised as the mage. I'd given up hope, because my efforts hadn't seemed to do anything; but hope flared back again.

Wary, but not yet overly alarmed, Nahag surveyed the villagers, dismissing them one by one and skipping over me to return to Caefawn.

"Is it you? What have you done?" Nahag jerked his sword out of Kith and began a strike toward Caefawn.

I grabbed as many of the captive spirits as I could and tore them free. The sword dropped to the ground, and the mage fell to his hands and knees with a guttural cry. Forcing my stubborn body to move, I walked forward. When I reached Nahag, I collapsed to the ground.

He was trying to hold together the gaps in his spirit with magic, but his power was a thin and pale thing now. He didn't seem to know how to reach the magic of the land, the magic I used. I saw his gaze focus on the lowland berserker, and Nahag began to crawl toward him.

"Hungry," gasped Nahag, his voice shaking. "I'm so alone."

Rook stepped forward, but I raised my palm and shook my head. I wasn't sure Nahag couldn't use the raider for something—I knew I could have. Rook met my gaze for a long moment and stopped.

Nahag still held part of the berserker. I found it mainly because he was trying so hard to hide it. I don't think he understood who was attacking him until I took it away.

He looked at me as if I'd betrayed him. Then he attacked with the remnants of his magic.

Damaged as he was, he was stronger than I, and better trained. And I was so tired. His probings hurt deep inside my head, and all I could do was keep plucking foreign essences off him like a demented cook. One at a time now, because the damage inside of me was growing.

"Finish the job, Aren," insisted my father, his face stern as he stood above my six-year-old self crying over a half-plucked goose. "Everyone has something to do here."

I'd dropped my staff somewhere. It was hard to fight off the visions.

I ripped and tore until the only thing left of Nahag's spirit was a shredded, sorry thing—all Nahag without any extra fragments. He'd quit fighting me for the last few pieces; either he was too tired or he just didn't care anymore.

I stopped because I didn't know what else to do.

We stared at each other, Nahag and I.

I don't know what he saw, but I saw what I'd nearly, very nearly, become. He'd been someone's son once, who hadn't had a friend to save him as Kith had saved my brother. He hadn't had Caefawn to teach him.

His cringing soul expanded abruptly within the bonds of spirit. For a brief moment it hesitated, but the fragile spirit could not hold it and the soul drifted away. The spirit lingered an instant, then was gone.

The mage closed his eyes. I looked at Rook and nodded my head. Rook's blade slid into the mage's neck. I wouldn't tell anyone the bloodmage had been dead before the knife slid home. The raiders needed all the credit they could get.

"People," snapped Wandel. I turned and saw the harper holding his shirt over Kith's abdomen. "If we don't get him sewn up, he's going to die."

I felt a jolt of incredulous joy that cut through the numb exhaustion and *wrongness*. Kith was alive? I crawled toward them, then remembered Wandel was supposed to kill Kith. I stared stupidly at the harper, who met my gaze and frowned.

"This village needs him." He sounded defensive.

I smiled at him with sudden euphoria. Wandel wasn't going to kill Kith. Not ever. He knew it, too; I could tell by the self-disgust in his voice. Neither Caefawn nor Kith was dead. At least not yet. There was an awful lot of blood on Wandel's shirt.

Caefawn staggered to Kith, favoring his injured knee. He sat beside the Wandel and touched Kith briefly. Without taking his eyes off Kith, he held a hand back to me. "Aren, I need your help."

I reached out and took his hand. He stiffened, as he had under the bloodmage's spell.

"Aren?" With the explosive swiftness I'd seen in him before, he turned toward me. The horror on his face made me want to cower away from him, but my body chose that moment to quit obeying me again.

Could he see how close I'd been to becoming something he hated? Could he see the taint left on me? I tried to pull back, but my body moved toward his gentle tug.

He took my face in his hands, and I could feel the touch of his claws resting against my skin. He'd taken his earring back from the bloodmage and rewoven it through his ear.

"What did he do to you?" There was fear in his voice, and something in me relaxed when I saw I didn't disgust him. The familiar grip of his tail reassured me.

My hand reached out and touched his jaw. His skin was smooth against my fingertips. He moved one of his hands from my face to catch my hand and flatten it against his cheek.

Wandel said something I didn't catch.

"I can heal his wound, but I need Aren to mend his spirit. Keep the pressure on *here*, while I try to undo whatever the bloodmage did to her." But I could see that it wasn't worry for Kith that drove Caefawn.

I'd always thought his flirtation was an attempt to obey the wishes of the mountain. The mountain who wanted him to mate so his race would continue and she wouldn't be alone. Motives I understood, both the mountain's and Caefawn's. I understood about loneliness.

I stood by the too-shallow grave as the men piled half-frozen dirt on Quilliar's body. He'd always wanted to be buried in the winter because winter graves were heaped high with rocks and stones rather than the sunken places where those buried when the earth was soft rested.

Warm lips touched my mouth gently. "No, Aren, don't go away." I was wrapped in Caefawn's arms, cuddled against his warmth. His skin felt soft against my hands. The warmth of his tail, still curled about my ankle, made me want to smile.

I opened my eyes and saw stark dread in his. *He loves me*, I thought.

And I was dying.

In my haste to regain control of my body, I'd ripped the ties between my spirit and my body. Nahag had already broken the bindings holding my soul. With Caefawn and Kith safe, I lacked the strength to hold myself together anymore. And, like Nahag, soon I would just drift apart.

"If you go," Caefawn said, "Kith won't live. He needs you to mend his spirit." His hands moved subtly on my back and neck, giving pleasure. He was doing it deliberately.

"Not just any emotions," he said with a speculative look, as if he could read what I'd thought about him. *"Only things that make your spirit want to stay with your body."*

The soft, fluffy end of his tail caressed my cheek playfully. Faran take it, he knew I'd used the half-frightening desire I felt for him. It hadn't worked as well against the fetch as it had against the ghost. But it left me feeling things that were frightening, embarrassing, and . . . wondrous.

"Aren." He crooned my name in a husky voice that spoke of dark nights and shared passion, calling me back. But his eyes were desolate. He believed I was going to die, too.

"What's wrong?" asked Merewich's voice.

I knew I was dying. And I was.

But . . . what if it was like with the fetch? What happened if I didn't believe it? What if—I thought, settling peacefully into Caefawn's lap—what if I was too stubborn?

Caefawn tucked my head under his chin, presumably because his tears weren't something he thought would hold me, body, spirit, and soul. Listening to his shuddering breath, I decided he was wrong. I would not die and leave the hob alone. Slowly, because it was all I could manage, I pulled a bit of magic from the land and began repairing the damage the bloodmage and I had done. It surprised me how little time it took.

"So," I said diffidently and a bit hoarsely, "How can I help you with Kith?"

AUTUMN
HARVEST

FINIS

At Merewich's insistence, Fallbrook held a festival to celebrate the peace between the raiders and the villagers. It was outside the town near an old snag the children decorated with brightly colored scarves.

Tolleck the priest opened the celebration by hailing the rich bounty the land had brought to us and our ancestors. The people caroused, danced, and sang to convince themselves that they'd survived. Wandel sang a lot of old songs praising the earth. The innkeeper played a fine fiddle, and the smith drummed. Poul danced with me.

I COULD STILL HEAR THE MUSIC, THOUGH THE FESTIVIties were hidden by a rise in the land. After happening upon Kith and Danci holding their own celebration, I avoided the private places and walked in the open with a silly smile on my face.

Kith, it turned out, had known from the first that Nahag had not been killed with Moresh because of the connection binding him to the bloodmage. When he'd kissed me in the stables, he'd meant it for good-bye because he knew Nahag was coming. With Nahag dead, Kith's body and spirit mended quickly. He'd been loosening up quite a bit, though I hadn't known how well Danci had been doing with him—hence my silly smile. The hug Poul had given me when we finished the dance added to my light mood. There were still a lot of people looking askance at me, but the death of the bloodmage had done much to raise my status—and that of the raiders. Besides, I had Caefawn.

" 'Tisn't exactly what I had in mind," commented the earth guardian, striding beside me as if he'd been there all along.

"Come, now," I scolded him lightly. "I just passed two people celebrating earthy things in the most traditional manner, and I'd be surprised if they were the only ones."

The Green Man laughed—a good thing. I didn't think he was the kind of person—well, elemental, then—to laugh if he were still planning to destroy all the crops in the valley. Caefawn told me he thought the earth spirit might overlook the irregularities in the festival because I had proven the village's good faith by killing the blood-mage.

"We'll do a proper ceremony after harvest," I promised. "Tolleck is already paving the way for it. If you have any suggestions, I'll be glad to take them to him."

"Nay, nay," he said, slowing his stride when he saw me skip to keep up. "I'd rather be surprised." He slipped me a sly grin. "But I think your fisherfolk better be careful or the river will be jealous."

I looked at him to see if he was joking, but I couldn't tell. We climbed to the top of a knob of land that jutted above the field of rye and the decorated snag. I found a seat on the ground.

"Are you going to mate with the mountain's servant?"

He didn't look at me when he spoke, his attention on the festivities below.

"If we survive until next summer, I suppose I will."

I didn't hear him approach, but I was relaxed enough that I didn't jump when Caefawn's hands touched my shoulders.

"Such enthusiasm from a bride-to-be," he commented dryly.

I widened my smile and leaned back against him. His feathered cloak dropped about me, bringing warmth against the slight chill of the night wind. He crouched behind me, his knees resting lightly against my arms.

"With hobs," observed the Green Man, "you seldom get exactly what you bargained for."

"I suppose I'll find out next summer," I answered cheerfully.

"If you survive 'til then," added the hob as his tail twined itself about my waist. He didn't sound worried.

I looked across the night at the fires below where the raiders drank cautiously with the villagers. If I let my eyes unfocus just a bit, I could see a few wildlings scurrying about.

"In the meantime," said the earth spirit, "there's a fetch to send on its way and a troll on Wedding Pass."

Caefawn sighed in contentment, and his arms slid over my shoulders until they were crossed in front of me and his chin rested on the top of my head. "That sounds like fun," he said.

About the Author

Until she learned to read, Patty Briggs lived a mundane's life in Butte, Montana. Shortly after her sixth birthday, she discovered there were dwarfs living in the mines and elves in the forests. The hob in the garage really startled her the first time she met him, but they've become great friends since. Sometime before her thirtieth birthday, the urge to share her discoveries with the rest of the world led her to writing. She currently resides with her husband and children in the Pacific Northwest. *The Hob's Bargain* is her fourth novel for Ace.